Eye of the Beholder

An Elissa Gabrielle Original

Eye of the Beholder

An Elissa Gabrielle Original

Peace In The Storm Publishing

Winner
Independent Publisher of the Year
2009, 2010, 2011
African American Literary Awards Show

PUBLISHER'S NOTE

PEACE IN THE STORM PUBLISHING, LLC.
P.O. Box 1152
Pocono Summit, PA 18346
Visit our Web site at
www.PeaceInTheStormPublishing.com

For Lawrence

Because you loved me,
nurtured me,
cared for me,
cherished me,
adored me,
believed in me,
and saw all of me,
when I was invisible.
There is no me without you.

PRAISE FOR EYE OF THE BEHOLDER

"Every now and then, God gives a talented artist a gift within their gift, a destiny-creating piece that illuminates so brightly it defies average definition. Elissa Gabrielle has brilliantly weaved a tale that is, simply put, for your eyes and heart to behold."

~William Fredrick Cooper
Award-Winning/Best-Selling Author of Unbreakable

"*Eye of the Beholder* is a love story crafted in a way that only Elissa Gabrielle can. In what is sure to be considered her greatest craftsmanship to date, Gabrielle effortlessly gives her readers an explosive experience of emotions through words and sounds that dance on paper. Think colors … vibrant colors that come alive in your mind as you experience the poetic prowess of her writing style. You don't want to miss this one."

~SD Denny, Author & Freelance Editor

"Smooth like jazz, this work of art, *Eye of the Beholder,* has a poetical feel that wraps around your senses leading you into a captivating trance trying to inhale all the words written on the pages. Very vividly written with imagery so strong that you are able to feel every emotion of the characters within as if you are one with them, this page turner is a must read. This instant classic is enthralled with love and pain, desire and passion, perseverance and encouragement, and a true pathway as to how the hardest of test and the biggest of doubts can be overcome with real love and strong faith. Elissa Gabrielle has managed to intertwine poetry and jazz together to bring forth a riveting tale that all walks can relate and feel down to the souls of their own being making them a part of the lead characters, Jerusalem and Jill."

~H. M. Trey, Author & Poet

"If the moon and the stars align Elissa Gabrielle will be a literary rock star. *Eye of the Beholder* marks in stunning fashion the return to readers the craft of writing that book lovers eyes should be awarded. A heartrending endorsement of losing trust, crossing lines and seeking forgiveness, *Eye of the Beholder* is a story of emotional deprivation beyond one's control, and searching for inner soul sustenance. Elissa Gabrielle has penned word by word and line by line from the beginning to the end poetic justice poetically in this novel. *Eye of the Beholder* is comparable in scope, texture, and depictions with the classics because of the strong wit and passionate intelligence."

~Alvin L. A. Horn, author of Perfect Circle

"If it's worth reading, it's worth waiting for...and I must say, *Eye of the Beholder* by Elissa Gabrielle is definitely worth the wait. Once again, Gabrielle reeled me in from the very beginning. I found the characters' names alone very intriguing and I wanted to learn every detail about them. Gabrielle makes her readers feel as if these characters are people they have met at some point or another in life. But, if you haven't met them, you certainly won't regret getting to know the latest cast penned by our beloved... Elissa Gabrielle!"

~Linda R. Herman, author of Consequences

"Elissa Gabrielle delivers a story of intimacy, love and hope with a healthy amount of romance crafting the ultimate love story in *Eye of the Beholder*. While it is not uncommon for Elissa to create relatable characters in every book she pens the characters in this novel are not only relatable but memorable. Being familiar with the author's work, just when I think she is incapable of penning a novel better than the one preceding, she does just that in Eye of the Beholder; it is indeed her best work to date and she is to be commended."

~LaLaina Knowles, Award-winning contributor to The Heat of the Night

"*Eye of The Beholder* is a love song in prose. And not just a love song that exists between a man and a woman but that lingers in the memories of children about their first love, their mother. Many are caught up in what is visual, what the eye can see, but *Eye of The Beholder* is about what the heart can see and overcome. This book should be set to a jazzy beat so the reader can close his or her eyes and allow themselves to be swept away. Gabrielle has poured her heart into the pages of this book and the reader will come away with the realization that love transforms and transfigures; allowing us to see true beauty."

~Angelia Vernon Menchan, Author, Publisher, Womanist

"Elissa Gabrielle's *Eye of the Beholder* takes you to another place and time. Vulnerability and hope are the backdrop of this riveting novel. Gabrielle's words are like cool water for a thirsty soul, each one dripping with lyricism and purpose. Eye of the Beholder will cause you to experience firsthand the transformative power of love."

~J'son M. Lee, Author/Editor

Sensual, spiritual and thought-provoking, Elissa Gabrielle craftily brings relevant subjects to life in the exceptionally-written *Eye of the Beholder*.

~ Loretta R. Walls, Author of The Majestic Dynasty

"Jerusalem and Jill are poetry in motion, as Jerusalem weaves his life story of discouraging events to an undercurrent of floetry and jazz that you can hear as a backdrop. Jill is the artist, drawing from her personal life to add fuel to who Jerusalem is becoming, not allowing him to wallow in his current condition, with her true compassion and love for what she does. *Eye of the Beholder* draws you into the world of these two people from the very first sentence, carrying you with them from their pasts into their present."

~ Sharel E. Gordon-Love, author of the award-nominated The Putting Away

"Poetic, Lyrical, rooted in urban life and harsh realities. Elissa Gabrielle has done it again with this graceful novel, *Eye of The Beholder*, full of love, redemption and hope."

~L'Nora, Author

"Elissa Gabrielle writes with incredible boldness and sensitivity. Her characters are believable and have left a lasting impression in my mind. *Eye of the Beholder* is a wonderful read."

~Toriana Jones, author of Good To Have You Back

"When reading *Eye of the Beholder* by Elissa Gabrielle, you come to know the characters as if you grew up with them. Elissa Gabrielle weaves into *Eye of the Beholder* the memories, the family members, the tragedies and the triumphs that shaped the two lover's will and perspectives on life. With *Eye of the Beholder*, you get more than a love story. You get a life story."

~Joey Pinkney, Author and Book Reviewer

"Eye of the Beholder by Elissa Gabrielle is epic storytelling and to sum it up in one word, it's simply poignant."

~Jessica A. Robinson, Award-winning author of the Holy Series

"Eye of The Beholder is yet another fine example of Elissa Gabrielle's intrepid and brilliant pen. When she inks it...it is written, launched, and ALWAYS on target."

~Marc Lacy, Author, Poet, Lecturer

"Everything has its beauty, but not everyone sees it."
~Confucius

"My music is the spiritual expression of what I am – my faith, my knowledge, my being. When you begin to see the possibilities of music, you desire to do something really good for people, to help humanity free itself from its hangups …
I want to speak to their souls."

~John Coltrane

Chapter 1

Jerusalem

Introspection

I wake to the sound of my own voice howling a blood-curdling scream into the cold, brisk air which fills my bedroom. The sound, even though it comes from my own body, startles me; causing me to sit up straight to regain my mentality and composure. I'm scared beyond belief; to the point of feeling my own body shake and tremble in fear beneath me. "It's a night terror, not current reality," I tell myself, but my mind could care less about the distinction as it relives the pain.

The chill in the air is offset by the warm beads of sweat dripping from the terror-filled adrenaline pumping through my body, drenching me from head to toe while warming me and causing my temperature to rise. My heart races and I inhale deeply, trying to catch breath that escapes me. The source of my screams, sweat, and tears is the same recurring invader plaguing my mind, from time to time, over the years without rhyme or reason. It is a mental sensation I have not been able to shake since the day I saw her in the hospital more than two decades ago. A mind-altering intruder of mine is more vivid and real than any nightmare a person could ever have, simply because it is my reality instead of being a product of an over-active imagination. Even in the realm of dreams, reality trumps fantasy. It is my mind's way of reliving the beginning source of my pain and my soul's way of reminding me never to forget.

The Evian water bottle on the nightstand next to me finds its way cleverly and productively into my hands, as it routinely does when my mind starts playing tricks on me during the night. I gulp down its purifying contents without missing a beat. Yet, no matter how hard I try to soothe the savage beast of my past, the water cannot drown the images that linger in my head no matter how fast or how hard I choose to swallow. Even as I quench the fire of my exhausting night thirst, I can't extinguish the fire ignited by my dreams—the contents of which refuses ignoring.

I still see her. I smell the scent of her Chanel No. 5, as if she is standing right next to me and I remember *that* day, as if it were *today*. I'm lost in that moment in time. My night terror ensures that I will never forget that day or *her* for that matter; despite how many minutes, hours, days, years or decades that pass. *That* day will always be *today* and she will always invade my dreams.

When the beginning of my *end* began, I was ten years old. That is the moment in time that changed my life—the point of definition known to me as the *history* of my life.

A ten-year-old does not possess the wherewithal to appreciate the blessings that make up life. A ten-year-old lives in the *here and now*; unaware of the need to smell the flowers of life along the way, or of how good life really is. If I had have known then, what I know now, maybe my life wouldn't be attacked routinely by night terrors clubbing me over the head while begging me to be thankful for what I currently have. Maybe, if I had have been a little more grateful, *she* would still be here. My dreams impose that mentality on me. They make me pose that inquiry to myself each time I awake in cold, night sweats remembering *that* day. Even as an adult, I know that rationale has no basis in fact, and was not the case then or now, yet my nightmares still make me wonder. In the instance of wanting to blame someone other than God for the fact that sometimes *shit happens* in life, my dreams still make me want to point the finger of blame at myself. That is what children do. Their minds often place blame on themselves instead of on the foundations concerning the cycle of life.

Even though I am an adult, remembrance of my mother is still through the eyes of a child. I do not see her weaknesses; a mother is Wonder Woman in the eyes of her child. Mothers are invincible; as such, I will forever see her in that manner. I couldn't see that she, just like all human beings, had the capability of being vulnerable. My mind cannot comprehend that her life was what it was intended to be—as God made it.

I look at things concerning her through the eyes of a child missing his mother; and all I can see is invincibleness; as such, all I can do is wonder what I did wrong that might have caused her to be taken away from me. Through the eyes of a child is how I see things when it comes to my mother. The view lies in the eye of the beholder, and the day it all began and ended still invade my dreams.

It began innocently enough. There was a carnival at school and Mom agreed to make cookies. I sat in the kitchen as she pulled the cookie sheets out of the oven, one by one. There were at least five dozen, if not more, and the aroma filled our house in a manner that only home-baked sweets can. I could not sit still because the smell was making my mouth water. I reached for one as she placed the cookie sheets on the top of the stove to cool.

"Can I have one?" I asked, as my hands hung midair in an attempt to have the first bite of what I knew would be pure, sugar-filled heaven. She had a way of making the best cookies in town; at least in my opinion, even if I was a little bias.

Her…

My Mom was the epitome of grace. I realized it then, I yearn for it now. The King of kings kissed her and turned her skin bronze; it was always aglow. Her deep, dark, penetrating almond-shaped eyes made my father weak. Full, thick, jet black hair; she wore it in a side sweep on special occasions, but mainly tied it up under a soft, satin scarf. Dad loved that. The sight of her face alone was enough for him.

Her lips were full, like the upper petals of an orchid flower. Dad's eyes danced with excitement whenever she pecked him on his cheek. He loved her so. We all loved her so.

And, when the kiss was planted on him, he would always reply, "A kiss from my angel, sweet love of my life."

"Can you have one?" She raised her eyebrow, as if she had

been waiting for the exact moment in order to put class in session. "What have I told you about that word, 'Can'? 'Can' means do you have the ability to have a cookie. We both know you have the ability to have one. What you really want to ask me is, 'May I have a cookie?' By asking, 'May I have one?' you are really asking if I will *allow* you to have one. That is what you really want to know, isn't it, son? You really want to know if I will *allow* you to taste one—not if you have the ability to taste one—isn't that right?"

Mom smirked while continuing to stir batter for the next batch of cookies for the oven.

Hungry and wanting a cookie instead of hearing her insistence of teaching me something at every twist and turn, I rolled my eyes. I just wanted a cookie. She could have kept the English lesson to herself. Sorrowfully, I looked down at my Buster Brown shoes and beige corduroy pants. I smile when I think about how my mother dressed me in the early eighties.

"I guess so. So, can I have one, Ma?" My response was respectful, but to the point.

"Yes, you *may* have a cookie. However, as you eat it, I want you to remember the difference between the two words, son. Just by virtue of being alive, you *can* do many things in life. In addition, while those things are important and satisfying, recognize that what's more important are the things at which you *may* have to be a trailblazer; the things that life *may* restrict or dictate because of who you are. Those are the things in life that I want you to concentrate on, and not the things that life says you 'can' have, but the things that life takes a pause in telling you that you 'may' have."

At the time, I didn't hear anything she said other than, "Yes, you 'may' have a cookie." Now that she's gone, I wish I had paid more attention to everything she had to say. I wish I had lingered a little while longer at the feet of her wisdom.

Bending over the counter top, I reached for a chocolate chip cookie cooling on the tin sheet in front of me. As I did, I noticed her closing her eyes and rubbing her temples with the tips of her fingers. I gobbled the cookie quickly as crumbs fell from my mouth. I didn't want to give her a chance to change her mind.

"You okay, Ma?" My words came as an afterthought, as I reached for another cookie. Instead of the usual smile that she normally gave me, she collapsed. Hearing her plump frame hitting the kitchen floor, scattering kitchen table chairs in the process, was startling. She shook uncontrollably on the floor and my feeble, ten-year-old mind tried to comprehend what was happening.

"Ma! Ma! Are you okay?" I screamed, awaiting a response, but none came. My eyes grew big and I gnawed at my fingers contemplating what to do. I picked up the phone and fumbled with the cord to the headset, which always seemed to tangle right at the moment that it needed to be straight. Taped to the side of the refrigerator was Dad's office number for emergency purposes and even at ten years old, I knew Mom lying on the kitchen floor constituted an emergency.

In all of what a few seconds had to offer, I saw everything in my life flash before my eyes as I called Dad. President Reagan was on television, interrupting Mom's soap operas with a special news report. The wood paneling and drop ceiling in our kitchen, wow, I saw every one of them. The brick that covered the back wall to our stove and the yellow, linoleum floors in our cozy kitchen; I saw it all, in slow motion, as my heart raced.

Crumbling before my eyes was my safe haven in Newark, where Mom and Dad kept the outside evils away and the goodness of heaven in. Ripped from my ten-year-old hands was life, as I knew it, as she lay helpless with only me to rescue her.

Life as I knew it, was being ripped from my ten-year-old hands as she laid there, helpless.

Seeing her body shake and contort on the kitchen floor, was the beginning of my end; it is the sight that introduces my night terrors, and the vision that causes me to sit up straight in bed, screaming and sweating profusely. My memory fast-forwards from that moment to the next memory like a badly edited movie. The next image I have is of standing at her bedside in the hospital, as the doctor told my father that my mother had a brain tumor and only had days to live. Cold and callous were the doctor's words as if reciting items on a dollar menu at a fast food restaurant. I don't remember much about seeing her lying in bed dying, but I do remember the tubes in her nose, the sounds of machines keeping her alive, and the sound of Dad's voice saying, "Make sure she is comfortable so that she can go in peace."

Chapter 2

Jerusalem

Pleading with My Savior

Unwrapping layer after layer with slow precision, the doctor peels the white gauze from my face. Unaware of the covering for several weeks, my eyes are weak underneath the bandages, causing me to open them slowly, adjusting to the overhead lighting. As each fold is removed, I am able to focus a little bit better on the only two moving objects in the small, make-shift hospital—the doctor removing my bandages and the nurse assisting his every move. Both dressed in Army combat uniforms in blends of tan, gray and green, the desert standard issue for soldiers in Iraq.

Fear instantly floods my senses, as I look around the large, metal structure posing as an Army hospital. Clueless as to where I am or how I got here, terror takes second chair to the intense pain I feel all over my face. The skin around my head is dry and tight as a glove and my face feels engulfed in flames. I run my tongue inconsolably across my brittle and cracked lips, which are the only part of my face that is exposed. Longing for a sip of water, I try to sit up, but the doctor forcefully holds me in place. His attempt to restrain me gives the first, real indication of pain in my injured chest and ankle.

"Whoa. Not so fast, soldier. Calm down, Sergeant Jones. We didn't know when you would finally come around to the land of the living, but we're glad you finally joined us again."

Removing the last layer of bandages from my eyes, I blink quickly, wanting to speak. I need to ask questions about where I am and how I got here, but my jaw is still constrained by the bandages. I sense Lieutenant Morgan moving faster, anticipating my need to speak.

"Private Brooks, do you mind giving Sergeant Jones a few of those ice chips over there? He must be dying of thirst."

Placing the tray she had in her hands on the table beside me, the Private does as she is told, grabbing the pitcher of ice from the other side of my bed. I could hear it all. Military training, when done right, makes you a person who has the ability to see and hear with your ears. I've learned to tap into this skill and need it now more than ever. I have to see with my eyes, see with my ears, I feel it. Life is changing. She empties a few pieces into a glass and then removes one chip and runs it across my lips. Pressing deeply into my chapped lips, saturating them with the cool ice, I feel relief as I slowly close my eyes and exhale aloud.

"Sergeant, you are in an infirmary in Iraq. You were brought here shortly after your accident. I know this must all be a little scary for you, but don't worry, we will take good care of you. You slept through the worst part of it, probably due to all the pain medication. But we will have you up and feeling like yourself in no time."

Lieutenant Morgan continues to speak while removing the last of the bandages from my face and examining his handy work. The nurse puts a few more ice chips in my mouth and slowly the fire within my throat begins to subside. I manage to speak through the pain.

"What happened to me?"

"Do you remember anything at all?"

"Not really. I vaguely remember that my reserve unit back in Jersey was called to active duty and that we were shipped here to help out, but I don't remember much of anything after we set up camp."

"Well, considering all that you've been through, it is not uncommon to block out what happened, but it will come back to you. An Iraqian sniper shot you. The other two soldiers in your vehicle didn't make it, but you survived; the sign of a true soldier. You wouldn't give up!"

As the doctor utters the words, the nurse tries to retrieve the tray full of cutting utensils, but drops it to the floor. The crashing sound startles me and instantly my mind rewinds to that near fatal moment.

The desert was hot and the humidity flanked our Humvee like an over-sized blanket. There were only two vehicles on the mission and I was the lead. Each of us strategically tried to focus on our surroundings, searching for the enemy. "Situational awareness" was the running joke in the midst of the desert. *Always be aware of your surroundings.* We laughed amongst ourselves as we stared at what appeared to be nothing but dust and sand dunes. Suddenly shots rang out from nowhere and everywhere at the same time. Metal bounced against our vehicle, along with threats shouted our way.

One of the sand dunes seemed to come to life as several Iraqian soldiers ran from out of nowhere straight toward the front of the Humvee. They were on a suicide mission and their aim was directly focused on the front of the vehicle and the soldiers' heads in the two seats directly behind the front window.

I jerk in my hospital bed, mimicking the movement I remembered of the driver of his vehicle weeks earlier. My body continues to tremble as I relive the moment that the vehicle lost control and flipped several times before bursting into flames. As if in a trance, I could suddenly smell my flesh burning the same way it did when I was in the passenger's seat. While confined, the Bible verse I chanted echoed in my head. I prayed one of the prayers of Jabez. *"Let your hand be with me, and keep me from harm so that I will be free from pain."* My mother named that boy my brother, here second son, Jabez and I instantly went back to her, then him, when I prayed. Free from pain, I pleaded with my Savior. From my hospital bed, my lips begged – through a whisper – the same mercy it had on the day I was wounded.

"Your faith saved you, Sergeant. You are lucky to have it. That and your buddy, Sergeant Thomas, both of them are contributing factors in your being alive today. You are a very lucky man."

"Right now I'm feeling anything but lucky," I replied, as the doctor applied ointment to my face. It begins to sting and I cannot help flinching at his touch.

"This is nothing. I am sure it feels a lot worse than it actually is. You are healing quite nicely. In a day or two, we will be able to release you to go back to the states."

I ran my fingers across my face and instantly knew that it was a figment of its original form. I could feel that the right side was the same as it had always been, but the jagged, rough skin on the left side was the first indication that my once strongly, chiseled facial features were just a memory. As my fingers dug into craters and raised skin from my jawline to my lip, I knew, without a visual, that I would never be the same.

Doctor pulled my hands away from my face.

"Still needs time to heal. You cannot touch and feel your wounds this way, you'll only infect them."

"Do you have a mirror, Doc? I'd like to see the damage." I implored for the only tool that could confirm what I already knew.

"Okay. But remember, you're alive. That is all that matters. Wouldn't you rather have a scar and be alive, or no scar and be dead?" Lieutenant Morgan tried to be encouraging, as he reached in a drawer and passed the mirror to me.

The doctor did not realize the magnitude of his words. A scar. As far as I was concerned, my whole life had been a scar, only now I had a physical mark to brand me in remembrance.

Chapter 3

Jill

Not on My Watch

He wears his pride like a badge of honor, a look given through self-protecting eyes that I have seen before—years and years ago. The same masked look my sister wore daily to hide the deep pain she harbored. His eyes, just like hers, begged me to pretend not to take notice that it was all an act. I obliged; simply because I knew his heart needed me to do so.

His injuries are extensive. When I open the blinds in his room, allowing the sun's rays to expose the extensive damage to his face, I want to cringe. It looks so painful. But I know he needs me to pretend it doesn't look as bad as it really does. While he doesn't speak those words, my heart hears the language his heart is speaking. The flaking skin and raised red and blue molted flesh startles me, but my words treat him as if the flesh is normal. After all, outward scars do not define my patients. I know that. I just have to help them know it as well. Being a bridge to that reality starts with treating them like a human being instead of a charity case.

Pity is an unwanted companion to those with disfigurements. Janet taught me that.

Her life was my classroom. I sat in the front row.

Although she was the one hit by the truck that day, both our lives were forever changed. I witnessed the transformation in her—physically and mentally. Sometimes the mental is far worse than the chains of body limitations that restrain the physical. Janet's very spirit seemed to seep slowly out of her after that day. The crime of stolen youth was committed upon her and she was a victim twice over. Assaulted first by the hit and run driver that left her paralyzed in the street, and secondly by our parents who seemed to harbor a sense of embarrassment at her life sentence to a wheel chair. Which assailant was worse? That question remains unanswered in my mind.

Maybe some of my self-imposed guilt concerning Janet came from my being with her that day and a sense of remorse that it should have been me instead of her that ended up under the tires of that truck. Maybe my sympathy for her came from my seeing, minute by minute, her daily struggle just to be "normal" and accepted. Maybe my mind housed a need to be by her side because everyone else she trusted in life had written her off or let pity be their tour guide when dealing with her.

Hindsight is a bitch, and yet it never has the decent courtesy of giving answers to the big questions we want answered.

Kick ball. That simple game started the downward tumble. To this day, just uttering those two words causes my skin to have a chill to it. We were in the front yard, just Janet and me. It was one of those moments in childhood when our mother had forced us go outside just so she could get us out of her hair for an hour or two. I remember it as if it just happened even though it was about two decades ago. I kicked the ball toward Janet and missed my mark. As the ball rolled past her and into the street, she followed behind the large, yellow grim reaper that we called a toy.

"You kick like a girl!" I remember her saying that as she came to a complete stop in the middle of the street.

Those where the last words Janet uttered before I saw her body catapulting into the air and then being savagely ran over by the rear wheel tires of a Ford 150 pickup.

The driver never stopped. He barely even slowed down. My

sister was nothing more than a speed bump to him. An irritant in his journey from points A to B.

As red taillights faded from view, with tires screeching around the corner of our suburban street, I ran to her. It was too late. With damage done, Janet, as we all knew her, was gone. She lived to see many more days of life, but she never really "lived" again. Removed from the street, bandaged and nursed to the best health possible, something that once resided in her died on the street that day, never to return. There was no wake, no funeral, no moment of observation to mourn the loss, yet a part of her died.

Janet's stay in the hospital was a lengthy one, as doctors brought her mangled body to a point that it could function, with assistance, in a somewhat normal fashion. Our parents made adjustments for her arrival back to our home—an added wheelchair ramp to the front of the house and a new van that made it easier to transport her. They did all the outward signs to show they loved and supported their daughter in spite of her disability, but those outward signs did not translate over to their inward feelings. Those were more transparent and less rose colored. Our parents spared no expense in making her comfortable, but they also didn't spare her feelings when reminding her constantly how much of a burden it was to provide those accommodations for her. The burden was not financial, as we lived a very comfortable lifestyle in that regard. The burden was more of the perception of their peers.

Mother liked to live up to the Joneses, and having a wheelchair ramp just didn't go well with her finely landscaped front yard—an accessory that just did not match the ensemble Mother was trying to present for the behalf of the neighbors. Making room in the formal dining room for Janet's wheelchair seemed to take away from the fine china and the expensive dining table she loved showcasing twice a year. Those are just the top layers of situations caused by Janet's new living arrangement that rubbed my mother the wrong way—situations she voiced her dislike for, time and time again.

Stated in sly remarks given with a huff, Mother couldn't help herself nor did she try to. Father's comments were never verbal; they were subtle looks, glances and just an overall discernment from his eyes. The delivery method of my parents' resentment ran the gamut of extremes, which was felt by Janet. It seemed as if

Janet's very existence after the accident was at the very least a discomfort to my parents, if not a major embarrassment to their way of life. I watched her shrink to nothing inside. Once a bubbly, bright and outgoing child, she slowly turned into an emotionless puppet who desired nothing more than to be invisible.

A puppet—that's exactly what Janet became, and it hurt my heart tremendously as I watched it happen. The strings attached to her by our parents dictated her movements, her actions, her whole way of thinking. The very people, who were supposed to give her the wings in life with which to fly, were the ones that clipped those wings on the ends instead. Over the years, I learned that Janet's wheelchair did not restrain her—our parents did.

I guess in hindsight, Janet is the answer to my unanswered question, which is why I do what I do.

Watching her deal with life without actually living it changed me. To me, Janet's disability was a byproduct of her circumstances. It never should have defined who she was; but somehow it did. I tried to be her cheerleader in life, but it was a case of too little too late. After all, I was a child at the time, too. I was helpless to bringing about any major change in her life. But now, "helpless" is no longer in my vocabulary. Not in how I live life and not in how I beg my patients to live theirs. I choose to enhance life rather than watching it slowly die.

I've worked in several hospitals before calling the Veteran's Hospital my home. There is something about the possibility of breathing new life into men and women who had served our country that gave me a sense of pride. Our Vietnam vets came home to a country that treated them as outcast. The same feeling Janet received in our home. I feel a special kinship to our vets just as I did to Janet. I was determined not to let another soldier feel that same since of shame and despair based upon injures they received in support of our country. They will never feel that level of pain; at least not on my watch. So I guess, because of being a passenger along the journey of life with Janet, from the very start of my career, it all was predetermined; I didn't choose working with the Veteran's Hospital, it chose me.

Chapter 4

Jerusalem

Moment of Clarity

Over bandages, my fingers run across the bumpy road of scars and stitches that now compose my face. I'm not sure who I pissed off in the universe to deserve this kind of karma, but I have to deal with the cards I have been dealt. I've been doing that all my life. The mirror is unforgiving and relentlessly abusive; my future seems even less kind. I can tell that the doctor senses my despair because he exits—stage right—with quickness, his bedside manner in tow. He leaves the female Private alone with me to help me lick my wounds of initial shock and deal with the inevitable depression that is destined to overtake me—a task above her pay grade or rank, no matter how hard she tries to pretend otherwise. In the midst of her kind words and fumbled attempts, *she* arrives, cloaked in the pretense of being my physical therapist, my nurse, but truly heaven sent. Initially, I guard myself from her. The hideous sight that is my face is not something I am ready to share with the world – now or ever; nor do I want the emotional, psychological or medical pity of some physical therapist. I am above that falsity. I assume she is also.

Methodical are her actions, as she follows procedures in making me feel comfortable and saying all the politically correct words that a nurse should say.

"Sergeant Jones, this is a minor hiccup in your life. Recognize it as that and let me do my job and we both can go about our normal lives. I hope you do not want a pity party, because I am not good at hosting them. I am more about results. I'm about bringing you to the point you were at before you ended up in this bed."

Her take-charge manner is just what I need, though I pretend not to notice. I sit in silence, inwardly swimming in pity.

She opens the blinds in my room and within seconds, we wince at the encroaching light that begs for our acknowledgment and attention. With the sound of the blinds opening comes a sense of respect for the therapist's way of adding light to a very dismal situation.

"I'm Jill, by the way." Her introduction has the same pep in it as her steps from the window to my bedside. "And you are Sergeant Jerusalem Jones. Well, at least that is what your chart says. It's nice to meet you."

Rolling over in pain, I turn my back to her, staring at the wall. Instead of patronizing Jill and her efforts to get warm and cozy with me, I watch the female Private exit the room in the same silent manner that the doctor had.

"Besides that minor kiss of war on your face, we also have to work on that broken ankle and fractured sternum of yours to get you back up and running on the battlefield."

Did she just say, "Minor kiss of war?" There is nothing *minor* about the scar on my face. Did she not notice that the gash and third degree burns on my face stretches from my cheekbone to my lips? I turn over to face her and give her a piece of my mind, but the warmth in her eyes stops me dead in my tracks. Hazel, almond-shaped gateways sooth lips that want to spit sarcasm in her direction.

Jill walks from the foot of my hospital bed up to my waist area, and begins folding down the bed covers to get a better look at my leg. The gentleness of her touch and the smell of her perfume begin to chip away at the wall I have built up. A wall that a lifetime of unfortunate circumstances demanded I create. Her hands are soft and gentle. Her aura as luscious as her lips. Something about her tames me to my core. She is comfortable. Both in her curvaceous full-figured body and in the way she flirts with the outskirts of my soul.

Inquisitively, I watch her actions as she shoots question after question at me—relentless in her approach at trying to get me to talk. But I'm a soldier. I've mastered the art of evading for a living.

"So, are you originally from the Jersey area? Was that your home before Uncle Sam snatched you up and threw a uniform on you?" She speaks while massaging and bending my legs, moving. She is dedicated to her job. Her accent is thick, even to me, given the fact that we share the same native tongue of where we were born. I assume she is a New Yorker.

"Unfortunately, I've lived a little bit of everywhere; mostly for short amounts of time. Uncle Sam has just been the last one to house me."

"Well, depending on how you look at it, having lived in a variety of places does add a bit of mystery to life. It shakes things up a bit and keeps you on your toes."

She continues massaging my legs and talking, never allowing my negativity to take hold of her. It is clear that she was serious about not being a host to pity parties.

"So, do you have family? A wife, kids, brothers or sisters? Who should I be worried about suing me if I cause you too much pain?"

She moves away from my legs and lightly presses her hands on my chest area. I wince in pain, closing my eyes tightly. Softly, she rubs my arms, providing solace to what ails me. I exhale as she continues inspecting the fracture to my chest.

"You didn't answer me. Who do I need to prepare to protect myself against in the form of a lawsuit if I cause you too much pain?" She smiles while working, amused by her sense of humor.

"No wife. No children. No parents. Only a brother, Jabez; but he's not a threat to you or anyone else."

I close my eyes and relax into the pain. No sense in trying to fight it or Jill's questions either, for that matter.

Her manicured fingertips form circles along my shoulder blades as a tingling sensation of relief radiates through my upper torso. Squinting, I watch as a few strands of her hair effortlessly escape from the restraint of her ponytail and fall along the side of her face.

No wife. No children. No parents. My words echo inside my head and while Jill massages away some of my physical pain, I wonder how my father's chest must have felt as the bullets entered it. The shallowness of my breathing teases me as to what his last breaths must have felt like. The rigid constraints on my ability to breathe normally make me question if that is what my father felt. Was the feeling the same for him? It had to have been worse.

I close my eyes tighter, letting Jill's perfume and mere essence hypnotize me into becoming one with my thoughts. I hadn't thought about my father in a long time. Probably because pain— and trying to avoid it—has been a dance that I have been doing since the day my mother died, sprawled on the floor, in the middle of a batch of warm, home-baked cookies. But the moment before me took me on a stroll down memory lane. First Mom died. Daddy was gone shortly thereafter, and pain has been my nemesis ever since.

Unlike Momma, Daddy did not have the luxury to go peacefully in the still of the night. His departure was more urban than graceful—forcefully induced—the result of gunshots received in the line of duty.

Protect and serve. That was his motto. That is what he did. It was who he was. Yet, where did it get him? Lying on the other side of the dirt, with two bullets buried deep within his chest as passengers in his coffin with him forever—his badge of courage.

For a few minutes, I try to relieve my father's pain, trying to walk in his shoes as he gasped for his last breath of air. After all, his death was the turning point of my life since it led to the foster homes and despair. My childhood died when Daddy did.

The pain in my chest gets heavier as Jill presses harder and my abusive memories dance the same dance on my heart. Jill must sense my discomfort even in the absence of words; as if hearing what's not being said, she immediately stops her attempts at massaging my chest.

"Only one more area to focus on," she says, as she moves her hands up to my face, coupling my chin. My initial reaction is to back away from her. It is instinctive. I do not want her to focus on my flaws. Mortified, I'm sure, by what she sees, as I know I am, and I only briefly saw the damage to my face. Intensively staring at the aftermath of the explosion on my face, even if for medical purposes, has to be horrifying.

It is a moment I do not want to share with her or anyone else. With that in mind, I recoil further away from Jill. At least I try to.

"Now Sergeant, you aren't going to make me pull rank on you, are you?" She grabs my face tighter, holding it firmly in place. I can tell she has prepared herself for my resistance. "Soldiers make the worst patients…your determination to take charge of situations always override your need to sit back and let a woman do her job."

I can't open my eyes. I refuse to. I don't want to see the pity in hers. I am too weak to add yet another dagger into my psyche.

"You know, I've always had a great respect for soldiers. The way you all put your life on the line for your country is truly admirable to me. It's the same as a mother's love for her child. It's unconditional. It's hard to have anything but respect for that."

Jill's fingers gingerly move across my face with precision, examining the extent of my wounds. She continues talking, unfazed by what her fingertips feel on my skin.

A feeling of helplessness and insecurity overtake me. I'm vulnerable. A place I have been inwardly running from for years. I try to recoil, but Jill pulls my face closer to her…again.

"I've always thought that the true measure of a person came from what radiates from the inside. I make a living rehabilitating the outer shell of people and I pride myself on being able to heal the inner parts; as it is the inside of them that I find the most interesting and intriguing. That's where the true beauty lies."

Jill presses hard along the base of my scar, moving along each inch of it undaunted.

Is she always like this? I ask myself. The world delivers and zooms in on ugliness. How can she possibly be real in seeing past all of that? All of this? All of me?

Chapter 5

Jerusalem

Back Down Memory Lane

Lonely nights spent in my hospital bed are almost as irritating as the bandages and constant anesthetic wiping of my face to clean the burns. Once the doctors, nurses and physical therapists make their final rounds and I receive my last meal for the night, I am all alone with my thoughts. That is the worst.

The sterile walls and echoing ceilings haunt me relentlessly. My childhood comes rolling back in to view, whether I like it or not. Over the years, I have gotten good at suppressing the memories, until something ignites a spark, grasping my every waking thought of my standing on the frontline, like I did, back before the accident.

Loneliness is often the key. Even the stints in the orphanages, although shared with many other kids, still left me feeling alone. Each orphanage housed more than thirty beds full of children all waiting for the chance to go home with a loving family. Despair filled those large open-bay facilities. We all hid it well. We all felt alone. My only refuge was that I had Jabez with me—at least in the beginning. That gave me a little comfort at first, but our surroundings seemed to take more of a toll on Jabez than they did on me.

I still remember the way the light shone so brightly in his eyes and how it began to get darker and darker and finally fizzle out as our time there dragged on. As the first year passed without so much as a nibble of anyone wanting to adopt either one of us individually, let alone take us as a package deal, his spirit slowly died. I tried to take away his anger and insecurity, but his feelings of being unwanted seemed to be stronger in guiding him than my brotherly love could ever conquer. He was always starting fights with the other children in the orphanage. I knew he did it as a means to feel better about himself. Better than others. Bigger. Stronger. Putting down others seemed to allow him to escape the feeling of being unloved, which seemed to have controlled his every thought.

Yet, in the midst of all the anger bottled up inside my little brother, he still needed me. If for no other reason than to be a sidekick during his fights—either to break them up or to help him if he was on the losing end of the brawl—Jabez needed me.

After our parents died, I didn't like who he became, but at least we had each other. Well, that is until Mr. and Mrs. Hamilton walked into the orphanage looking to make *their* lives whole. Unable to have children of their own, the Hamiltons were a young couple in their late twenties. Highly religious and dead spent on making the world a better place by adopting a hard-to-place child, they chose Jabez. He was more than a politically correct statement of their righteousness or a poster child of what great people they were for adopting an underprivileged child. They really wanted him.

Good people. They really were. Why that placement did not work, I will never know.

I exhale, remembering the love the Hamiltons gave Jabez. Love I wish I had received for myself. Love I wanted the both of us to have and share together. While Jabez left the orphanage to the open arms of a couple that only had intentions of raising him in a home full of love and everything his heart desired, I remained where I was…invisible on the inside, and in a place that was filled with bodies, yet void of love.

Tears filled his eyes the day Jabez left.

"Why can't you go with me?" he inquired, as big brown eyes

stared back at me awaiting an answer.

"God knows what's best. We should never question Him." My reply was more for my reassurance than for his. "Besides, don't worry about me, I'll be fine. You're lucky, lil bro. Somebody wants you. Let's be happy about that."

He hugged me tight and that was the last time things ever felt warm and loving between the two of us.

I kept in touch with Jabez as often as I could after he left the doors of the orphanage. He had the best of everything—good schools, unconditional love—and all the material things a kid could ask for, but with each phone call or visit, I heard it in his voice and saw it in his eyes. He had died slowly on the inside. First, the suspensions from school, then there were the fights, trouble with the law, and ultimately running away and living an unnecessary life, but one his broken heart chose and forced him to live.

I never understood the path his life took. I still don't.

As I watched Jabez slowly spiral downward, I felt mixed emotions in wanting a bit of his opportunity for myself. He was wasting it. I knew I wouldn't if given the chance. He was my brother and I was happy for him, but a piece of me wished I had been the chosen one to walk in his shoes. He was outside the walls of the parentless-forced kiddy prison, and blowing away the fruit of God's gift, while I sat behind invisible bars, with only hope as my blanket of comfort.

I prayed for a chance to have a piece of happiness of my own. Even with my prayers, after Jabez's adoption, it was years before someone wanted me. I had just about given up hope of ever having a home of my own when she came and claimed me as her son. Her name was Miss Janice and I would join her, and the three girls she had previously adopted, in rounding out her illusions of being a "good" mom.

Miss Janice looked good on paper…as they say. Her heart was as big as the state of Texas because she opened her home to children classified as "hard to adopt" because of their age and the amount of time they had spent in the system. The misfits…they were her children of choice; she took them in and called them hers. She was the "clean up woman" as some had begun to call her because she picked up the baggage and dirty laundry in the form of kids that others did not want. And, for a short period, I bought into that same bullshit as everyone else when I first met her.

But not all that glitters is gold, and it only took six months for me to come to that realization. Miss Janice was much like the drill sergeants I came to meet later in life—all sugar and spice in the beginning to get you, and the devil incarnate once the deal is sealed.

My happiness at finally having a place to call home was shattered shortly after I stepped through the doors of her home. I found out her wrath the first time I stepped outside the line of being the good, robot child she insisted I should be. At that moment, my innocence was lost. A simple mistake of a boy taught me the lessons of a man.

I remember it like it was yesterday. That was the day I crossed over the threshold from boy to man. Beaten like a boy, but instructed in the artful skills of being a man that became Miss Janice's means of corporal punishment

It was a normal day like any other. The school bus dropped me off on the corner and I was tossing my football in the air as I walked home. When I hit the front yard of the home that I felt was my new refuge, I threw the ball, aiming at the side of the house and into the backyard to the left.

I missed.

She was home.

And she wasn't happy, as the ball flew past her head, sailing through the front window of her living room. My insides shattered, right along with the windowpane.

"Jerusalem Jay Jones! Bring your ass in this house right now!"

I knew I was in trouble when she used my full name. She never did that. Probably because it was not the one she gave me and was a reminder of my government-issued status to her.

"Yes, ma'am," I replied, running in the direction of the house, hoping my haste would help me out a bit.

"Don't 'ma'am' me! Respect for me and my house went out the window as your football came flying in." she stared at me. "You're just full of yourself and a shitload of testosterone today, aren't you?" Her eyes sized me up in a way that I had never seen before.

I looked at the table and saw a half empty bottle of rum sitting next to a glass.

Funny how I never saw liquor in the house during the visits from the social workers who were responsible for the checks she was given for housing me, I thought.

"I'm sorry, ma'am." I tried to pick up broken pieces of glass.

"It's too late for you to be sorry. As a matter of fact, I am going to make you eat those words. You're going to feel what 'sorry' is." She grabbed a hanger from the laundry basket on the floor next to the couch.

My eyes widened, as she raised her arm and swung down like an axe connecting to a block of wood. The pain was almost paralyzing. Mommy and Daddy never hit me. At least not like that. Not with a fierceness full of anger that made me want to forget I was ever born. I curled into a ball on the floor, taking it like a man. The only thing I knew how to do. I hoped my actions would make her stop, but they had a different effect on Miss Janice. Instead of making her feel pity for me as a child, my act of "taking" it like a man seemed to awaken something sinister inside her that I hadn't seen before, and something that I am sure those who had placed me in her care didn't know existed.

Only murmurs of pain escaped my lips, as the hanger connected with my heated flesh. That woman whipped me until she grew tired.

"Oh, you manning up now?" The whites of her eyes turned crimson.

Sniffles betrayed me. "No, ma'am."

She smiled and stopped beating me. As the welts on my back took form, I exhaled a sense of relief that she had put a halt to her attack.

"Since you are showing your manly instincts of respect, I want you to show me how much you 'really' love me." She put the hanger down and sat back on the couch. "Come show 'Momma' how thankful you are that she took you away from that awful orphanage." She hiked up her skirt and leaned her head back on the couch, using her hands to dictate that she wanted me to crawl between her legs.

I knew what she wanted. I had seen it in some of the girly magazines of some of the more experienced boys in the orphanage. But seeing it on the pages of a magazine and doing it were two different things.

"I'm not sure I can do it right," I said, as I moved closer to her thighs, getting a whiff of a day-or two-old scent that smelled like when Momma made tuna sandwiches for Daddy for lunch back in the day.

"You can't get it wrong if you start by tracing the alphabet with your tongue." She moved her underwear to the side. I will teach you. You will be a pro when I am done with you, and your future wife will thank me for teaching you some skills. I'll say the letters and you trace them with your tongue down there. A…B…C…"

I did as instructed. Feeling the skin on my back start to tighten with a sting from her blows that I had never experienced before, I knew I did not want to do anything to get any more of that. A…B…C… My tongue made the motions of each letter. We went through all twenty-seven in the alphabet.

"Jerusalem Jones? Do you spell Jerusalem with an S in the middle or a Z," the night nurse said, as she put a cuff around my arm, taking my blood pressure and waking me from my flashback.

"S, there's an S in the middle, not a Z," I said, noticing that my tongue was already moving unconsciously in the direction of spelling the letter out just the way Miss Janice had taught me to do as a child.

Chapter 6

Jill

Lush Life

Removing my shoes from tired, weary feet, I massage my toes. I've been standing all day long, running rampant between hospital rooms, floors, patients and treatments. It is part of what I believe is my calling in life. My purpose, if you will. A higher calling - most definitely. Mother and Father wanted me to be some sort of royalty in their eyes in the form of something and someone—like a doctor or lawyer—they could most assuredly brag about. A nurse? That's not exactly what they had in mind. I don't believe I can ever recall a time when Mother or Father said they were proud of me. Proud of whom I have become. Sure, I thought of furthering my career and becoming that doctor I had dreamed about many moons ago, the profession that would have made them proud; in that time and space where eight years of schooling seemed so easy and carefree, until reality greeted me with a smile and smack upside the head, along with a dose of humanitarianism once I discovered all the good a nurse could do. Goodness called and I humbly and eagerly answered the calling I heard from above. I followed that goodness, that humanitarianism around until I made my way to a place where both my skill and my spirit could soar all in one safe place and I could get away with calling it work.

Lush Life.

One of my favorite John Coltrane albums is *Lush Life*. The song, as well as the entire album, places me in a state of Zen. Somehow, when I listen to jazz, all seems to be right with the world. Everything instantly becomes balanced. Even when outside forces and circumstances that surround my life and the life of my patients deem otherwise, once I put that jazz on, I release most burdens. Jazz does for me what gospel does for the devout Christian or someone whom the Holy Spirit moves. Jazz. It is a side of me few get to experience—my love for it, that is. It is part of my daily existence, a place—a source, if you will—that keeps me sane in an insane universe.

Insanity.

Although I recognize this country must have soldiers fighting its battles, the aftermath seems, on some levels, insane to me. But God bless their hearts, as their slightly injured wounds allow them to go back to war. They are that dedicated to the cause. They are that loyal to their country. They fight, 'til the death. They fight until they cannot fight anymore. A sacrifice made on their behalf of the United States of America. We get to taste a bit of freedom each day. Caring for these soldiers confirms in my spirit, that freedom is never free. They pay for it daily, and oftentimes for the rest of their lives.

I think of him. Jerusalem. His energy is dismal, but something tells me there is more to his life than what I am getting from him. He is black; black like a lineage of African kings, black. Dark, velvety smooth in appearance. I wonder if others teased him as a child for, having skin the color of cocoa and as smooth as silk. It is beautiful; that skin of his, but children don't recognize the beauty of something like that. Children are ingrained with the American way of viewing Black. Even after the abolishment of slavery, America still has not abolished its way of thinking. It is historical—the hate that many of us have that translates into societal. With age and maturity, we learn and are aware of the presence over time. We learn that black is not evil. Black is not a sin. Black is divine. Yes, that is what we get if we're soul searching and being honest within ourselves. We recognize that a people, adorned with black skin, have conquered so much and when we take an honest, in-depth look at that, and appreciate it even from a sound place of introspection, we see that black is something to be especially proud of because it is exceptional.

He is exceptional.

I wonder if he knows it. I wonder if he realizes that he possesses the heart of a lion who wears the skin of his African ancestors.

Jerusalem Jones. Combat devastated one portion of his face. I peeled back the layers of the bandages and he lay there still and quiet; calm, like I was peeling back the layers of his soul. He handled it, and me, like a soldier. I know he's scared. I can feel it. I feel something else too. It's endearing. Anxious to see what he is all about.

I walk over to my marbled bathroom and turn the shower on. I smile when I smell the aroma in the bathroom. Although it's merely hot water running behind glass shower doors, my bathroom is filled with the many scents that come from a superior collection of bath essentials handcrafted by a woman who visits the hospital frequently, named Valencia.

Valencia has been selling handmade soaps, body washes, oils, candles and all things lovely and perfectly-perfumed for a woman's needs, when it comes to health and beauty. Having adopted a more natural lifestyle, Valencia's products are right on time for me and my life.

She's an Erykah Badu type – speaking of the light of the sun and the glory of the moon and how it connects to the stars. She doesn't eat meat. She feels it's disrespectful to murder one of God's creations for our greedy physical fulfillment. I don't think I disagree with her and her analysis on life but I'm not all the way there yet. I, like most of the world, am a work in progress.

Removing my clothes, I look in the mirror and I smile because progress is certainly being made. I step into the shower.

The shower feels good against my skin, along with hot, soapy, bubbles of an almond and honey mixture that Valencia makes for me. I rub it in, vigorously, the scrubbing bubbles opens up my pores and breathes new life into my weary body. I'm tired, but there is more work to do. My eyes focus on peach colored tiles in the bathroom, as I wash every inch of my body. I love the way this feels.

Taking the towel from the shower door—it's oversized and plush, cream in color with gold borders—I begin to caress the residue of water and stress from my fatigued body. It's a "good" towel, if there is a such thing; meaning, it's heavy and cost a pretty penny. I work hard; I shop harder.

I stare into the mirror. Fog and steam block my view. Instinctively and ritually, I use the towel to wipe some of the moisture that has collected and look at myself. I exhale at the woman in the mirror. I stare at my eyes, admiring the curvature of them. They are like big almonds. Teased as a child because of their size, now I receive compliments on them all the time. For a woman in her late thirties, I'm not half bad. Admittedly, it took a long time for me to say that, let alone admit it to myself. The pressures society places on women—the same pressures we readily accept without a fight—build up over time. They sink deep into the psyche of many of us, leaving us with feelings of inadequacy, feelings of not being worthy and not being good enough.

Once we get it. Once we learn to see ourselves the way God sees us, we are somehow born again. It's a revelation that only comes with the passage of time and the gift of wisdom. It took a long time, but somewhere around the age of thirty-six, I started to get it. As I look in the mirror while drying off, I bear witness to full hips, and thick lips and maybe just a bit too much around the middle. Attributes I once thought of as shameful but that I now embrace. I see soft ringlets of natural, honey-colored hair. I admire my full breasts. They are full—bountiful emblems of my sensuality and womanly prowess. Their presence was the foundation of much teasing for me as a child, now people are paying to obtain what I was abundantly given. Lips follow suit. Called a duck throughout my grammar school years because of the size of my lips, today, those two are objects other desire and often purchase. As I inspect the woman in the mirror, I smile at all of my perfect imperfections. I have no worries, other than staying healthy. I have learned to view myself the way God views me, and the sight that stares back at me is one that makes me smile. Have mercy.

I dress and step outside of my brownstone and make my way to my car, on my way to see Janet, my sister. This nursing home, which is also an extended living facility, has been Janet's home for several years now. After her accident, our parents were embarrassed beyond shame behind their perfect little daughter, who wasn't so perfect anymore; so they financed this place as her permanent residence in order to keep her out of sight and out of mind. Evidence that money can make anything go away…even a less than acceptable child. Mom and Dad still visit Janet, but it is not enough, and even Janet can tell that it is done out of parental obligation instead of their unconditional love. So, I make sure I give her love several times a week to ensure her heart is kissed in a manner that has no conditions attached. If she weren't so disabled, I'd take care of her myself; but she is, so I can't. Her care requires more than my best wishes and sisterly love can provide.

Believe me, it's not from a lack of trying. I've tried.

I tried.

I remember the day she left.

"Mom, where's Janet going?"

"To a place that can take care of her."

"We can take care of her here, Mom!"

"Watch your tone, young lady!"

"Mom, you're just ashamed of her is all!"

Smack.

She smacked me dead in my face. I'll never forget the disrespect that accompanied that smack.

"Don't ever speak to me that way again, Jill!"

"Trust me. I won't!"

My father walked in.

"Jill! Respect your mother!" he shouted, as the nursing assistants hauled my sister away like old furniture on its way to Goodwill.

"Why don't you show some respect for your daughter, Dad!"

I stormed out. I kissed Janet on her cheek.

"Janet, I love you. Soon as I can, I'm going to take care of you, I promise!"

"Jill, it's okay." Janet slurred the words, but she still uttered them.

Janet had been a bit slower because of the accident. Brain damaged? Yes. An invalid? Absolutely not. An embarrassment to the family? Most definitely…at least in the eyes of my parents.

Chapter 7

Jerusalem

Number 56

A little, skinny-armed, light-skinned black boy is what I remember about Larry growing up in Newark. Lawrence Assange. The children in the neighborhood always wondered where he got that funny last name. He didn't think anything was strange about it. I didn't understand that back then, but I understand that now. What we're born with is what we know, as a matter of fact, it's all we know. Assange was his last name. The kid with the skinny arms.

He could run so fast. We threw footballs for what seemed to be ten days a week outside of our homes; right in the middle of the street. We grew up on opposite sides of the block and became fast friends when we realized what true friends really were and what friendship really meant. Even though it took us a while to appreciate what we were to each other, thank God, we eventually did.

Back in the day, while the girls thought I was too dark, they all loved Larry. The sun kissed him lightly and mercifully; unlike me, whom she kissed all over—repeatedly, it seemed. His light brown eyes made the girls go wild. I have to admit, I envied those eyes of his even though I never let it show. His crooked smile seemed to work wonders for him along with soft, curly, brown hair that showed no mercy on anyone. Another attribute of his that made me a green-eyed monster to my friend at times.

"Man, throw the damn ball!" I yelled to him, as he held the football hostage.

He kept backing up and doing his best imitation of Lawrence Taylor. Yes, that was his man. While I loved football since my father was a die-hard New York Giants fan, and my mother was one by default, I was really a basketball fanatic. Magic Johnson was my hero. No one in the world could tell me that I wasn't going to play for the New York Knicks or New Jersey Nets; point guard to be specific.

"Hold up! Wait a minute! I'm trying to show you how Lawrence Taylor would do this, boy! Now, watch and learn," he told me, as he did something that made the rest of us boys out in the street pause and laugh. Larry was a clown. My best friend.

"Lawrence Taylor doesn't throw the ball, dummy!"

"Yeah, well, if he did, he would do it like this!"

He finally threw the ball and I ran backwards to catch it, and I did. Sweat poured down our faces and we smelled like two-day-old pastrami and cheese sandwiches as we made our way back to my front porch.

Jabez came downstairs and sat on with the rest of us. That was the posse;— Larry, Jabez, Leroy, Kenya and me. Kenya was the African boy from down the street. Neighborhood kids teased him so badly that we felt we had no choice but to let him into the posse.

Since the dawn of time, people of color have been led to believe that their skin is too dark, hair is too kinky, feet, nose, lips, butts are too big. We're lead to believe that the Mother of Civilization, Africa, is a place that houses savages and Aids and malnourished children who need the white man to save them.

As such, and to our ignorance and demise, we fall victim to those misconceptions. It happened in our childhood and poor Kenya, we called that boy names something serious. "African Booty Scratcher" was the main one, but over time, I saw how those words affected Kenya so I stopped. Shit, Kenya and I were about the same color. I urged the other kids to stop also. As we got older, we slowed down.

God bless Kenya.

Jabez, my little brother, was a true buzzkill in every sense of the word. I loved him dearly, but truth be told, he would rain on a good parade every chance he got. If the posse wanted to go left, Jabez went right. If we wanted to go get ice cream, Jabez wanted pizza. If Mama baked fresh, homemade chocolate chip cookies, this fool pouted because he wanted sugar cookies. I'm not sure how he became the way he was, he just was.

"What up, y'all." Jabez gave us all dap. He drank from a Styrofoam cup, the sweetest red Kool-Aid known to man. Mama had a way of mixing cherry and tropical punch in the biggest pitcher. She added just the right amount of sugar, lemon slices and ice to make you addicted. Everyone on the block loved Mama's Kool-Aid; almost as if nature gave no other option. Once we saw Jabez with a cup in hand, we all inquired.

"Mama made Kool-Aid?" I asked, looking up at him as he gulped down the contents of his cup as if there were no tomorrow.

He stood up so we could all see him drink. He was a jerk that way. Ashy knees stood out as his red basketball shorts stopped just above them.

"Yeah," he responded after he downed every last drop in his cup.

"Bet! I'm gonna get some," I yelled, as I stood to my feet. I looked to the posse. "Y'all want some Kool-Aid?"

They all yelled in unison, "Yeah!"

Jabez stopped me on my way into our home. "Yo, Jay. Mama can't afford to be making Kool-Aid for all your friends."

I wanted to punch him right in the face, but just as I was about to tell Jabez a thing or two about himself, Mama came outside. Her face was shining so bright with the most radiant skin I'd ever seen on a woman. She looked like an Indian; one of those Native American women with dark features and long hair. Her eyes were dark and piercing and she had a smile that could warm the heart of the devil without trying. In her hands was a pitcher of freshly made Kool-Aid and a stack of Styrofoam cups. The posse's faces lit up.

"Thank you, Ma'am!" everyone yelled and Jabez stood there, shit-faced and jealous.

Mama handed everyone a cup and we all stood up and allowed her to pour our cups and fill them to the rim.

"You boys must be so thirsty," she said, as she poured each cup to the brim. "It's a hot summer out here this year; you boys need to stay hydrated."

We downed those cups of Kool-Aid, stood up, and waited for her to pour more.

Flustered and aggravated, Jabez walked into the house and slammed the door behind him. I could hear him murmuring to himself, but I couldn't make out the exact words.

"I'll talk to him, Jay," Larry volunteered as he turned to head towards the house.

"No need, Larry, you sweet little boy. Thank you for wanting to help. Jabez is just the baby of the family and he doesn't want to share his Mama is all," Mama said aloud to Larry, stopping him in his tracks.

"Okay, Ma'am," Larry replied as if relieved not to have to intervene.

"But, thank you, Larry for being such a good friend," Mama added.

"Anytime, Ma'am."

"Let's head out and throw the ball a little more. The block party is tomorrow, so they will be getting ready soon and closing off the street," I told the posse.

"Bet," Larry said, we all headed out into the middle of the street.

Larry threw the ball hard and fast, and backed up in such a way that we all knew he was grooming himself for greatness later in his life. That kid was ten years old with the heart of a thirty-year-old. He lived, breathed, ate and slept Lawrence Taylor, number 56 of the New York Giants. Because of his fascination with the pro footballer, we gave Larry the nickname "LT."

Growing up, LT did not have a father. He was an only child and leaned to my father for guidance on serious matters in life like homework, becoming a man, dealing with girls, what to look for in colleges and last, but not least, how to become the next Lawrence Taylor.

My father taught LT how to tie a tie. He taught the rest of the posse how to do so, too, saying every man needed to know how to tie a tie. He also showed us how to take care of our dress shoes, how to polish them and how to place them in the closet so that they wouldn't get ruined or dirty. Dad schooled us on how to take care of a woman and often talked about how it was so very important to keep a woman happy—one woman.

"Having one woman that treats you right and loves you with all of her heart, that's what a real man wants. You'll hear a lot of nonsense as you get older about how having many women is what it's all about; that's not true, young men. Find that one woman that was created just for you; love her to death, and she will love you more than you can ever imagine. See Mr. Parker down the street? Remember when his wife ran after him with that knife? See that is what happens when you do not love a woman right. Remember my words young men."

We all laughed at Dad's words, but I never forgot them.

"So, you leave the states for a year, leave me hanging, and this is how you come back? *Maaaaan,* you have got to find a safer hobby!" LT smiles and gives me dap the best way he can, while making sure to overlook my hospital bed. Secretly, I loved him for his small gesture.

"Yeah, good to see you, too, good brother." I crack a half-hearted smile.

LT leans in to prop up my pillows. It's subterfuge and I know it. He's really leaning in to get a good look at me without being obvious. Again, I appreciate the gesture. He always managed to look out for me over the years. Sometimes his actions were obvious, other times clandescent in delivery. We've been friends for over thirty years and I often think God placed him into my life because he knew I would need him. A reason, a season, or a lifetime…we don't always know the category of our needs, but God does and He supplies accordingly.

"I know you're doing your inspection, LT. I promise I'm good. Just happy to be alive," I tell him to reassure him.

"You're always good, Jay. Even in those foster homes, you were good. You're strong, but I'm here to make sure."

Looking up at LT, I still see the same little, skinny-armed kid. He's older now. We both are. A brief stint in the NFL almost went to LT's head that is until the New York Jets cut him due to a leg injury. His chances at celebrity status at the hands of a pig's skin died. He commentates on the local television station as a sportscaster now. It pays the bills and has garnered LT some notoriety, but I know he's heartbroken about not being able to hear his name screamed from a crowd from the fifty-yard line. His ego was too big to allow him to play arena football, and his talent would have considered that a crushing blow, so commentating would have to do. As his friend, I offered the only solace I could. I reminded him that at least he had the opportunity to go pro, something most young, black boys would never be able to say. I know my words and that reality were both only consolation prizes to a life he felt robbed of being able to capture. Being "close" to the goal only matters in the game of horses, not in real life.

"The doctors and nurses say I'm lucky to be alive."

"Well, we don't believe in luck, now do we, Jay? You're blessed. I'm happy to lay hands on you now. When I got the word that you were injured in Iraq, man…that was rough."

"Tell me about it."

"So, what's the prognosis?"

"Doc says no major internal damage. No loss of limbs, praise God. And I still have my mental faculties in order."

"That's questionable." LT chuckles.

"The most damage is to the side of my face where I'm bandaged up."

"I see the bandages."

"The one nurse attending to me, Jill, won't let me feel sorry for myself. She's a tough cookie. Reminds me of my mother. Pretty… angelic almost, but takes no nonsense. I was starting to believe the ghost of my mother was reborn in this girl. Ha!"

"Well, this Jill is right. No pity parties here, partner. Besides, you dark-skinned brothers have been back in style for a while. It's almost as if ya'll got nine lives and can do no wrong. The ladies love y'all. I mean, Blair Underwood, Idris Elba…dark skin reigns again…you will be fine as far as appearance is concerned. Hell, that scar coupled with a war story or two might just get yo ass some added panties thrown your way."

"You know you ain't got no sense, but it's 'bout time dark brothas are back in style, man! When we were growing up, all the girlies wanted LT! They loved your high-yellow ass and they could not get enough of those light brown eyes of yours! All the rest of us with some added color could get, back in the day, were your leftovers! So excuse me if I say, it is about time for the rest of us get to be a main course for a change. But, on the real…I'm scared about what my face looks like. I don't want to look disfigured. That scares me."

"Don't be. You'll be fine. You've gotten through much worse than this in life, Jay. This is a pebble on the road, that's all."

"It's more than a pebble; it seems like a boulder. But I hope and pray that you're right, LT."

"I'm right, Jay." LT walks toward the window, opening the blinds to let in some sunlight.

Adorned in a New York Giants 56 Jersey, jeans and timberlands, LT, makes his way to the chair next to my bed, he grabs the remote from my nightstand and takes a seat. He flips through the channels until he finds something that we both find entertaining— rap. We grew up on hip-hop and loved it just as much as we did sports. We often debated who was the greatest rapper of all time. Today is no different.

"You see this shit right here, Jay? Why do these fake-ass, wannabe rappers get so much airtime?"

"It's what is hot right now."

"This shit is not hot, man. Where is Big Daddy Kane when you need him? If he came back out right now, he'd shut this shit down."

"True. But we still have Nas, so all is not lost."

"Truth. But you know the greatest of all time, Tupac, would rule right now if he were alive."

"Correction…Biggie was the greatest of all time, and he would definitely be running it."

"Man…whatever, Jay. Yo ass is delusional."

"Listen, pretty boy, don't get mad at me. You know it's the truth."

"Jay, I'ma let you have that since you're recovering; but as soon as you're better, we'll get back to this." LT rises to his feet. "You hungry, man?"

"I haven't had much of an appetite lately."

"Okay, but you know you gotta eat, right?"

"Hurts to chew with my face on the mend."

"Right."

"Let me run and get you a chocolate shake from White Castles!"

"Word? I could go for that."

"Bet. I'll be right back."

As LT makes his way out of my hospital room, Jill walks in. Passing by him, she smiles at LT. He returns the smile. She moves closer to me in all white scrubs and her soft-brown, curly, natural hair cascades down around her shoulders. LT looks back at her as he leaves the room. I know what he's thinking. My friend is such a whore.

Chapter 8

Jill

What's New?

Entering Jerusalem's hospital room, I pass by a brother with a bright smile. It was welcoming and inviting. He looks so familiar to me, as if I've seen him before. For the life of me, I can't put a name to his face and I don't have the slightest clue as to why I think I know him, but nonetheless, he is familiar to me.

Shaking the eerie connection, I approach Jerusalem's bed. The warmth of the sun's rays illuminates every inch of the room allowing him to say good morning to a beautiful day. This is a first. For all the time he's been here, Jerusalem would never allow me to open the blinds to let the smile of God flow throughout the room. Not without a subtle fight or sigh or some indication that he did not want to see the light of day. He normally just lies here in a dark room, most days. No television, no radio, nothing…just a dark, dreary, lonely and isolated hospital room. He was adamant about leaving the blinds closed, so I'm curious as to what may have changed his mind today.

"Good day, soldier." I make my way to his bed.

"Hello, nurse."

"I told you to call me Jill."

"Right, Jill."

"How are we feeling today, soldier?"

"As the old folks would say, 'fair to midland'."

"That's good. Today, we're going to have some fun. The doctor says you're strong enough for physical therapy, so you'll be up and on your feet starting this week. It's time to get you walking and moving with full strength. It's time to remove all the cobwebs from your bones."

"Ouch!" he says and cracks a slight smile.

Am I seeing what I think I am seeing? I say to myself. I know I haven't seen him smile since he's been here.

"You smiled." I say as I straighten the bed around him.

"It's barely a smile."

"Well, barely is better than none at all. Vast improvement, soldier. Your bandages will be off soon and you'll be back to a Kool-Aid smile in no time."

He chuckles. "You said *Kool-Aid.*" he adds as if commenting on an inside joke to himself.

"I did."

"Funny."

"I try."

I check Jerusalem's vitals and his heart rate is a bit elevated, but not to the point of true concern. His blood pressure is good and steady. I proceed with mild physical therapy on his arms and hands, and he is responding so well. He has big, strong hands, but they're soft, and kind.

"Be right back," I say, leaving the room. I walk out to the nurses' station and return with my CD player that I had bought from home. I figured I'd take it upon myself to add some culture and feeling to Jerusalem's room. My thoughts are totally off protocol, but I've never been one to follow *all* the rules.

I plug in the CD player and hit play. John Coltrane's "What's New?" begins to play— soothing and mesmerizing.

"What's this?" Jerusalem questions.

"Coltrane."

"You like jazz?"

"No. I breathe it."

"I see."

"What about you?"

"I'm more of a hip-hop head."

"Nice. Jay-Z, Biggie or Nas?"

"Nas and Biggie."

"Sweet. I love John Coltrane and Miles Davis. I hope you enjoy," I say as I begin to massage his arms again.

"I'm sure I will."

"You're coming back to normal so fast. You're really making progress, Jerusalem. Be proud." My hands continue to massage his shoulders and neck area. I can feel his blood flow reacting to my touch.

"Thank you." He says as he turns his head away. I can sense that he's ashamed of being in this situation, so I change the mood immediately.

"You're so brave to do all you do for your country. I thank you for your service and your sacrifice."

His eyes light up, but he still looks away as I raise and lower his arms.

"Young, strong man with the heart of a lion. You are selfless to endure so much. I admire that."

I make my way down to the foot of the bed. His eyes follow my actions even though he tries to act like he is not interested in what I am doing. I inspect his legs and feet. Doubtful eyes oversee my actions. My fingers caress his wounds of war. The doctor was able to remove all the embedded shrapnel from his shins and calves. He's healing beautifully and my fingers linger on the doctor's handiwork.

Lowering the bed, I prop the pillow under his head and back to make sure he's comfortable.

"How does that feel?"

"Okay."

As I make my way back down to his feet, his friend reappears with a huge cup of something and a straw. He says hello again and I return the gesture with a "Hi" of my own and get back to the business of my patient.

Lifting Jerusalem's legs to make sure circulation is functioning normally, I ask, "Feeling okay, Jerusalem?"

"Yes."

I run my fingertips up and down his legs to make sure he can feel my touch.

"Can you feel my fingertips?"

"Yes." He responds in a shy like manner.

"Good." I smile back, acknowledging that my touch has made him a bit uncomfortable. "I'll let you get back to your guest. We'll go out for physical therapy after lunch."

"Okay, but aren't you going to check my face?" Jerusalem inquires nervously.

"Not right now. Besides, I know you're on your way to perfection soon enough." I smile and walk toward to the door.

"Oh, Jill. This is my best friend, LT…I mean, Lawrence. Lawrence Assange."

Lawrence extends his hand to shake mine. "Pleasure's all mine, Jill."

"Thank you. It's nice to meet you, Lawrence."

Today is Theresa's birthday. She's another nurse on the floor. Balloons all around the nurses' station and treats galore are strategically placed within eyesight of every place I turn my head. Funny how when you're watching what you eat, everything you want to eat seems to be watching you. I see those brownie bites to the left and they are digging my flow. They're silently whispering for me to come and have a taste and enjoy because after all, I'm a hardworking woman who deserves a chocolate treat every now and then. I smell the fudge.

Glancing to my right, I witness tiny finger sandwiches, and my favorite—turkey and provolone on rye, and I'm ready for lunch now. In pursuit of a more Zen life and healthy lifestyle, I've managed to give up a majority of animal fat and most sugars as things that I put in my mouth. I'm not quite a vegan, but am a little bit more than a vegetarian since dairy doesn't visit my lips that much anymore either. I feel great because of the life change I have made. That change was more spiritual than anything else. Nevertheless, every now and then, I indulge. When I do, I don't feel bad about it. I know that I have dedicated, what I pray is the last half of my life, and Lord-willing more, to eating right, exercising and taking care of myself and others. Compassion runs through my veins; it's simply who I am. I'm proud of the woman I've become. So slipping into guilty indulgence is a treat I give to myself every now and then.

Taking a paper plate, I grab one of those little pieces of heaven—that turkey and cheese finger sandwich—and make my way down the assembly line of food. I scoop a small portion of salad onto my plate, grab a napkin, and put not one, but two of those fudge brownie bites onto the napkin. I plan to enjoy this sweet and delectable treat.

I hand Theresa a card I made for her this morning. In my spare time, I create greeting cards, with my poetry written inside. I am a poetry fanatic to the core. I love words. I love sounds. So, between poetry and my daily and nightly dose of jazz, I'm content. Both bring my soul to a place of ease. I hope my words bless her. I felt blessed writing them for her.

Donning burgundy scrubs, with pink and white Nike sneakers, Theresa looks up to me, and smiles. I'm five-foot-nine, compared to her plump, round, five-foot-four frame, yet I can feel her appreciation rising to meet me face on. She has a big smile, wide, and carefree and cheeks like a baby. Her bone-straight, jet-black weave compliments her round face well. She's been a pleasure to work with. The flowers I ordered for her should be here soon. She deserves the love. Theresa is probably twenty-plus years older than I am. I'm guessing she's in her mid- to late-fifties and I've learned about the human spirit, patient care and compassion from her. She's been a role model in showing me how to pay it forward.

"Thank you, baby girl!" she yells as she takes the card. "You probably wrote something in here that will make me cry, right?"

I smile. "Perhaps."

"You're so sweet, Jill. God bless you."

"All my love, Theresa. I hope you have a wonderful day."

We embrace and I sit down in front of my laptop and alternate between eating my sandwich and updating Jerusalem's chart.

When I bite into that turkey and cheese sandwich, I felt like Sophia from *The Color Purple* and softly whisper, "I know dey iz a God." Being far removed from meat doesn't take away the fact that it really tastes good, especially when you haven't had any in so long.

The phone rings at the nurses' station and I answer since everyone else is either dealing with patients or socializing with Theresa and giving her birthday greetings.

"Good afternoon, Trauma Center…" I answer in a robotic tone.

"Hey, girl."

"Hey."

"Jill, it's LaLaina."

" LaLaina, why are you calling me at work?'

"I called your cell phone, but it went straight to voicemail."

" LaLaina, that's the idea. I'm at work!"

"Yeah, yeah, yeah…listen, me and Deseree were talking, and—"

"Oh, Lord." My eyes begin to roll as I start to imagine what that could lead to.

"Let me finish. We've decided that you are too tight, too square, too corny, too lonely and too consumed with work."

"Is that right? Well, I love you, too."

"You're going out tonight. It's Friday night and I already know you're not working this weekend. We also know you're not indulging in anything but poetry or jazz or both and a good meal, so we have it all covered."

"Oh my, God…" I take another bite of my tiny sandwich and shake my head.

"Yes, 'oh my, God' is right, Jill. You have to live a little. Have you looked at your rocking body outside of those scrubs lately? The yoga is most definitely paying off, girl."

"I have not."

"Well, you should look at yourself. Oh, and Deseree and I were wondering when's the last time you got some?"

"Got some what?"

"Oh, never mind, Jill. We're picking you up at your house at eight o'clock tonight. No questions, no excuses, just be ready. Wear something hot and sexy and sprinkle it with tight and cute."

I can't help but chuckle. "I guess I have no say so in the matter, LaLaina?"

"No, you don't."

"Okay then, I'll be ready at eight. But I don't want to stay out too late because I have yoga in the morning and I need to go check on my sister and I may want to check on a few patients tomorrow and..."

Click.

"Hello? LaLaina?"

The dial tone greets me on the other end of the phone.

Whenever my two best friends, LaLaina and Deseree, come over, I don't bother locking the door because they never knock. LaLaina even had her own set of keys made. She's the wild one. Deseree isn't as presumptuous and does at least have the decency to knock on the door or call before she comes over; you know, she has manners.

"This is the best I could do," I whisper to myself, as I stand in front of the full-length mirror. I didn't feel like flat ironing my hair, so I opted for a bun. It matches my form-fitting, turtleneck, black dress. Oversized earrings compliment the outfit well—gold with a gold clutch to match. I am wearing black, patent-leather pumps and this is me for the remainder of the evening.

I sit at the center-island in my kitchen and wait for LaLaina and Deseree to arrive. It's eight o'clock and my front door opens.

"Hey, girl, yooo hooo!" LaLaina yells. She is loud and ghetto, but I love that about her.

She walks in wearing a freakum dress—in all red, from the dress to the lipstick to the earrings to the come-and-get-me heels. I'm not sure if LaLaina has a modest bone in her body. She's a size twenty-two, but carries every inch of her skin as if its caviar in motion. She wears a small, cropped natural 'fro and it is a look all her own—a perfect symbol of individuality and pride that demands acknowledgment from all within her view.

Deseree follows behind LaLaina wearing a silver, button-down Ralph Lauren dress that stops right at her knees. She has killer legs and showing them off has always been a smart move on her part. Her hair hangs just below her ears in a fierce bob and the red highlights offset her cocoa-colored skin to perfection. My girls look good tonight.

We all stand, hug, kiss, and make our way out the front door and into my truck. Because I drive a Chrysler Aspen, whenever we all travel together we do it by way of my truck. It's sexy, classy and big and roomy enough to make for a comfortable ride wherever we go.

We pull up to Cocoa Brown's, a spot in New York City known for great soul food, eccentric poets with dope rhymes and beautiful jazz ensembles on key dates each month. Lord knows I'm tired as the day is long, but this should be fun.

The short Mexican man takes my keys as we valet park and make our way into the venue. We frequent Cocoa Brown's a few times throughout the year, usually on nights when jazz musicians own the night with sounds of beautiful saxophones that duet with pianos and bass. It all makes for a beautifully composed evening with poets, their words and vibes feeding our minds, and traditional soul food with a contemporary flair that nourishes our bodies.

By the time we leave this place tonight, we will be satiated and well fed in many senses of the words.

We take our seats and the place is packed. Scented vanilla candles invade my nostrils. I also take notice of a hint of jasmine and lavender in the mix as well; all are pleasing and make for an alluring ambiance. Cabaret style seating has us all close to one another, but it's not overbearing; we're just in tune with each other's rhythm, and immersed in each other's aura. The pulsating vibe that floats between all of us leaves everyone feeling and witnessing a connection that transfers from person to person. Creating a strong and unique energy, one only felt by being in this place and at this time. You have to see it, feel it, touch it, smell it and witness it to believe it.

The waiter takes our drink order and my poison of choice for the night is a chocolate martini. Chocolate is something I'll never turn down for it owns me; I seek it daily in whatever form I can get it and devour it once in my grasp. LaLaina's ghetto ass orders a corona with lime and Deseree puts in an order for an apple martini, plus crab cakes, and onion bloom and Buffalo wings as our appetizer. She looks at me as she places the order, tugs at the server's apron and says, "I forgot, please add on a spinach dip to that for my vegetarian friend." We all laugh.

Maybe it's the energy in the room, maybe it's the strong connection of being amongst my friends, or maybe it's just the lingering memory of his hands when I was massaging them earlier today…but whatever the reason, I think of him…Jerusalem, and wonder how he's doing.

Chapter 9

Jerusalem

It Takes A Village

"**G**et your ass over here now!" she yelled to me.

One of my foster mothers. I despised referring to *her* as a mother. She was nowhere near a mother. She wasn't *my* mother by any stretch of the imagination. My mother was beautiful. She was an angel that left my brother, my father and me too soon.

It's funny how life works. My mother was an only child and my father was an only child, so Jabez and I had no aunts or uncles around to save us from being separated. No one was there to rescue us from the inevitable turmoil that we faced after our parents' death. I think about those years quite often. I can't help, no matter how hard I try, but press rewind on my mind concerning that time. I think about this foster family, this alleged "Mother" in particular. Ironically, I learned some valuable life lessons while in her "care."

Known around the way as Brenda, she had five of us packed like goddamn sardines in a small bedroom. Two sets of bunk beds and one twin-sized bed jammed to fit into that tiny room on the second floor of a three-family home in Newark. This time around,

I was moved to the downtown area, also known as the "Neck of Newark."

Portuguese people occupied this side of town. Their restaurants were on every corner and they owned several bakeries throughout what seemed to be a separate town; a different world from the city of Newark where I grew up. There was community here.

When I was a child, we had more community then, and we lived on a block where Mrs. Johnson, Mrs. Rivers and even Mr. Howard were all of our fill-in, temporary parents while Mom and Dad were away at work. When I was a child, there was still a belief that "It Takes a Village to raise a child," and that mentality pretty much kept us youngins out of trouble.

I remember that village. I remember the Portuguese one. I remember Brenda.

Brenda…

She was not Portuguese, but she loved the men just as much as she loved her pork, rice, potatoes and any other food that would stick to her ribs, her gut, or her arms. Brenda was a heavy-set woman, not built and curvy like I remember my mom to be. Brenda was massive, commanding attention by her presence when she entered a room. She rarely left the apartment because of her size, but that didn't stop her from having all she wanted, including the Portuguese men and the Portuguese bread from the corner bakery. Both of which she over indulged in.

"Jerusalem! Boy, you are way too fast. I can't catch up with your ass, but when I do…I'm gon' beat you 'til the white meat shows!" she yelled. She was so slow. Fat ass.

On this particular day, she was highly upset with all her foster children. Hindsight is always twenty-twenty and as clear as day, so when I really think about this moment, I believe Brenda was out of dick, and perhaps, freshly baked Portuguese rolls.

"Jerusalem!"

"Yes, Miss Brenda?"

"Didn't I tell you to go find Hector?"

"Yes, Ma'am?"

"Well, then…where is he?"

"He said he's not coming today. He's with his woman."

"His what?"

"His woman…he said."

"Oh, he has a woman now, huh?"

"Yes, and she's really pretty too, Miss Brenda. Not like you. She's not loud, either."

"What did you say?"

Miss Brenda had fire in her eyes when I made that comment. But, it was only truth telling. When I look back, I can see why she slapped me into next week.

Pow!

Miss Brenda hit me so hard I saw stars. It was at that moment that I was, reminded, once again, of the power of love or maybe even lust, but I knew then, what I know now, and that is, do not play games with a woman's heart.

Lying in this hospital bed, trying to recover from what the war in Iraq has physically done to me, I believe this time of rest is also a time of healing from the effects of what life has offered me. My mother used to say, "God never gives us more than we can bear." I can hear her saying that and it often repeats, the sound of her voice and the words of wisdom she spoke. I repeat them, "God never gives us more than we can bear." I just wish He didn't trust me so much. Life has been a lot for me to bear.

My mother also said, "If He brings you to it, He'll bring you through it." Well, He's brought me this far, so I suppose I'll get through this. I miss my mother. I miss her words of wisdom, her comfort, her love. I miss her.

I think about her and Dad quite often. Like my nurse Jill, my mother loved jazz music; played it all the time. I never heard her listen to too much else. When she was in the kitchen making homemade biscuits or frying chicken, the memories I have are of her swaying side to side or nodding her head, up and down and she was immersed in the rhythm of the jazz that reverberated throughout the room.

Dad loved to watch Mom. He was so in love with that woman. He would come up behind her and smack her bottom, grab her from behind and kiss her on the side of her neck. She fell so comfortably in his embrace. She would smile—big, and bright—as if she felt the warmth of the sun kissing her on the side of her cheek. Soft giggles would escape her; the love within her laughter would permeate the entire household and we all felt it. I watched the two of them a lot. I saw a buoyant woman in my mother—happiness, joy and contentment were in her eyes all the time. I witnessed the beauty of black love daily. Unlike what we hear about today, I know it was real because I am a product of that love, that black love.

Studying my father paid off for me while in the Neck. Sure, I was only twelve years old, but Miss Brenda sent me to get Portuguese rolls. Stephen joined me. He was another foster kid in the same home as me. We shared the same clothes, the same bedroom and the same chores for Miss Brenda.

When Stephen would tell me about his upbringing, I actually thought he was better off in foster care with Miss Brenda. He was a frail, small Puerto Rican boy. Looked like he hadn't eaten in years. With a drawn in face and skin that was olive in appearance, he was fifteen years old, but you would never know it. My guess is that he was malnourished. I wonder where he is today.

Miss Brenda sent us out to get bread to go with dinner. We only ate the leftover bread, but she kept us fed. In retrospect, and after having been in and out of foster care for so many years, I'd say that Miss Brenda did make sure that we were clean and nourished. For all her flaws and short comings, she at least accomplished those two things when it came to her foster kids.

"Come on, Jay," Stephen yelled. "You know Miss Brenda needs her fresh bread so she can have it with her rice and beans." Anxiety oozed from his worried little mind.

"I know. Hold on!" I shooed Stephen away with my hand because Yelena was staring me down. Yelena was a sixteen-year-old girl from the neighborhood who had been trying to get my attention since I moved into Miss Brenda's house. Blessed with long, thick, black hair and a pair of tits that sat up high, she was stunning for a sixteen year old. Her caramel skin was silky and smooth and I could not take my eyes off her. I often wondered what she wanted with a twelve-year-old boy, but I never had the nerve to ask.

We played the game of staring at one another whenever we ran into each other. She was in high school and I was still in grammar school, so most times, I'd see her in the mornings on the way to school or in the evenings while looking for bread and gathering men up for Miss Brenda to fuck for the night.

Her white shorts were tight and stopped right under her apple-shaped bottom. She wore a soft, pink T-shirt and white sandals. With lavender painted toes, her hair was pulled into a ponytail right on the top of her head. Big MC Lyte gold earrings hung from her lobes and she sucked on a lollipop just like an around-the-way-girl. She was a perfect vision of lust for any boy; myself included.

"Hey, Jay."

"Hey, Yelena. How are you?"

"I'm good. You look nice today."

I smiled, and popped my collar a bit.

"Thanks, so do you."

I turned to look at Stephen's half-dead ass and told him to take everything back to Miss Brenda.

"Stephen, I'll see you at home."

"But…" his mouth was wide open as he tried to protest.

"Stephen, I'll meet you later." I did not take my eyes off Yelena as I spoke.

"Okay."

I walked over to Yelena and she took my hand. I inherited my father's height, so even at the tender age of twelve I towered over the other twelve year olds in the neighborhood. Maybe that's what she found appealing about me."Come over to my house," she said in a soft tone that sent a slight shiver down my spine. Her clear-colored lip-gloss made her lips shine, as she spoke to me.

"Um, aren't you going to get in trouble?" I inquired, as we held hands and walked toward her house.

"No, Papi. No one is home."

She called me Papi. I liked the way her tongue rolled as she said it.

"Okay."

"You play video games?"

"Mos Def."

"Good. I have some."

"Cool."

We entered the first floor apartment where Yelena lived. Bars covered the windows and screen door. I never saw anything like it before. There were also many locks on her front door and my mind wondered if that was to keep people out or in. In hindsight, it was probably a measure for both. The small apartment was very clean and more than a dozen pictures of Jesus and rosary beads hung from the wall units in the dining area. Figurines and statues of the Virgin Mary and other biblical figures were all around the home. It was a very eclectic sight to me: clean, holy, biblical and bars on every window.

She sat me down on the sofa and asked if I wanted anything to drink.

"Kool-Aid, Jay?"

"Sure."

"I like cherry, Jay."

"Me too," I said, as she approached me with a plastic cup full of Kool-Aid.

"You like cherry, huh, Jay?" She kissed me on my cheek.

"Yeah. I just said I did."

Is she dumb? I thought.

"Want to pop my cherry, Jay?"

"What?"

Yelena removed the cheap cup from my hand and placed my hand over her crotch. Even through her shorts, it was warm down there.

"My cherry is here. Do you want to pop it?" She stared me dead in the eyes waiting for an answer.

I felt my senses heighten. Tingling sensations ran through my blood and I felt my body betraying me. I couldn't control what was happening and she knew it. Part of me knew she was counting on my body's betrayal.

"You a virgin, Jay?"

"Why?" I asked her. I did hear guys around my old neighborhood talk, so I knew what she meant.

"Because, if you are I want to be your first."

"Word?"

I was scared shitless. I needed my dad around. I needed to ask him what to do. I wasn't ready mentally, but my body was running around in circles at a hundred miles per hour. My imagination went into overdrive.

"Yeah," she revealed, as she took off her shorts. As they slide down her hips, I saw her thighs and pretty legs. Her skin looked so soft and I could feel a desire in me growing to touch her. Her panties were white lace and she placed my hand on her panties. Told me to take them off her.

"Pull them off, Jay," she demanded in a soft but controlling manner.

I swallowed hard as I followed her every command.

Her panties hit the floor. My heart soon followed. Confused. Anxious. Scared. Excited.

She took off her T-shirt and bra. Her nipples were chocolate and hard which made my heart skip a beat as I looked at them. Tootsie rolls from the corner store that sold penny candy is what I thought about when I saw them. But they did something to me no piece of penny candy every could. Glancing down at my crotch, I saw why I was in so much pain. My penis was rock hard. Solid as a damn rock. Yelena saw it through my jeans. It aroused her. She looked and smiled.

"Papi, that dick is hard for me, already?"

"Yes," I whispered.

"Don't be scared," she told me, helping me to my feet.

Yelena began to take my clothes off. She kissed my lips and neck and the feeling was electrifying. I had never felt so good in all my twelve years of living. The way her tongue danced around my nipples made fluid leak from my penis. She grabbed it. She stroked it. The feeling was so good; I didn't want her to stop.

Yelena got on her knees and placed her clear lip-gloss covered lips around my dick. She sucked it, licked it and loved it, as if it belonged to her. I was going crazy with excitement, as she worked me over like a teacher giving a valuable lesson to her most prized student. She was the teacher. I was the student.

"Let me stop before you come too soon." she rising to her feet.

"Yelena."

"Yes, Papi?"

"That felt so good."

"I know, Papi. Now come with me. Lay on your back on the sofa."

I obliged.

She climbed on top of me and inserted my dick inside her. She guided me every step of the way. I remember her sugar walls gripped my dick so tightly, and her insides were so wet. The room spun hard and fast, and my body jerked. Yelena jumped off me quickly and white liquid gushed from the tip of my young manhood.

She placed her mouth to the eruption and sucked me dry.

Chapter 10

Jill

Jazz

I find myself lost in the flow of the high-hat. It is systemically in rhythm. I'm digging the way ol' drummer boy is fine-tuning his skills tonight on the drums. I feel him. He moves me. That message he's trying to emote. I love how he's not stingy with his vibe, instead he shares it with the other band members on stage. The skills of each musician dances with the others. The saxophonist is fierce as he receives energy from the pianist, and the bass player is simply and utterly amazing. Together, they are unison. Together they are as one. Purely entertainment for us club goers this evening, but I understand what's happening on that stage. Because I understood jazz from an early age, I get that this is so much more than entertainment. It's a way of life.

I'm a jazz enthusiast. A jazz connoisseur. I live, breathe, eat, and sleep all things jazz. Jazz is my husband. Poetry, my lover. We all get along just fine. When I give too much attention to one, the other runs its fingertips up my thigh and sends a gentle reminder to me of why it, too, makes me feel good. Natural highs.

"I bet if you had a child, his name would be Jazz, right, Jill?"

LaLaina questions through alcohol-soaked, crimson-stained lips.

"Probably. But, listen—""Nope," Deseree says, cutting me off mid-speech as she places her hand in front of my face. "You're not going home. In fact, you're not even ready to go home. See, you're not even tired."

"Ha!" I laugh. Getting up from the table, I rise to my feet. "Deseree and LaLaina, I'm simply calling the hospital to check on a patient. I'll be right back."

"Wait a damn minute. You're leaving jazz to check on a patient? Oh, okay, Jill, um, yes, you're going to need a vacation soon. You're pathetic!" LaLaina yells.

"Call me what you want, and like I said…I'll be right back."

I make my way to the entrance of the club. I see it near, but just like with any horizon, it always appears to be close within reach, but in reality, it takes forever to reach the intended destination. I'm still walking and it seems as if the front entranceway escapes me with each step. Maybe I've had too much to drink, or perhaps I'm a bit tired, but I can't get to the doorway fast enough.

The first bar at Cocoa Brown's is on my right and I can see the doorway. Crowds of people surround the bar, and contrary to what the media will have you believe about swarms of black people all gathered in one spot, I believe it's safe to say that there will be no shoot-out this evening. It's all about love, jazz, poetry, drinks and a good time had by all. The crowd is definitely grown and sexy; surpassing the age where having a big mouth and a big gun makes anyone feel like the bigger person.

A tall, chocolate, bald-headed black man rises to his feet as I approach. I pray he isn't a bouncer, needing to card me or ask me anything. As much as I love this venue and what goes on for the hours that I am in attendance, I'm truly a loner at heart, an introvert and I am not quite anti-social, but I have my small circle of friends I'm digging and not really trying to add to that mix.

If it ain't broke…

"Excuse me," he smiles.

Wow, he's incredibly handsome. I'm taken aback.

"Yes?" Brown sugar is physically appealing, but I still have to make my calls.

"I noticed you the moment you walked in. I needed to tell you that you are absolutely stunning," he extends his hand. "I'm

Avery. Avery Washington."

"Nice to meet you, Avery." I return his smile, and take his hand in mind, not wanting this to feel like a *Lady Sings the Blues* moment.

"Do you have a name?"

I chuckle. "I do."

The tall man with the shiny, chocolate, baldhead blushes and smiles hard. He doesn't know what to say, but he's not going to walk away. Not anytime soon, apparently. Part of me wants him to walk away, because I have things to do, but I'm intrigued by his presence. Seduced by his smile.

"Oh, you want to know my name?" I laugh.

"Yes," he laughs along.

I scan him from his tailor-made suit down to the top of his gator shoes. He gets an "A" for effort, but I won't verbally let him know that. I can only pray that my eyes go along with my plan.

"Jill."

"Well, nice to meet you, Jill."

He moves in closer to me.

"Likewise. So, listen, Avery, I'm sorry to cut this short, but I have calls to make. Again, it was a pleasure meeting you."

"Yes, the pleasure is all mine."

I walk away, but I'm not foolish enough to believe that he's not looking at me as I walk away. Feeling intrusive eyes on me, a little extra pep in my step accompanies me on my journey to the front of Cocoa Brown's and I dial the hospital.

The brisk, cool breeze makes me regret my decision to leave the table where LaLaina and Deseree both surrounded me and kept me warm, along with the delicious Brandy Alexander that soothed my taste buds. However, duty calls, and I need to check in on a few patients who require special attention. Don't get me wrong, the nurses I work with are all very capable of attending to our collective patients; I simply know that my level of compassion for a few of them is on high and well, this is who I am.

Standing in the cold, I witness the beauty of an illuminated New York City skyline. It's breezy, but nothing else is as stimulating when compared to this. Taxicabs zoom by and cars ride alongside them, as late night cyclists try to avoid losing a life, as they bob and weave in and out of traffic. The hustle and bustle here is electrifying.

It's late, but the moneymakers, the deal breakers, the movers and shakers are all hurriedly walking by, as if they're going to miss something if they don't keep up with the city's pace.

The phone rings and Tatiana picks up. She's one of the best nurses on the eleven-to-seven shift.

"Hey, T, it's Jill."

"Jill, why are you calling here so late? I'm starting to believe you think we can't do our jobs!"

She laughs, but I think there's an air of truth to her statement.

"I know you can do your job, I just need for you to prop Mr. Williams' pillow behind his head and under his neck. He sleeps better when this happens."

"Uh huh. Anything else, boss?"

"My new patient, Jerusalem Jones."

"Right, the burn victim."

"Right."

"He's so quiet. No television, no lights, nothing. He's a nice man, but he doesn't want anything."

"I know. That's why I'm calling. I left my CD player in his room. Do me a favor and put on disc number two. It's John Coltrane's "Lush Life" and I know it will help to soothe him. In the kitchen, there's some honey chamomile tea in the cabinet. Make him a cup, put lots of honey and some cream in it. Almost make it like a dessert, T, I mean really sweet."

"Girl, you are too much!" Tatiana yells.

"I know. And you know I thank you for this. He'll sleep well. I'm really learning him. But he's going to wither away and die if he doesn't have something there to nourish his soul. Put Coltrane on, and if he says something, you tell him that I said to drink the tea, and listen to Coltrane."

"Aye, aye, Captain!" Tatiana laughs and yells. I can almost see her through the phone saluting me from behind the nurses' station desk.

"Oh, T…"

"Yes, Ma'am.

"Give him a couple of chocolate chip cookies, too. His mouth is just about fully functional. He'll enjoy them."

"Will do."

"Okay, girl. Bye."

"Bye, Jill. Get some rest."

"I will."

Making my way back inside, Avery opens the door for me. I can't believe he waited for me to return. I can sense he wants something, but I don't entertain the thought. I don't know this man from Adam. I walk just slightly past him, as I make my way back into Cocoa Brown's. He takes off his jacket and drapes it over my shoulders. Thank goodness, a man of substance, otherwise this jacket would not fit around my size fourteen frame. I look up at him.

"Thank you so much."

"Cold out there?" he walks with me.

"Yes, sir; it is."

"So, Jill, what do I have to do to get your phone number?"

"Ask."

The corners of my mouth turn upwards in a smile.

"Okay, may I have your phone number?"

"No."

He looks at me with sad, puppy dog eyes.

"I understand."

"I'm just not looking to date right now, Avery."

"Me either."

"You're not?" Confusion masks my face.

"Not really. Don't get me wrong. You're a beautiful woman and I can tell that you are a gracious woman just from being in your presence for only a few minutes. I was captivated when you walked in. However, after talking to you, I'm intrigued, that's all. You're alluring. However, I'm not trying to date. I would love to get to know you though."

"Right."

"Right, what, Jill?"

"Give me your phone."

He hands over his phone and I take it from him.

I input my cell phone number and tell him, "Although I don't believe that excuse, because I love poetry, and that was pretty poetic, I'm giving you my telephone number. Please don't abuse the privilege."

"Well, I am honored and I promise I won't. I'll walk you back to your table and let you get back to your girlfriends."

"Thank you."

We approach the table and LaLaina and Deseree are all smiles, as they see me give Avery back his suit jacket.

"Again, Avery, thank you."

He takes my hand and kisses the top of it.

"Talk soon, Beautiful."

I take my seat and the venue has switched from jazz to poetry and the whistles and chants coming from the crowd hype the situation. I feel butterflies fluttering through my veins, as I'm so ready for some dope wordplay.

My phone rings and I lean in to the middle of the table and softly answer, "Hello?"

"Jill, it's Tatiana."

My heart sinks.

"Is everything okay, T?"

"Yes!"

"Okay, good. What's going on? I'm in New York City at Cocoa Brown's. Can't talk long."

"You got some nerve," she laughs. "Jill, I had to tell you that your patient, Jerusalem…honey, he smiled from ear to ear when I gave him your marching orders. I have never seen him smile! Never! He's killing those cookies and asked for another cup of tea. I swear, I don't know how you do it with these patients of yours."

"That makes me happy, T, thank you."

"No, thank you, Jill."

Oasis Dawn is on stage now and she's one of the most dope poets around. I've seen her perform often and felt I received a treat each time. She never has anything prepared; she simply flows when she gets in her zone. We all wait with anticipation as she takes the mic. She speaks about being in love and yearning for her lover all day and night. She speaks with a fiery-passion that I sometimes wish I had—a real, down, deep longing and love for

someone.
Like a river…she flows.
"your body's
silently
screaming
anxiously
yearning
for me
waking my muse
you try to
defy it
define it
deny it
lie to me
yet
I hear through the roar of your stare
It's moaning
begging loud and clearly
talk
that
shit
to
me
Papi
I'm fluent in the language you speak
I see you
need you
I
can't
reach
you
like you're ten miles away from the sun
I got this real strong need to love you everywhere
and after that
I still won't be done
in my dream I was loving you
every place that you wanted me to
let me take you there
yearning

so thirsty for your power
I feel so weak
thoughts of you are draining me
like It's 4 o'clock in the morning
and I whisper
"I love you"
as I peak…"
The crowd goes wild.
He ate the cookies.

Chapter 11

Jerusalem

The Art of War

And just like that, I was gone. Ghost. I disappeared. I enlisted.

I questioned God for many years while in the foster care system. I wondered why the God Mom and Dad so dearly loved would be so stingy as to take them away from me. Mom and Dad worshipped this God and adored Him amazingly. I remember the days.

We weren't in church seven days a week, but Mom and Dad made sure we knew the Lord. They believed that children who grew up fearing God would become good people. Mom and Dad were good people, so if I had to use them as a benchmark for the truth of their sentiments, then their beliefs were true—God-fearing people are good people. At least my parents were.

After getting in so much trouble at my last foster care home, the State decided that from age seventeen to age eighteen, I would live in a group home. I was terrified at the thought of moving once again. After all, I had been in five different foster homes from the age of twelve, with the last one being the most horrific. My foster mother at the time used me as her personal playboy, her boy toy and while the molestation didn't take place daily, the times it did, left me disgusted for days on end.

I lashed out in high school so much that the high school officials sent me to The Academy; a place for out-of-control students. Those students who disrupted class, stirring up shit non-stop, getting into fights all the time and those who appeared to have emotional issues were all sent there. I think I qualified, at the time, for all the reasons to place me there. Their reasoning in my sentence was justified.

Even in the midst of my terror, and while dealing with my turmoil, I often thought of Mom and Dad—her scent, the beautiful smile on her face and the flowing hair that cascaded down her back, along with my remembrance of him, kept me sane and grounded. I thought about his discipline and everything that he taught me by way of his words and even those lessons he shared in complete silence. I learned so much by the power of his silence. It spoke volumes. He was a decorated officer for the police department and I admired that so much about him. All of the children in the neighborhood loved him and looked up to him.

We walked home from the corner store one day. My father had such a serious sweet tooth. It was ridiculous. I really believe that's the reason why my mother was so good at baked goods. She knew her husband could not control himself when it came to daily and nightly sweets, so she got busy in that kitchen with the best desserts I've ever had in my life. Chocolate chip cookies, sweet potato pie, banana pudding and so many other delights.

"Dad, why did you become a police officer?" I innocently asked while not missing a step along our journey home.

"I wanted to protect the community. I wanted to protect women, beautiful women like your mom. I wanted to protect children, like you and your brother."

He took a bite of his oatmeal cream pie.

"I want to be just like you when I grow up."

"Well, I don't play basketball too good, son."

"I know. I'll be a great basketball player and when I'm too old for that, I'm gonna be a soldier like you."

"Well, I'm not quite a soldier. Just a police officer."

"You're a soldier in my eyes, Dad."

My father grew silent with my last comment.

We continued up the block until we almost made it home. Jabez ran up to us and my father handed him an oatmeal cream pie.

"Thanks, Daddy!" Jabez yelled. My father knew that he had to have something for that boy, with his spoiled ass.

I thought about my brother, Jabez, daily. The State separated us. I asked every single goddamn day where he was. No one knew. Only that he was with a good family. I was happy for him. I wanted it to be me. I wanted us to be together. I missed him. He was all that I had left in this world. He was the only other person on earth who had Mom and Dad's blood running through his veins. I loved him. I needed him. No one would tell me anything. I often wondered if Jabez thought of me. Was he safe at night? I cried a lot. I cried every night. I lashed out every day. He was a beautiful boy. Spoiled rotten and mean as hell, but I loved him. He didn't need to be separated from me. It was too soon. I needed to be there to mold him. To help shape him. He wasn't ready to be on his own.

The day I turned eighteen, I went straight to the Broad Street recruiting office in Newark, New Jersey to enlist. I had dreamed about becoming a decorated officer in the Army. I knew my father was looking down on me and I wanted to be just like him. After my dreams of being the next Magic Johnson shattered like broken glass by foster families who wouldn't even let me shoot hoops after school, I knew I would never go pro. The Army was the next best thing. I could escape this God-forsaken city and the many cities surrounding it where I had lived the past six years and be on my own, and travel the world. I would be on a quest to find Jabez, find me a good wife, raise a family like Mom and Dad did and get back to normal.

Miraculously, LT and I managed to keep in touch throughout the years even while I was in foster care. We never managed to end up at the same school, but he never gave up looking for me and he never let me spend one Christmas alone and he never forgot my birthday. I attended Central High School way across town, while LT attended Ridgefield High. His school recruited talent who were good in sports from the local grammar schools. I begged and pleaded to go there, but my foster mother never heard a word I said. My caseworker's load was so heavy that when she made her once-a-year appearance, she didn't even know my name.

I would stay after school some days and wait for LT. He knew that on most nights I wouldn't get enough to eat, so he would catch the bus over to my high school and we'd go out to eat at Sherry's on Clinton Avenue. Italian cheeseburgers and fruit punch are what we had most days, and we talked shit until it was time for me to head home. I wanted to cry every time I left LT, but I didn't. I kept my tears on the inside. I knew Mom and Dad had sent my best friend my way to keep me as safe as he could. It is upon reflection that I know the power of the Lord. Although I've had the life from hell, He blessed me with LT. I also realize that as bad as things were, it could have been so much worse.

"Yo, LT, you find anything on Jabez?" I asked as I took a bite of my cheeseburger.

"Nah. Last I heard, he had been adopted by that family. He is not in foster care anymore."

"Are you serious?"

"Yes, Jay, I'm sorry, Bro."

"No worries."

LT looked at me as if he could sense that I had died another death. I'm sure it was written all over my face…the look of defeat.

"Jay, we'll find him. I ask around all the time. My mother is asking, too."

"Thanks, man."

LT reached in the pocket of his varsity jacket and pulled out an envelope. He handed it to me. I wiped my hands, as ketchup covered my fingers, and took a quick sip of my fruit punch.

"What's this?"

"My mom wanted you to have this. She tries."

"How's your mom doing, LT?" I'm not sure if I really wanted the answer. LT's mom had struggled with emotional issues, as we grew older in our teens. Not sure if it came from the pressures of being a single mom or the fact that she had no husband. I never asked why.

I looked inside the envelope and there were two twenty dollar bills inside.

"Man, I can't take this."

"Take it, man. That fucking foster care family ain't doing right. Hide this. Use it for food, socks, whatever you need, man."

"Okay, man, but I promise, when I get older, I'll pay you back."

LT took off his varsity jacket. He handed it to me.

"Here, man, it's getting cold out, Jay. Take this."

"I can't."

"Take it. Coach will get me another one."

"Thanks, LT."

We continued eating Italian cheeseburgers and drinking fruit punch. I felt like shit, but it also felt like Christmas, getting that jacket and that money. I knew, at that moment, that I had enough to eat in case things at the foster care home had gotten any worse. I also knew that I'd be warm for the impending winter.

The military…

I was caught taking food out of a local bodega and it wasn't the first time. The judge gave me a choice: join the military or serve eighteen months in jail for petty theft. The judge didn't buy my defense, but I told him, "Hunger will make thieves of us all, Your Honor."

God bless LT and God bless that judge who reminded me of who I was at the core and that I needed to somehow follow in my father's footsteps.

Sitting in the chair, alongside the window, I think about LT and he walks in. I must have conjured him up with daydreams about our teens. He walks over, and gives me dap. I look out the window; the leaves have changed on the trees. Burnt orange and warm brown leaves take the place of ones that were once lush green. There's nothing like those beautiful fall colors on the trees and the leaves that fall to the ground. The air is crisp outside, I imagine. Many good fall seasons growing up in Newark. LT was there. We had good times out in those streets before life changed.

Life is ever evolving…

"Wait! You're out of the bed. And what is this you're listening to?"

"Ha. Ha. Yes, I am sitting up. How about that?" I smile as I look up at LT. He stands beside me. He helps me out of the chair.

"Look at you standing up, Jay," LT says with delight.

"I'm getting stronger. I'll be kicking your ass in some one-on-one soon enough out there on those courts."

"You wish," LT smirks.

"Listen, pretty boy…we're getting older now. Besides, those looks ain't never saved you from my wrath on the court. Get ready."

"I'll be ready, soldier. So, what's this you're listening to?"
I smile.

"Oh, jazz. My nurse makes me listen to music. Man, she won't let me sit here in the dark anymore."

"Ha, ha! Good. I like this nurse. Which one?"

"Jill. The tall one out there. Pretty curly hair."

"Oh, she's fine!"

"Yeah, you stay away. She seems to be a good girl, LT. Don't corrupt her."

LT has always been a ladies' man. From the early teen years to when he went pro, and all the years in between; even up until this day, LT loves the women. Always had, always will.

"No, not at all. I'm just saying…"

"Well, don't say, LT."

"Wait, Jay?"

We look at one another.

"Nah, LT. I'm good. She's my nurse, that's it."

"You like her, don't you?"

"NO! Man, I'm trying to get my face fixed and get up outta here." I lean on LT, as my leg is a bit weak.

"Here, Jay, sit down."

LT helps me to my seat. I'm really happy about the progress I've made in therapy. I can feel myself getting stronger day by day. I'm on my feet, strong, walking and I do feel like there is light at the end of the tunnel.

"You're doing well, Jay."

"Thanks, man. Long time coming. Can't wait to get out of here."

"What are you going to do once you get out?"

"Get a job. Find Jabez."

"Still no word?"

"No. I stopped looking. I was fed up. I was over in Iraq for two tours. I couldn't do much while I was there, but now it's a different story."

"I haven't heard anything, Jay, I'm sorry."

"I'm gonna find him. Mark my words."

"What type of work are you looking for?"

"Not sure. I hope the government takes care of a brother. I've heard some horror stories and seen some as well. We fight for this country and some of us end up homeless. I remember I couldn't wait to go to the army and do the right thing. I wanted to serve like my dad did in his own way. Now my face is all fucked up, I can barely walk, so I better have something coming my way for all I've done. I know you heard about Congress being in a dead-heat. Soldiers dying and their families couldn't get the money from the military to cover funeral expenses because the country is divided? It's a shame. The government shutdown. I pray they take care of me."

"No doubt."

"Sergeant Killen, a brother I served with on my first tour, has PTSD. I heard he's living on the streets."

"Man, that's a damn shame."

"I know. Tell me about it."

The smell of something intensely sweet captures my senses and breaks my attention. I feel her. I sense her. I smell her. Jill.

She walks up behind LT and speaks to him.

"Oh, how are you? Checking in on our soldier, huh?"

Her voice sounds like an angel.

"Yes, Ma'am. He's doing well. Thank you for taking such good care of him."

"That's my job."

She leans over to me, and hands me a hot cup of tea.

I reach for it. I smile.

"Your smile is getting wider, soldier. Your face must be making miraculous recovery under that bandaging."

"Yes. I can feel that it is."

"I made it sweet just like you like it."

"Thank you." I can't manage to speak too much around her. I don't know if I'm nervous or afraid, but I keep the conversations minimum with Jill unless she questions me. She does have her moments where she questions me to the point of forcing me to open up, even if just a little.

"Jill, thank you for getting Jay out of that bed and into this chair. I'm digging this music you have him listening to."

Jill props the pillow behind my back and rubs my shoulders softly. I pretend that I don't enjoy her touch.

"Music is good healing for the soul. Excuse me, what's your name again?"

"Lawrence. LT for short."

"That's how I know you! Aren't you a sportscaster?"

"Yes. Thanks."

"Your career was cut way too short. I'm a Giants fan myself, so you playing for the Jets and all don't mean much, but I was sorry to see you get cut so soon."

Ouch. Not sure how LT is going to take that. She has a bit of spunk in her blood, I see. *Sports fanatic maybe?* Her approach was sweet, but tough. The same way she's been with me. The grace of a ballerina, just like my mother. Beautiful upon sight, but has an air of toughness about her. Wonderful combination.

"Yes, Ma'am, I was cut way too soon." LT moves away and looks out of the window. He mentally licks the wounds of his failed pro career in silence.

Jill gets closer to my face and checks my eyes. Her soft brown eyes are shaped like big almonds and mine can't help but swim in hers. Her curls dance a jig around her honey-coated face. Her soft hand rubs the unbandaged side of my face. Her hand travels down my arm and across my chest. I can feel my heart beat faster.

"Your skin is warm. Do you feel okay?"

"Yes."

"Open wide. Let me take your temperature."

"Ah…"

She pulls out the thermometer and smiles. "You're good, soldier. Healing quite nicely."

"When will he get out of here?"

"Soon, LT. We don't want him out there too quickly. But soon."

"Cool. Time for my boy to start to live his life."

"I agree, LT. Just let me have him a lil while longer to fix him up."

"You got it. And, thanks again for taking such good care of my friend."

"It's my job."

Chapter 12

Jill

You Don't Know What Love Is

I dread Thursdays. Every Thursday, my parents request my presence for lunch or dinner. These two people procreated and birthed me and I'll forever be grateful to the Creator for the gift of life. I've never been terribly religious, and I'm sure that has something to do with Mother and Father pretending to keep up with the Joneses, even in a Catholic church every Sunday at 9 a.m., Janet and I were dressed to perfection. Mary Jane shoes on our feet, exquisite bows in our perfectly brushed hair and the best dresses Mother's money could buy. Her and Father showed us off every Sunday to their highfalutin' friends.

I respect my parents; they worked hard to get where they are in life. Mother's father was a white man who disowned her and my black grandmother, but when he died, he left Mother a fortune. I suppose the guilt of abandoning your brown, love child got the best of him and the only way he thought to repay her was to give her part of his fortune. My Mother never recovered from the rejection, I don't believe. She took the old man's money and made some very smart moves, including purchasing the beautiful estate in Nyack, New York, where I grew up.

She also invested in my father.

My father has always been a wannabe. Granted, he is a lawyer, and a damn fine one at that, but rumor has it that my mother groomed him and molded him into the man he is today. Not hard to believe. She's aggressive that way. He filled her need, her void to have the perfect family. My father looks the part. Exceptionally handsome, the Creator lined the stars up in harmony when he was born. Although in his fifties, Father could pass for forty, easily. Curly cropped hair and a tall, slender frame, his salt and pepper goatee turns the heads of women of all ages when we're in public. He has that soft, rich and buttery skin, the tone of butter pecan ice cream—light but not too bright, his hue fits him well. If he would only come out of that rigid shell and live a bit.

So caught up in the aesthetics of every damn thing, they both fail to live.

I lost respect for them slowly as I was growing up, based on their actions and their reactions to almost every situation. The nail in the proverbial coffin for me was how they whisked Janet away. I'll never forgive them for it. Never!

The only reason they have me over once a week is for the looks of it. How would the neighbors and their country club associations feel about them disowning one daughter and being embarrassed about the other? My role here is for show and show alone.

I'm proud of the fact that I'm a nurse in an urban environment who takes care of veterans who have sacrificed their lives for us on a daily basis. But no, that's not good enough for Mother and Father. When I am here for dinner, and their friends stop by— something their friends do every week while I am here—for the whole show and tell thing, Mother always makes it a point to tell the neighbors that I am going back to school one day to become a doctor. I used to disrupt the flow and correct her until Father put me in my place about the shame it would cause the family should they know that my career stops at being a nurse in the ghetto. I would further shame Mother and Father if the neighbors were to find out that I love to write and recite poetry and that I am a jazz enthusiast. Little does Father remember that my love of jazz came from him, at least in part.

When Mother was at work, running one of her corporations,

Father would be at home blasting Miles Davis and Charlie Parker. I listened. I learned. I fell in love with it. Father loved it, too. She caught him one day and told him to turn it off. She replaced it with classical music. He listens to classical now.

"How's work, Jill Marie?"

"Great, Mother."

"That's good to hear," my father interrupts.

I take a bite of the poached salmon in white wine sauce. The maid, Carolina, pours another glass of wine for me. "Thanks, Carolina."

"You're welcome, Jill Marie."

"So, thought about any medical schools, Jill?" Father questions.

"No." I continue picking at my salmon without raising my head.

"But, you're still interested in becoming a doctor, right?"

"Right now, I'm very happy taking care of my patients. I'm going to take a vacation soon in order to write some poetry and listen to jazz and study the history and origins of the genre."

Mother chokes on her wine.

"You what?" she yells.

"Yes, Mother. I'm even thinking about going back to school to study Cultural Arts and minor in Jazz. It's fascinating."

"You're just going to continue to waste your life away, is that it?"

"Mother, I'm in my thirties and I'm doing fine. I'm sorry you don't approve."

"I'm very proud of you, Jill. I just want to see you do better with your life," Father chimes in.

"I've never been pregnant. I've never even smoked a cigarette! You two are pathetic! I graduated college in three years with a 4.0 GPA! How about this…the next time we meet for dinner, we meet at the assisted living facility where you have thrown my sister away like last week's trash!"

"Watch your mouth, young lady! You're out of order!" Mother yells.

"NO! You're out of order!"

Carolina tries to diffuse the situation and pours water for everyone. She makes a lot of noise and the short, stout, older Spanish woman who has been my mother's maid for God only knows how long, tickles me.

"So, next week, you're going to spend time with your daughter, Janet…remember her?"

They both look at me as if I have two heads.

I get up from the table and take my purse in hand. I make my way out to the huge, mahogany doors and head to my truck. I don't look back; I simply get in, and speed off.

Tears flood my face, flowing faster than I can wipe them away. I'm having trouble seeing the traffic before me so I pull over. Coltrane's "You Don't Know What Love Is" plays and the song is more than appropriate at this moment. I can't stop crying. I hate my parents, but I love my parents because they are…my parents. I wish there was something I could do to change their mentality, but that would be like trying to conjure an apocalypse and I simply don't have the power to do that. They've managed to feed those deadly sins they wear like badges of honor and they feed those beasts daily on every level imaginable.

It's one thing to be convicted and firm in your beliefs in life; I certainly am and I don't back down too often from them, but then it's a completely different thing to be convicted and dead ass wrong. Mother and Father are totally fucking wrong. They have been for a very long time.

I pray for their souls.

Arriving at the assisted living facility where my sister Janet resides, I smile as I get out of my truck. She would die laughing if she knew what I just did to Mother and Father. They deserve it. Mother is a fake, Father is a spineless bastard, I am their child and that's incredibly sad and extremely funny at the same time. I thank the Creator that I didn't turn out like either one of them. Who I am today can be attributed to the Creator having His way with me. I am poetry in motion, an iconoclast who loves to challenge the status-quo, who loves to break the rules when they need to be broken and reexamined. I love life and I want people to live life to the fullest. Free-spirited, yes, and proud of it. Very proud.

My hair is wild today. A natural, big, Pam Grier afro that is starting to hang a bit because of the length. I have a white lily pinned in over the right ear. The mascara I put on this morning left my lashes full, thick, and luscious, but because of the tears, I am now cleaning my face. I laugh as I look in the mirror – me resembling a raccoon. I see my mother's eyes. They are big and bold. I wear Father's skin very well. I am their child. By design. I am their child.

I reach Janet's room, and she smiles as I stand in the doorway.

"You look beautiful, Sister," she says, as I approach her and kiss her on the cheek.

"How are you feeling?"

"Good today, Jill. Loving the new menu. I do miss Carolina's cooking, though."

"I just saw Carolina."

"How is she?"

"Good."

"Mother and Father?"

"Oh, Janet. They are Mother and Father. Have they been by?"

"No."

"Well, I'm here. Look what I have?" I pull a Snickers from my purse.

"Yes!" Her eyes light up like a Christmas tree.

I look at Janet sitting in that wheelchair. Her dark brown hair hangs low, almost to her waist. That's what happens when black women leave their locks alone. It flows. She's dressed in one of the sweat suits I bought her last week. She loves those pink and white Nike's, too. She's still beautiful, even as she ages, and even in that wheelchair.

I admire her courage. She faces so much rejection daily— mainly from her body—but she's always so upbeat; even with a mind that doesn't work at the best capacity. She has the spirit of the Creator in and throughout her.

She's one hell of a woman. My sister.

I break it off and give her half and she begins to eat her half, just like we did when we were little girls. We would sneak out to the back sunroom and the deck and would hang out there at night and eat chocolate. Carolina would clean us up before we came back inside so Mother wouldn't have a hissy fit about the chocolate and the fact that we would gain weight if we ate too much of it.

Life was good back then.

Chapter 13

Jerusalem

So What?

"Come on, Mr. Jones, only five more steps left." The physical therapist tells me. He practically yells those words to me. I think, *easier said than done*, but I don't say the words aloud, I simply think them. This physical therapy has been going on for weeks now and is getting the best of me. Funny how life works out, though. Simple things like walking we take for granted with each step, yet, I'm learning how to walk again and while gaining strength with each step, this shit is hard. I've always been a strong man; I learned how to be the best kind of man from the best kind of man out there, my father. Shrapnel in my legs and being in a hospital bed so long have made this otherwise strong man, very, very weak, in body and in spirit.

"Soldier, two more steps left!" Phil, my physical therapist yells. The look in his eyes is one that is familiar to all soldiers. It's the eye of the tiger. We all possess it. He wants to make sure I don't lose it. Sweat drips from my forehead and my nose as I make these steps. Just a few weeks ago, I stood on my two legs like a stroke patient. Wobbly and unstable is what I was, and I could not walk on my own. Today, I am walking and climbing stairs. And while in my teens I may have questioned the presence of the Lord, but at this moment—walking, climbing, regaining the eye of the tiger—I know, without a doubt, that God is real and ever-present in my life.

His jet-black hair lays flat on the top of his head. When we first started this session, he had it moussed up, or whatever it is that white boys do to get that Tom Cruise look. He has those blue eyes the women in this place seem to love. He's tall, and from miles away, you know that Phil is a soldier. It's undeniable. Hard to explain with any real rhyme or reason, it's just one of those things that are obvious upon first glance.

His hair, after our sessions, is usually in shambles. Normally, a man would not notice this about another man, but the difference in Phil is like night and day. Cracks me up every time.

He's strong enough to lift me when I fall, which I haven't done since the early weeks of being here. I'm normally average about two hundred thirty pounds at six-foot-two, but since being here, I believe my last weight-in was about two hundred ten pounds. But I'm not complaining. Jill has been getting on me about eating more and I so desperately want to tell her that it's somewhat hard to eat with half of my face bandaged up, but I don't say a word to her. She's tough. She's passionate. She has earned my respect. I simply do the best I can, and honestly, my best is not good enough for her. She demands more.

Her not so subtle demands have me where I am today. I must attribute credit to her. Although she is not a physical therapist, she pops in here during physical therapy to coach me along. She's like a cheerleader in addition to being a nurse. She yelled when I fell, and helped to get me off the floor. When I couldn't get up and was so weak, she got the wheelchair for me and helped Phil to place me in it. When we returned to the room, she rubbed me down. It was at this time that Jill started to give me hot tea and made me listen to John Coltrane. She would stay after her shift was over, sit in my hospital room, and read books to me—poetry mainly. She did read a couple of cheesy romance stories that I fell asleep on.

Jill kept opening the blinds to let in the sun. For the first few weeks, I didn't want any sunlight in; I just wanted to sit in the dark. I didn't watch TV. I didn't eat. I was simply a rock on grass, only wanting to think about the people who meant the most to me—Jabez, Mom and Dad. I was often haunted by the Iraqi children I saw being blown up as casualties of war. Nightmares greeting me nightly and during my afternoon naps about my brothers—those fallen soldiers who came home in pine boxes. I may have lost my will to live a time or two, but then she happened. Jill. She gave me hot tea. Sweet hot tea. She read me poetry. She played jazz. She got in my face. She yelled. She rubbed my legs. She catered to my wounds. She nourished my body and my soul. She brought me back to life with words and sounds.

This last step is torture and I am having trouble making it.

"Come on, Soldier! You got this!" Phil yells. He yells so loud. I'm tired now.

"Come on, Son!" You can make it!" Dad yelled as we ran. Every summer, Dad would take Jabez, LT, and me to Weequahic Park in Newark. It was huge to me as a kid. Dad trained there. No gym, no fancy treadmills, nothing like that. He'd use the outdoors to get the body he wanted. At a very young age, he taught us the power and importance of physical fitness.

"Dead Man's Hill" in Weequahic Park was steep. Dad trained daily in eighty-degree heat sometimes, to conquer that hill. LT and I, along with Jabez, also accepted his challenge to conquer Dead Man's Hill. We would need to run up the hill to complete our session for the day. The hill had three-hundred-feet of incline surrounded by trees and grass. It was a man-made path, with no benches or rest areas in sight.

Dad was already at the top of the hill as he showed us how to run it and pace ourselves to reach the top without stopping. Jabez made it to the top shortly after Dad, standing with that stupid smirk on his face. He always had to be in first place with his spoiled-rotten ass. He smirked and chuckled as I struggled to get to the top. LT was right ahead me, out of breath, but he made it.

"Come on, Son!" Dad yelled, as I was about a third of the way there.

I wanted to give up.

"Come on, Soldier!" Dad screamed. "Pace yourself! Don't look at the road, look at me!"

I looked up at him and didn't pay attention to the road. I stared at him as I slowly, but surely, climbed Dead Man's Hill.

"Eye of the Tiger, Son!" he yelled and reached out for me. He didn't move forward or change his position to make it easier for me; he simply reached his hand forward and yelled, "Eye of the Tiger, Son! Come on, you got this, Jay! Look at me; don't look at the obstacles before you! Look at your father!"

Once again, I looked up at Dad. He was within reach. I made it to the top of the hill and grabbed his hand. He grabbed me by the top of my neck and hugged me.

"I love you, Son. Remember, when the road of life gets rough, don't look at the hurdles before you look at the light at the end of the tunnel. If you don't see a light, look for God." He told me those words. They ring true to me at this moment.

"Jerusalem Jones, Soldier, Iraq war veteran and hero! Take that last step! Take it now! You're so close to victory!"

Jill appears at physical therapy. She's wearing dark framed glasses and her hair is pinned up with ringlets hanging around her face. Burgundy scrubs and pink Nike's complement her appearance.

"Soldier?" she questions.

"Yes!"

"Are you gonna take this last step or are you going to give up?"

"Taking the last step!" I yell, out of breath, ready to take a nap.

"Then take the last step!" Jill orders.

Phil supports my back, holding it slightly. He's pushed me incredibly hard today. Instead of wondering why and wallowing in self-pity, I take the last step. I see Dad at the top of Dead Man's

Hill. I see his hand reaching for mine. I look at Jill. I see her determination for me. She's taken this on as her own challenge. I hear her words.

"You're a soldier, Jones. Last step!" she whispers that in my ear as I climb the last step.

"That's it, Jones. There's nothing in this life that you cannot conquer." she continues to whispers to me.

The other physical therapist comes over with a wheelchair and I prepare to sit in it.

"No, Jerusalem, we're walking back to your room," Jill tells me.

I want to cry.

She takes me by my arm and walks slowly with me. A hospital gown with sweats and sneakers adorn my body, and my face is half-bandaged as I walk down the hospital corridor. It is the first time in months I've walked this far and practically on my own. Part of me feels a sense of embarrassment by how I look, but that part gets suckered punched by the sense of accomplishment that I have with each step I take.

Jill wipes beads of sweat off my face and holds me securely. Standing next to her, I never realized how tall and statuesque she is. She has to be about five-foot-nine and smells like a piece of heaven. I inhale deeply, becoming intoxicated by her smell and her determination to help me over one more hurdle.

"You did well, Soldier," she says in a soft, calm voice. "You did well and I'm proud of you."

I smile. "Thank you."

We make it to my room and I see a White Castle's cup with a straw on the table. It must be LT.

"Yo! LT!" I yell for him, as I don't see him in my room.

"LT is not here, soldier," she tells me.

"Oh, but I see the White Castle's cup."

"Large chocolate shake."

"Oh?"

"I got it for you on the way in today. I know how much you love them."

I smile. "You didn't have to."

"I know."

"Why did you?"

"Because you love them; right?"

"Yeah, I do."

Jill escorts me to my bed, props my pillows and sits me down. Slowly and gently, she removes my sneakers and sweatpants and begins to rub my legs down with force yet with finesses. She covers me with warm blankets she had delivered by a nurse's aide.

"Thank you, Candy. Please bring in Jerusalem's lunch."

Candy brings my tray and Jill sits that in front of me on the table next to the chocolate shake.

"You have one hell of a sweet tooth, Jerusalem," she smiles.

"I do."

"I'll give you some time to eat and then I'll be back to read to you."

"Okay."

She stops by her CD player and puts on some jazz.

"Jill?"

"Yes?"

"Who's this you're playing for me today?"

"Miles Davis, the *Kind of Blue* album. The first song is "So What?""

I smile.

"You'll love it."

"I'm sure I will."

I watch Jill as she leaves my room. She's curvy, honey-coated and passionate about what she does. Not pretentious in the least, just genuinely sincere. She fills out those nurse's scrubs to perfection and while I take my head out of the gutter, I enjoy a bit of Miles Davis, a chocolate shake, warm blankets and remember the eye of the tiger.

An hour later, Jill resurfaces.

"How are you feeling, Soldier?"

"Actually, pretty good."

"Good. You have to meet with the plastic surgeon again this

afternoon."

"Not looking forward to it."

"Why?"

"I don't know."

"Well, don't be nervous or scared. He's going to get you looking like your old self again. He's extraordinary. You'll be on your way out of here in no time."

I don't respond. The thought of someone else tampering with my face is hard to deal with.

"Why Miles Davis today?" I change the subject and question my stunning nurse.

"Because he is one of the masters. The first song "So What?" is how you have to look at this phase of your life right now. So what, you got injured in the war. You made it through. So what, you have to deal with physical therapy. You're walking again. So what, you have to have plastic surgery, you still have a face. If you listen to the song, you'll notice Davis is able to give the piece periodic lifts in color and tension level. His horn is almost saying, "So what." That's how you must view life right now, Jerusalem. Lift…peaks and valleys because one without the other is neither and just like any hardships you've overcome in life, so too will you get through this."

I smile and sip my chocolate shake.

"I'm digging Coltrane and Davis."

"Good boy."

She smiles, rubs my hand and gets up to walk away.

Chapter 14

Jill

Spiritual

I've discovered that no matter what life hands my way, regardless of what lies before me—the hurdles, the trials and tribulations—somehow, some way…jazz seems to soften the blow. The blows have been many—some light to the body and some hard, strong, fierce and unrelenting, yet—I've managed to persevere. *Was it the jazz that got me through it all?* I'd be safe to say that my Creator was responsible for bestowing an abundance of grace and mercy on me, but the jazz, the soothing melodies singing sweet rhythms and calming narratives into my soul, supported the efforts.

John Coltrane's "Spiritual" plays loudly throughout my home. The surround sound in my bedroom is set up so that even if I'm downstairs in the kitchen, I can enjoy the sounds of the greats: Coltrane, Davis, Mingus, Ellington and even Red Garland, the Tenor Conclave and the others who've made this genre exceptional. This Coltrane piece, in particular, speaks to me today, as it is appropriate for where I am in life on the journey the Creator has given me.

I cherish this life. New chapters abound.

Around the age of thirty-five, I took a hard look in the mirror and began introspection; a journey into my soul, an honest, in-depth look at my spirit, and what I discovered was liberating. I needed to get my spirit, soul and body on one accord and in order for me to do that, I needed to remove toxicity from my existence and I did just that, by any means necessary.

Tossed by the wayside, and thrown out like two-day old trash, were toxic people, toxic places, and toxic things. Along with that, I threw parts of my spiritual anatomy into the proverbial compactor because I knew that in order for me to grow, in order for me to become what I believed the Creator intended for me to be, I needed to get out of my own way. That's probably the hardest part of self-discovery, realizing that we don't have all the answers and oftentimes we are our own biggest enemies, our own problems. I've learned too that many times in life, we have solutions and we're looking for problems when in reality what we need to be is simply be…to live life and go with the flow. It's the best way to be, to live our best lives is to fight like hell to get to a place of Zen.

Not a fan of organized religion, and I make it a habit to stay clear of church folks, I am very spiritual and apply biblical principles to my life daily. A woman may fall many times, but she's only considered a failure when she accuses someone of pushing her. I've never been pushed. I will never fail. Everything I've been through in life, all that I have endured, has transformed me into everything I am; including those stumbles and falls. Those value in the valley moments, when a soul has to be refined, of which I place no blame, has made me stronger, wiser and better, and continue to provide strength and life lessons that can only come from having been taught by trial and error. I chose a life that chose me. It includes failures, victories, and that yin and yang that makes life flex up and down in rhythm to keep a person humble and in proper alignment. It has peaks and valleys, joy and pain because one without the other is neither. It is that sweet victory that lies ahead awaiting my grasp because I've acknowledged what it took to get me here, including getting out of my own way... I am the sacrifice and I'm a woman behind mine.

I'm at the part of Coltrane's "Spiritual" where he goes to work on the saxophone. The crescendos he delivers in most of his work always provide a pivotal height and climax for me. Today, it serves as the point in my routine where I plank the floor. Planking is something I dislike. No actually, I hate planking, but I've added it to my in-home yoga workouts and even my strength training.

I grew up with a mother who was slender and petite to a degree and a father who is exceptionally good-looking. I, however, was blessed or cursed—depending on your views and perspectives in life—with what I think was passed down to me through genealogical lineage. Blessed seed, indeed, I carry the weight of my ancestors in the fullness of my lips and in the heaviness of my hips.

Depending on the day, and the shoes I have on, I am five-ten or five-nine. And, I'm a perfect fourteen on my very best day, but a sixteen sometimes and in most realities. Mother stayed on me like white on rice about my size as I became a teen. I pray to the Creator that she never meant to hurt me with her judgmental views on my size, but when those words come from the mouth of the woman who birthed you, it stays with you long after the blows are delivered.

I expected to hear things from outsiders; it's simply how our society is designed. Hearing it from Mother changed the game for me. She's probably the reason why food and appearance has been such an issue with me for most of my life. Through introspection, I came to realize that I am wonderfully made as I refer to Psalm 134 and that many women nowadays are paying to get what the Creator has blessed me with naturally—full lips, full breasts, long legs and full hips. I have pounds to lose, but I'm not trying to. Spirit, soul and body, attempting to get that all on one accord assures me that I am on a mission to gaining health as opposed to losing anything, in particular, my weight.

Heading to the shower, I remove sweat-soaked clothes and look at myself naked in my bathroom mirror. I like what I see. Triple-D-cup breasts don't sit up as they used to when I was twenty-one, but they work for me. Turning on the shower, I can smell the jasmine incense and vanilla candles that I lit earlier in the day; placed all around my house to keep the atmosphere calm.

Avery Washington. He's tall, handsome and throughout our phone conversations, seems to be a decent guy. I am equipped with the knowledge that all men who approach me are looking to reach the promised land as quickly as possible, so while I accepted his invitation for dinner this evening, after he asked multiple times, I know what he wants, and he ain't getting it, unless of course, I want it equally.

I know my worth…

Mr. Washington wants to meet at JE's Restaurant in the heart of downtown Newark. It's classy, with a sister who plays the hell out of the piano. I do hope he made reservations or else there's going to be one hell of a wait on this Saturday night. Nice spot, his selection shows he has nice taste.

Actually, Mr. Washington wanted to pick me up, but it's way too soon for him to know where I live and to be comfortable enough to be in my home.

It's a brisk early-winter night, so I opt for a long sleeve Bodycon dress in a beautiful plum color that stops at my knees and hugs all my curves. Very understated in its design, but these dresses are meant to allow the body to speak. A bohemian multi-colored necklace that hangs to the top of my breasts with a matching bracelet is really all I need. I braided my hair in big braids with coconut oil and curling crème, and sat under my dryer for an hour. When I took the braids out, I had a big curly mess on top of my head. A run through it with my fingers, which gave me the perfect look that I was looking for. Soft pink lip-gloss, a little mascara, my faux fur mink jacket, and it's a wrap.

I get out of my champagne-colored Chrysler Aspen truck and park just across the street from the restaurant. I put quarters into the parking meter, enough for two hours of fine dining, and make my way across the street. On either side of me, I see a sneaker shop and a men's suit shop, all with designer suits in the window. The location screams of the eclectic nature of Newark. Something for everyone.

Spotting Avery standing in front of the restaurant waiting for me, I walk toward him with a smile.

"Well, hello, beautiful girl."

He smiles back. He looks sharp in a lavender, button up and black slacks. He has a mean shoe game going and his watch spells class.

"How are you?" I smile and lean in to hug him.

"I'm great. So happy you decided to give this brother a chance."

"You got it."

Wow, he smells good.

Avery holds the door open and tells the hostess that he has a reservation for "Doctor Avery Washington for two."

"This way, Doctor Washington."

I didn't know he was a doctor.

"You left out that little detail, *Doctor Washington*," I say, as I take my seat.

"I was saving things for us to talk about." He smiles.

"I'm a nurse."

"I'm a Ph.D. in Africana Studies. I work at the University of New York."

"Impressive."

"Do you like soul food, Jill?"

"Most definitely. I've been here before. Not in a long time, though."

"I love their short ribs."

"I think I'm going to have the roasted chicken, Avery. That looks good."

"Whatever you want. I want you to enjoy yourself."

"I know I will." I smile.

The server comes to our table and she looks at Avery and smiles. She dismisses me with a quickness that I often see in black women. We inherently hate one another. The divide is historical, it is societal, and it comes from generations of us not being good enough on so many levels. That hate, we're born with it, and it's sad. It's generational.

"Would you like to start off with drinks?" the server asks.

"Sure. The lady will have…" Avery looks to me.

"I would love a Brandy Alexander."

"Nice choice, Jill." He smiles at me and looks at the server.

"I'll have Crown Royal on ice."

"Great. I'll be right back with your drinks."

Avery looks at me like a man who likes what he sees. He is making me blush on the inside, but I don't reveal that to him. He rubs the top of my hand.

"Thank you again for coming."

"I'm happy to be here, Avery."

Our server returns.

We order our food and take sips of our drinks. Avery makes a toast to "New Beginnings" and I'm sure he means every word of that.

We feast on our respective meals and I dive into my sweet potatoes and collard greens. I haven't eaten like this in so long. He's killing those short ribs. I love a man who can eat.

"I love a woman who can eat," he says and I chuckle.

"What?" He smiles and questions.

"I was just thinking how much I love a man who can eat."

"I eat well, Jill," he smirks.

"Well, since you're treating, I'm gonna throw down."

We both laugh.

"More where that came from, Jill. I'm like putty in your hands. Have me any way you want me."

"Wow."

"What?"

"Nothing. So, tell me about your teachings, Doctor Washington."

"Well, I've been a professor for about five years now. I teach about culture and politics and old world studies regarding African Americans and people of African descent."

"Interesting. I've always wanted to study culture and jazz."

"Is that right?"

"Mos def."

"So, why didn't you? Or have you?"

"My parents wanted me to become a doctor."

"You don't seem like the type to listen to anyone." He laughs.

"I try to march to the beat of my own drum, but I wasn't always this way."

"Life's a journey, Jill."

"You're right."

Avery takes a sip of his Crown Royal.

"Tell me about you being a nurse."

"I love what I do. I work at the Veteran's Hospital. I help soldiers day in and day out."

"Noble profession."

"Thank you."

Avery begins talking about his career, his hopes, goals, and the dreams he has for his life and how I could fit into that equation. I glance at my watch and look at the sweet, fat-faced woman playing the piano, instantly I remember it's dinnertime at the hospital. I wonder if Jerusalem is eating dinner and listening to jazz. I want to call the nurses' station to check in on him, but that would be rude.

"Jill? Earth to Jill? Are you listening?" Avery interrupts my thoughts and concern for Jerusalem.

"Yes. I'm here. I'm sorry. Just thinking about one of my patients."

"Okay, no problem. Who's the patient?"

"Oh…an Iraq war veteran. Just hoping he's eating tonight."

"Very nice of you. You must love your job."

"I do. I really do."

Avery begins to tell me about his students, which ones are doing well and ones that are simply trying to breeze through the course. I think about Jerusalem and the progress he's making. As Avery's voice trails off in the background of my mind, I remember how I whispered in Jerusalem's ear, "You did well soldier. I'm proud of you." I can hear Avery speaking, but my mind is focused on the way Jerusalem smiled back at me then. Life is going to be very good for him once those bandages come off.

Chapter 15

Jerusalem

A Song in My Heart

Doctor Rodgers makes his way over to me. His white medical coat is ultra-white today, almost looks brand new. I've become so strong lately and in all actuality, so sick of sitting in that hospital bed that today I'm sitting in my chair and looking out the window. Music is playing, and as my nurse, Jill, would say, "I have a song in my heart." Her words the other day struck me so, and stayed with me. I couldn't figure out what she meant by that but she said it's from an Ella Fitzgerald song and she softly sang some of the lyrics. She said that because she is—on many levels—an eternal optimist, having a song in our hearts means that we're living, loving life and moving through with joy in our souls.

So, for as nervous as I am, I choose to have a song in my heart.

Doctor Rodgers begins to speak to me about what I can expect after the surgery to my face. The left side of my face was severely damaged, this I know, and there are third degree burns throughout, but he seems to be quite confident that he'll be able to fix me up pretty good.

"Mr. Jones, I do believe that once I'm done with the first procedure, you'll really be pleased."

"The first?" I question with astonishment.

"Well, fixing your face may take more than one surgery, although I've gotten so good over the years and medical technology has advanced in ways you could only dream of, so there is the possibility that maybe one surgery will do the trick."

"Hope so."

"You will have some scarring to your face and it will never be one hundred percent the same as before, but I can get it pretty close."

"I appreciate that, Doc."

The butterflies in my stomach are at an all-time high. I can't quite express that to him, or to anyone else, because I'm a soldier; but this soldier is scared.

"So, Doc, when will the surgery take place?"

Doctor Rodgers fixes his horn-rimmed glasses, rubs the side of his Caucasian face, and looks at me.

"Shortly. We're going to get the O.R. prepped now and you'll be down for surgery about one o'clock this afternoon."

I look at the clock on my wall and see that it is a quarter to twelve, so just a little over an hour remaining. I knew the surgery was today, but I think somewhere in my psyche I suppressed it. I didn't want to think about it or deal with it.

"Great, Doc. How long for healing? And when will these bandages come off?" I question, unsure if I really want to know the answer.

"Good question, soldier. Your wound is severe; you will have to undergo debriding, which is the removal of dead tissue, prior to reconstructive surgery. We're going to do a little bit of skin grafting and the graft is placed on the area in need of covering and held in place by a dressing and a few stitches. The donor site is also covered with a dressing to prevent infection from occurring. Recovery time from a split-thickness skin graft is generally fairly rapid, often less than three weeks."

"Donor site?"

"Yes, soldier, we're going to take just a small piece of skin from your buttocks." The doctor smiles.

"Are you kidding me?"

"Not at all. Listen, soldier…for all you've sacrificed, a little piece of skin from your ass is the least of your worries. I also predict in about two weeks you'll be very happy."

I laugh.

Doctor Rodgers laughs too.

"Yeah, a little skin from that boy's hide on his face, huh?" LT walks over to Doctor Rodgers and me. He laughs. He moves in close to pat me on my shoulder. He extends his hand to Doctor Rodgers and introduces himself.

"Hi, Doc, I'm Lawrence, Jay's best friend and brother."

"Nice to meet you, Lawrence…hey, wait a minute. Aren't you the sportscaster on television?"

"Yes, Sir, I am."

"Good meeting you, son. I remember when you were drafted to play for the Jets."

LT smiles. "Is that right?"

"Yes, son. My team is the New York Giants. Wished you had gone with them. They probably would have protected you a bit better."

"Ha, Doc, you just take good care of my friend, Jay."

"I will, Lawrence. He's a fine, young man. He'll be good to go in no time."

"From your lips to God's ears," LT says and shakes Doctor Rodgers' hand.

"Yes, to God's ears," Jill says as she walks into my hospital room. "Afternoon, gentlemen. Doctor Rodgers, Jerusalem's labs are all charted and our soldier is ready for what I hope will be his last battle."

She smiles and looks at me. Then she shakes LT's hand and greets him with a smile.

"Hello, LT."

"Hello, Jill. Thanks again for taking such good care of my boy. You got him listening to jazz and drinking herbal tea. I never thought I'd see the day."

She smiles and laughs.

"Nothing wrong with being exposed to new things, especially if they help to make us better people," she replies.

"Amen," LT says and walks over to the window.

"Doctor Rodgers, I need to discuss a few other patients with you if you have a moment."

"Of course, nurse."

Jill and Doctor Rodgers walk together out of my hospital room and I once again notice the curvature of her physique. She has on baby blue scrubs today and white sneakers. Her hair is pulled up high into a bun on the top of her head and those dangling earrings compliment her soft and beautiful face very well. She looks back at me as she exits the room and smiles.

Have mercy.

LT takes the chair next to me and we begin to chat. "You know this is going to be a piece of cake; right, Jay?"

"Mos def."

"So, when it's all said and done, you're going to look like a broke down Blair Underwood with a scar? Oh, the ladies are going to go wild. You know they love men who look like they are up to no good and that scar is going to scream Bad Boy to them! Ha!" LT bends over laughing.

"Shut up, punk!" I throw a dirty napkin at him. "LT, man, I pray this turns out right."

"It will, brother. You'll be fine. Hey…listen, Jay, I came over to discuss a bit of housekeeping, you know, business with you."

"What's up, LT? You good?"

"Definitely. So you know I'm still living in that spread I bought when I got drafted."

"Right, man, I know. Ain't been there in a minute, but I got you."

"Right. I remember your father always telling us to do right with our money. Even when we were little boys. He said…"

"Live on half of what you make." LT and I say that in unison.

"Well, since your father was like my father, really, he was the only Dad I ever had; I took his words to heart."

"That's a beautiful thing."

"So, Jay, at the same time, I bought an income property right outside of Newark. Actually, it's not too far from where I'm staying. It's a duplex. I was renting both sides out. One side pays the mortgage. My tenant is still there."

"Smart man, LT. You've always have been…well, except for those crazy women you got caught up with, but I digress."

LT laughs and I chuckle.

"You got a point, Jay, but anywho, the other side of the duplex is free. My tenant retired and moved to Florida last month."

"Word?"

"Yes, Jay, so take it."

"Take what?"

"The duplex."

"Man, I can't do that. Soon as I get out of this hospital, I'm going to find work. I'm requesting to be honorably discharged. I can't do this shit anymore."

"I remember you told me you were leaving the military which is why this works out so perfectly. Take the duplex, man. Small kitchen, just for you. I upgraded everything in that joint. Three bedrooms, two and a half baths, basement with washer and dryer. Small living room with dining room. It's perfect for you, Jay."

"Damn, LT, how can I ever repay you?"

"Man, if it weren't for you, your mom and dad, and that lil shit, Jabez, I would have never had a family. Shit man, I may not have become the man I am today if it weren't for your Dad. Your family saved my life. No one will ever be able to convince me otherwise."

"Bet. I'll take the duplex. What's the rent?"

"Man, didn't you hear me say the tenant pays the mortgage?"

"LT, I can't do that, man."

"Just take care of the taxes and utilities and of course, if you want cable and all that you gotta handle that on your own."

"Of course. Man, LT, for some reason, I feel like I'm beginning my life over again. I actually, for once in my life, look forward to living. Thank you."

"Jay, it doesn't stop there. There's an assistant head coaching position for basketball that is opening up at the University of New York. Quiet as it's kept, they are getting rid of Dunkelmann."

"Man, Dunkelmann and those University of New York Chasers suck. They're like 0 and 6, right?"

"Yeah, something like that. Jay, I've been talking to the coach and my connects at the university. Told them all about you. That you're an Iraq war veteran who played basketball throughout your Army career and that you're pretty good. Told them you got your degree while serving. They love your story. I think you'll get the job."

"Are you fucking kidding me?"

"Nah, man. This is real shit."

"Damn, man. I have to find a way to repay you, LT."

"I already told you. My life is what it is now because of you, Mom and Dad and that little fucker, Jabez. Jay, have you been able to find Jabez?"

"Nah, man. I searched and searched. Looked all over social media while I was in Iraq, and Germany and everywhere else. No signs of him."

"I ran into Kenya the other day and asked him and he said no he hadn't seen Jabez or heard anything about him. I know we talked about this before. I am just hoping and praying is all. You know Leroy is locked up down south somewhere."

"Damn! That's fucked up. I miss my brother, LT."

"Me too. When you are one hundred percent, we're gonna find him."

"That's a plan, man."

LT leans in to give me a hug and I hug him back in return.

"I love you, man," LT says and pulls away. He gets up from his chair and looks out of the window again.

"Alright, you two. LT, I need to take Jay now. We are headed to pre-op and then down to see Doctor Rodgers and get some of his magic." Jill says as she walks in. She moves in close to me, leans down and looks me in my face.

"You ready, Soldier?"

"Yes, Ma'am."

"Take care of my friend, Jill."

"He's in good hands. I'm going to take good care of him," she responds to LT.

LT walks out of the room and says, "I'll be here when you get out of surgery, Jay."

"I know you will."

"Candy, bring the wheelchair in for Mr. Jones and some warm blankets and socks."

"Yes, will do."

Candy returns to Jill with the items requested. Jill places the socks on my feet. Her soft hands are so gentle when they touch my skin. She's meticulous, even when placing socks on my feet. She doesn't miss a beat. She takes one of the warm blankets and lays it over my legs. She takes the other and wraps it around my body. I feel like I'm wrapped in a cocoon, and I feel secure.

"Warm?" she questions.

"Yes, very. Feels good."

"Good."

"Thank you." I smile.

"There's that smile again." She smiles and looks at me. Her hand covers mine. "You're going to be brand new in just a few weeks. Okay?"

"I believe you. I'm looking forward to coming out from under these bandages."

"In no time, Jerusalem."

"Thank you again."

"You'll be ready for a new chapter in your life," she tells me and wheels me out of the room.

Jill's hand touches the top of my shoulder, as she wheels me to the elevator. Her touch is soft and reassuring. The scent of her sweet perfume penetrates my senses. She backs us into the elevator. The reflection from the elevator doors allows me a bird's eye view of her full frame. Her long legs are curvaceous in those nurse scrubs. Jill's big almond-shaped eyes are clear and wondrously alluring, as she glances at me through those same elevator doors. She smiles. She knows I'm watching her.

"I have a song in my heart," I tell her.

"Is that right?" She smiles.

"Yes. Stayed with me."

Jill begins to hum the tune to the song. Her heavenly voice soothes my spirit. It's calming. I'm scared to death about the future of my appearance being left solely in the hands of a man I just met. Yet, as she hums, my fear is quieted. She sings words about greeting someone with a song in her heart. Something about it being a hymn to Your grace and touching my hand. She hums again, the sweet tune, and sings again about heaven and rejoicing and how a song like ours came to be.

Good God Almighty.

Cold and sterile is how this room feels. I suppose it is typical for an operating room. Laying here on this operating table, my body trembles. I'm so nervous. Fighting everyone as a kid in the tough streets of Newark, to fighting off men and women who were supposed to care for me while in the foster care system, to fighting off enemy combatants in the U.S. Armed Forces…all should have prepared me to deal with the fear and anxiety I am facing at this moment. But it hasn't. The fear is just as heavy and just as real as it was each of those times. It's just me and fear and this hard table.

I think about my father. I wonder if the fear I'm facing is the fear he faced that night he was gunned down.

Jabez, LT and I would stay at the YMCA on Thursday evenings. My dad worked late nights on Thursdays and since my mother had died, there was no one at home anymore on his late nights to care for us. Sure, Monday, Tuesday, Wednesday and Friday we were good. My mother kept me in the kitchen nightly, as she cooked so I learned my way around a pot or two. Dad would get home from the police station around five in the evening. He always scheduled his patrol duties and work hours to the needs of our family.

My mother was a homemaker, but so much more than that. She was our counselor, our teacher, our friend, our comforter and lawyer when we needed to get out of trouble. Our mother was light, sun, love, and laughter, who wrote poetry. My mother adored that record player next to the dining room. She loved jazz and reading. Although she stayed home, her presence was integral to the survival of the three most important men in her life. When she died, I played her records and made dinner for our family four days a week.

Dad never wanted us to be home alone until eight in the evening, so he signed us all up for YMCA after-school activities. Yes, he even signed up LT. LT's mom had grown to love the bottle more than her son at times, and she seemed to be changing right before our eyes; so my father sort of took LT in, even though he didn't live with us, the time he spent with us only really left room for LT to go home, shower, and go to bed.

We waited on the corner for an hour or more after we finished at the YMCA and there was still no sign of my dad. The YMCA was way across town, so after school we'd catch the school bus over there. Well, the time had come and gone for a school bus to come and rescue us in the absence of my dad. So, we did what any kid would have done. We started to walk home.

Walking home meant two miles or so, but we just talked shit and walked and it made the time pass. Jabez bragged about how Mom spoiled him like a baby and LT sulked at the fact that while his mom was still alive, that our mom was more of a mom to him. I changed the subject, because talking about mom was hard for me.

"Yo, punks, when I grow up, I'm gonna marry Apollonia! Did y'all see her in *Purple Rain*?

"Yeah, I did, but she ain't got shit on Lisa Lisa from Cult Jam," Jabez chimed in.

"Word, but I may be old school, but Vanity and Jane Kennedy both gonna be my wives when I get older," LT said, as we tossed the football back and forth.

After what seemed like hours, we finally reached the end of our block. Police cars appeared in front of our home and I ran up to see what happened. Jabez followed closely, along with LT. I ran to the nearest police officer, one that I recognized from a dinner in which they honored my father a few years back. He hugged me and sat me down on my porch.

"Officer Culligan, what's going on?" I asked as my eyes moved side to side looking at all of the commotion around me.

"Well, Jay, your dad was shot in the line of duty."

My heart sank. Jabez started to cry and threw all kinds of tantrums as he paced up and down the street. LT went to console him.

"He's in surgery now. Son, I know how strong you two boys are. I know the kind of men your daddy raised you to be. I don't think he's going to make it, son. He was shot three times in the chest."

Tears poured uncontrollably down my face.

"Can I see him?"

"They won't let you in the room, but I'll take you and your brothers to the hospital right now. Do you have any family?"

"No, it's just me and Jabez and my dad. Oh, and LT."

Officer Culligan grabbed me and summoned LT and Jabez to get into the police car. We all cried in the backseat as we made our way to Beth Israel Medical Center. We were able to look through a tiny window on the door of the operating room and I saw my dad on the table. Blood-soaked clothing was ripped from his chest. He had tubes in his mouth and one doctor had two things in his hands that looked like irons and he put those on my father's chest and yelled, "Clear!" to the nurses. My dad's body convulsed and the doctor repeated that same "Clear!" thing.

After a few minutes of looking through the window, the doctors and nurses walked toward the door. I'll never forget the look on that White doctor's face as he told me, Jabez, LT and Officer Culligan that my dad didn't make it.

As I lie here on this operating table, I wonder if my father had the same fear then that I can't shake right now. I wonder if he was as brave as I remembered him to be when he laid there losing his life. Knowing my father the way I did, and loving him how I do, and admiring him as he was the only hero I've ever known...I think my father braved it to the very end, and that's what I'm going to do now. Show the measure of true strength; just like my daddy, but with a song in my heart.

Chapter 16

Jill

My Man's Gone Now

Yesterday, I forced myself to take a mental health day; while spending half the day in the gym and part of my afternoon with Deseree and LaLaina, as we treated ourselves to manicures, pedicures, and facials, wouldn't necessarily be classified as mental health, rather more like in need of mental health, it was still refreshing.

Every six to eight weeks it seems, the hospital gets a new round of patients and by the grace of our Creator; many of those patients are able to walk out the door. Unfortunately, many do not. We are often providing hospice care to those veterans who are on their way to their own victory, to meet their ancestors, their loves that have gone on before them, to rest in eternal peace with our Creator.

It's a sad reality every two months or so, of having to tell family members the true state of someone's condition. No family, who is true family, ever has hope that is lost. At the most crucial and heartbreaking times of their lives, their hope is always renewed; it's always at an all-time high. It's beautiful to watch people who survive and move forward in life with just their faith alone, and most of the time, all they have is their faith because the facts prove otherwise.

So, every couple of months I take a day just to renew and refresh my own spirit so that I can be the best healer the Creator intended me to be. Every so often, I take that day to recharge my own battery, to get my spirit, soul and body on one accord. Some days are easier than others.

Today, I am grateful for yesterday. Yesterday, I was with two women who love me unconditionally and take me for who and what I am. I don't have many people in my life who do that, except for Janet. Those girls don't judge and if they happen to correct me when and if I'm in the wrong, it's simply out of love and the desire for me to be happy and better.

Today, I am grateful for their non-judgmental views of my life and me because it provides a sense of balance. There's no balance here with Mother and Father. It's always a feeling of not being good enough, thin enough, wise enough, or having had made the right decisions for my life, or not being in the place and time they want me to be and not becoming the person they had hoped for.

It's Thursday, and today is our day.

I opted for lunch as opposed to dinner because I promised Avery that I would have dinner with him this weekend. He's really laying it on thick, and while I haven't given him much of my time, he has proven to be a much-needed distraction. I guess I can't get tired of hearing how beautiful I am and how he wants things to progress at a more rapid pace. What woman wouldn't want a well-educated man fawning over her? Right? I probably need a vacation to clear my head.

I pull up to the one hundred foot driveway and turn into the circular path that is laid with brick. I remember when Mother and Father had this driveway done many years ago. They paid a grip, I am sure, to have this triple border with diamond inlay. Mother has style even if she lacks in other areas of her life. She indeed has an incredible sense of style and taste. My childhood home… it's to die for, visually speaking, of course.

I didn't have those stories growing up like many of the people I know, like Deseree and LaLaina, who can remember times when their mothers made spaghetti with hot dogs because they couldn't afford beef. I can't recall a time where the lights were cut off.

There was always food in the refrigerator—our stainless steel, custom-designed refrigerator. The thread count on my bedding was always superior and Mother would never shop at one of those big retail stores where you could get everything under the sun that you needed for your home. She shopped upscale.

Janet and I had the best that Mother's money could buy and she would never let us forget it. LaLaina would tell me stories about how her brothers would have to share pants when they were in high school and that many times, if their mother, who was a single mother, ran out of money, they'd have to share shoes too. LaLaina jokes about them being in church seven days a week, and while there was no real money at home, her mother made sure she paid her tithes. Mother and Father tithed so much at the Catholic Church in our neighborhood, that they have a room in the church named after them, and a scholarship fund in their name as well.

Those good White Catholic folks don't give a damn about my black mother and father, but mother will never see that, because they smile in her face as she's writing checks, but she can't turn her back to them. Growing up in that Catholic Church wasn't about God at all. It was about keeping up appearances and going with the proverbial flow. There was nothing Godly about church, home, or Sunday grace, for that matter.

Deseree would tell LaLaina and I stories about how when we were in college, she had to get on the equal opportunity education program which was designed for low income minorities who did well in school to have a chance at going to college. That's where we all met. In college. The three of us instantly connected and have been the best of friends for years.

I would have never met a LaLaina or a Deseree growing up in Nyack, New York where Mother and Father made our home. I thank God for BET, Yo MTV Raps and radio so I could connect with whom and what I felt was most comfortable. I am grateful that my Father did sneak in jazz music when Mother wasn't around, because it probably kept me sane. Listening to WBGO jazz radio made me fall in love with sounds and reading Maya Angelou, Nikki Giovanni, Amiri Baraka, Anais Nin, and Khalil Gibran made me fall in love with words.

Words and sounds.

Stepping out of my truck, I toss my scarf to one side and raise my shades off my face. Carolina, with her tiny, plump self, runs out of the house. She's the sweetest Latina woman I've ever known. She practically raised us, Janet and me. She let us eat chocolate when Mother wasn't watching. She got me those books that I wanted to read so badly. She snuck them to me. She taught me how to dance salsa. She introduced me to Latin jazz and the greats like Tito Puente, Celia Cruz and Poncho Sanchez. Carolina taught Janet and me how to cook. She said the way to a man's heart is through his stomach and through his eyes.

"Mantener a su hombre feliz, Jill and Janet. When you get older, keep your men happy. Cook for them. Dance for them. Look good for them. Men love with their eyes."

Janet and I would always giggle at Carolina, but I get it now.

"Senora, Jill," she says and reaches up to me. She has tears in her eyes. She always does, every time I come. "I miss you, baby girl."

I kiss her on her round, Latina face. She smiles. Her thinning jet-black hair sits on top of her head and she looks like a Spanish angel in her maid's uniform. I can't understand for the life of me why she still has to wear that stupid ass maid's uniform after all of these damn years, but that's Mother for you.

"I miss you too, Carolina. You're good?'

"Si, si, mamacita. Come, I cook for you."

"Oooh, what did you make, Carolina?' I smile as we walk into the house together.

"Arroz con gandules and some fried pork. I know you miss that pork, Jill. You're not eating enough. Losing too much weight, Senora."

"Carolina, I need to lose more."

"No, your man wants you to be a woman always, Jill. A woman. Man loves curves, lil belly, yes?"

I laugh.

"I love you, Carolina."

Carolina reaches up to kiss me on the cheek and takes my coat.

"Your parents are in the dining room waiting."

I dread this moment each and every Thursday, but something about me remains compassionate, so I'm here each and every Thursday without fail. It's the right thing to do. I walk into the dining room and it is just as dope as always. Mother could be an interior designer if she didn't think that profession was for lesser people. She's got good taste.

I take a seat at the other end of the extraordinarily long, mahogany dining room table. Carolina comes in to prepare my plate. My mother smiles, slightly and Father looks happy to see me. I return the smile with no real enthusiasm, and take a sip of the sweet tea Carolina has poured for me. Carolina knows that most of the week I'm eating grass, so when I come on Thursdays, she tries to fatten me up. I don't stop her. I know it is done out of love. I humbly accept her love.

"Drinking too much of that sweet tea will put pounds on you," Mother says as she sips on her lemon water.

Carolina coughs as to cause distraction and places a napkin in my lap.

"Well then, let me have another glass of tea, Carolina." I say to get under Mother's skin.

"Where did you get that sweater from, Jill?" Mother questions.

I decided on an ivory sweater with oversized sleeves and a rustic brown belt. The cowl neck on the sweater makes for a nice look. It's chic, yet comfortably casual. Blue form fitting jeans and honey bronze leather boots tie it all together. My hair is natural and flowing freely all over my head. Caramel-colored lip-gloss and stained glass hoop earrings complete my ensemble.

"I got it from the thrift store near the hospital. Do you like it?"

"Looks cheap."

"Why, thank you, Mother."

"You look nice, Jill." My father says to ease the tension.

"When are you going to start dating again, Jill?"

"Dating someone now."

"Really? Who? Let me guess. You want to keep it real so you're dating some wannabe rapper thug?"

"Not at all, although that doesn't sound like a bad idea. His name is Doctor Avery Washington. He's an Africana Studies professor at the University of New York."

"Oh my. You have to bring him over for dinner." The excitement in her voice makes my skin crawl. I knew, by his profession alone, he would please my mother and that bit of bigotry on her part appalls me.

"Not that serious."

"He sounds like the perfect catch."

"I'm sure *you* think he is."

We take bites of the incredible meal Carolina made for us. Classical music plays softly in the background and I look at my watch to check the time. My eyes peer to the walls at the framed pictures of Janet and me. We'd take professional photos each and every year when we were younger. Mother insisted upon it. We looked like we could be models for some high-end department store. Cute. I smile.

"Well, thank you for lunch, but it's time for me to go."

"So soon?" Father questions.

"Yes. I have to check on my patients."

"I thought you said you took the day off?" Mother questions.

"Yes, I am off, but I will call to check in on them."

"Oh."

"Then I'll go see my sister. Oh, and thanks for visiting her last week. The nursing home told me you did."

"Are you spying on us now, Jill?"

"Not at all," I say as I get up from my seat. "But I did tell you that if you didn't visit her, you could forget about me ever coming back over here. I guess you got the point."

I walk over to Father and kiss him on the cheek.

"Mother."

"Jill."

I begin to walk out of the dining room and into the foyer. Carolina walks up to me. "Senora, tell me about Doctor Avery." She smiles and raises her eyebrows in a girlish manner.

"Oh, it's nothing just yet, Carolina, but if it gets somewhere, I'll call you." I wink at her.

Carolina reaches up and grabs my face, kisses me on either side of my cheeks, says, "I love you," and puts my coat on me, just like she did when I was a little girl.

"Love you, too."

Once I get into my truck, I call the nurses' station to check on some of my crucial patients. I think of Jerusalem and his progress. He's two weeks out from his reconstructive surgery and the bandages are still on as he heals. I know that's driving him insane. He's walking like a champ and has even picked up a few pounds along with his appetite picking up. He really can eat.

"Hello, Kaye?"

"Hey, Jill."

"How's Mr. Thomas in 2C?"

"He's doing well; the family is in there with him now."

"Good."

"How's Jerusalem Jones doing? He's up and about like a champ these days."

"Oh, Doctor Saunders discharged him this morning. He's all packed up and gone."

"What?"

"Yes. Doctor Saunders ordered the discharge this morning and his brother, I think, came to pick him up. His brother is fine as hell. Damn."

My heart sinks and then resurges to a lump in my throat.

"Okay, thank you, Kaye. I'll be back on Monday. I'm going to take tomorrow off and this is my weekend off anyway."

"No problem, Jill. You could use the break."

"Yeah."

I place the phone down in the passenger seat and turn on the CD player. Nina Simone's "My Man's Gone Now" comes on and it is so appropriate for this moment. I think of him—Jerusalem, and wonder how's he's doing. He's come such a long way and I'm thankful to the Creator for his healing—mind, body and spirit. But a part of me is devastated and I'm not sure why. I mean, we try our best to heal patients and that's our job. It's our goal. It's why we do what we do. So I should be happy about Jerusalem's release. I should be happy. I just never guessed he'd be leaving so soon. Well, such is life.

The night has drawn near and I have yet to tell Avery where I live. Although he insists on picking me up, I always meet him at the destination of our choosing. He desperately wants to move things to the next level and I am not sure what's stopping me. But I'm just not ready yet, and that's the best way I can explain where

I am in this time and place.

We've been at the restaurant for about twenty minutes, I haven't said much, and honestly, I don't feel like eating. I would much rather be in my bed eating some rocky road ice cream and watching something salacious on TV or reading a good book. Avery and this dinner and all this pretending that I'm doing tonight is for the birds.

"What's wrong, Jill?"

"Nothing. Why do you ask?" I question him as I sip on the water.

"Well, you're not talking much and you're not eating much. And, don't get me wrong, you're beautiful, but I've never seen you with a scarf on your head."

Oh shit, right, I do have my scarf on.

"I mean, your dress is banging and it does match your scarf. Guess you're going for a different look today?"

"Well, I was writing a bit of poetry earlier…"

"Ha! Oh, you're one of those types, huh?"

"What do you mean?" I'm pissed about the way he just cut me off and laughed at the idea of me writing poetry.

"Well, do you light candles and incense too?" He chuckles and takes a sip of his red wine.

"I do, as a matter of fact."

Avery talks about being a scholar and I drift into another world. I think about the time when I read Jay some poetry out of one of the collections I had picked up on clearance in a local bookstore. He didn't like those poems that much because I had started him out with the best who've ever done it, like Sonya Sanchez and Maya Angelou, so the lightweight poets in the collection I was reading from…well, he could tell the difference. In the short time since I had introduced him to poetry, he had acquired an exquisite taste for the best and anything short of words spun with mastery lost his attention. He was nice about it, though.

"Okay, so, Miss Jill. You read poetry. Do you write it?" Jay inquired after a few lines from the bargain collection.

"Yes, I do, Nosey Jones."

He laughed.

"Well, you're reading all of these poets to me, let me hear *your* poetry."

"Oh, I couldn't."

"Yes…you could. Please. I would love to."

That was the first time anyone had ever asked to hear my poetry.

"If you're not comfortable reading it to me, let me read it."

"I…I…I think I'm comfortable."

"Good girl. And let me hear something that is not about you saving the world and being in a place of Zen. Let me hear your innermost thoughts. I know you have a body of work as diverse as you seem to be."

Wow, the way he read me. I was astonished. I smiled and pulled my notebook out of my bag.

"See, you have an entire collection of poetry over there. Why you holding out on me? Oh, let me guess…you're reading your poetry to the *other* brother down the hall with the messed up face and shrapnel in his leg. You're catering to him because he's worse off than me?"

He laughed and I did not find that funny.

"No!" I tapped him on his hand as if I was punishing him.

"Okay, just making sure you're not betraying me with a soldier who's worse off than me."

"I would never betray you."

There was an awkward moment of silence between us and I pulled my notebook out and found a poem I would feel comfortable reading to him. He smiled and anxiously waited for me to say a verse.

"Come on, Miss Thang. Don't be scared."

"Hush." I smiled.

"Okay, I found this one. It's called, "Only In My Empire.""

"Get it, girl," Jay says as he lifts his hand and snaps his finger. "Ouch," he whispers as he lowers his arm.

"See there, Soldier. Let me finish healing you before you start pretending to be some flamboyant homosexual."

"Ha!" he laughed.

"You ready?" I questioned. I was nervous, but ready.

"I'm ready."

These Visions of Grandeur
Promote deep-seeded, uncultivated feelings
That sorrowfully soar throughout my soul…

Awaiting you...
Debating you...
Resisting you, yet missing you.
Is it wrong to love you?
Because damn... I do.

And my sweet Visions of Grandeur
Have me struggling in a world where
Time and Space and Reason and Righteousness
Have No Place
It's just you and me and we...
For we are a set of free spirits yearning.

"Oh, oh, oh, you got skills, I see!" he yelled and smiled.
"You gonnna let me finish, Soldier?" I questioned and smiled. I was so embarrassed.
"Okay, stop blushing and finish. Show me what you got!" He smiled even wider.

And My Love ...
I want to lock you up in my Empire for days
To complete this fantasy... this craze
Nah... Hell No... It is truly beyond that.
To fulfill what is so unfulfilled
To both you and me and we.

He interrupted again. "You know it's hard for me to smile this hard with these bandages on my face, right?"
"Jay!"
"Okay, okay, okay, go ahead, Miss Angelou."

Perhaps we should alter the rules,
Transform the Earth
To have it rotate on our axis
Because this world as we know it
Is not designed for what we believe...
You needing me and us needing we...
And you and me carouseling thru this galaxy,
Making eternal history,

Exploring the possibilities – infinitely
This mesmerizing infatuation is beyond my understanding.
It Will be next lifetime, sweet friend.

And my Visions of Grandeur ...
With my wet-sticky-day-dreamin'
Envisions a time where
You will journey to a light at the end of my fantasy/fallacy
And penetrate so deep that you will caress my soul...
And touch my spirit with the endowment that God has blessed you with.

And I grab a hold of visions and refuse to release them into this world
Where vultures and rhyme and reason will devour them.
Cause it does hurt like hell...
To not possess you the way that my entire being needs to...
How every breath I breathe needs you...

So let me just hold on...
And never let go,
Knowing that if I step back into this harsh reality,
I will realize that I confused it with fantasy.

It was only after I looked into your eyes,
That I saw Paradise...
And every woman wants that.
Suddenly I realized,
That you could be my Savior in disguise.
Is it wrong for me to love you?
Cause right here, right now, baby,
Damn...
I do.
And my heart won't allow me do
anything other than love you.

"Oh My God, Jill! You're incredible! That was superb. So much feeling. So much depth. Reminds me of my mother in a weird way," he said as he took a sip of his tea.

"How so?'
"She wrote poetry."
"Sweet. Does she still write it?"
"She died when I was a kid."
"Oh, Jerusalem, I'm so sorry."
"Thank you. I loved her very much."
        "What happened, if you don't mind me asking?"
"Never really knew, but the way she collapsed, I think it was an aneurysm in her brain."
"I'm so sorry."
"Thank you. I appreciate you."
Awkward silence once again infiltrated that space between Jerusalem, the patient, and Jill the nurse, but it was liberating and welcomed and freeing…it was salvation.

"Jill? Where are you?" Avery asks.
"Oh, I'm sorry, Avery. I am so tired. I think I'm going to call it a night."
"But you barely ate your dinner. Are you feeling okay, baby?"
Did he just call me baby?
"I'm fine. Just got a bit of bad news today. I just want to go home and rest. I appreciate dinner. Hey, as a matter of fact, it's on me this time."
I reach into my purse and hand him eighty dollars in cash, rise to my feet, pat him on his shoulder and leave.
As I make my way back to my truck, I think of him, and his words, "I appreciate you." I remember his laugh. Simone's voice strums to my inner pain while "My Man's Gone Now" plays on repeat and I shed a tear as I make my way home.

Chapter 17

Jerusalem

Kind of Blue

Law enforcement officers pledge to serve the public and put their lives on the line daily. When they pass away, whether from circumstances in the line of duty or otherwise, their funerals should reflect honor and respect for their service and dedication. My daddy deserved the honor and respect he received at his funeral.

For years, I've held onto his memorial flag case. I have always referred to it as "Daddy's Flag Box." It is solid walnut with an heirloom walnut finish. The case opens from the front with a hinged lid. I open it and see two of the most important things in my life— the flag that draped my father's casket and my mother's wedding ring.

Throughout my years in foster care, I was able to hold on to one thing—this box. I guarded it with my life and my life *did* depend on it. This walnut box with the heirloom walnut finish kept me sane. It's the only thing I have of my mom and dad that means the world to me.

I take the flag out of the box. It has not faded, nor withered over time. I've held on to "Daddy's Flag Box" for twenty years, along with my sanity. I unfold the flag and remember the day. I think about the day my daddy was laid to rest. For years, I could not deal with his death and I suppressed memories of the day. I would talk to myself in school and in those hell-hole foster care homes, and even in the group home and I would tell myself that we'd meet again—Daddy, Mommy and Jabez. I convinced myself that their absence was only temporary and I would see them again one day. Another thing that kept me sane. Just the thought of putting my eyes on my mother's beautiful face once more made me happy. It gave me hope. I yearned for the opportunity to play basketball with my dad once more, or to run up "Dead Man's Hill" to grab his hand as I made my way to victory. I prayed to see Jabez again and deal with his selfish ways with his spoiled ass. I kept the faith. My faith, even in my younger years, kept me holding on. If I had not thought about the three most important people in my life on a daily basis, I probably would have ended up in jail or dead; or both, respectively.

I inhale the scent of the flag and remember the day.

Dignitaries and even the Mayor of Newark and councilmen and the like were at my father's funeral. There were so many police officers there in uniform and everyone who attended had the saddest look on their faces. At the time, I thought only Jabez and me, and even LT were the sad ones because we had lost a father. I realize now, those police officers lost one of their own. They too, lost someone who meant the world to them. My daddy was awesome like that. He had that effect on others. People loved him because of his heart. He was authentic and actually gave a damn about the people around him.

Jabez and I wore black suits given to us by one of the police officer's wives. We had suits at home that mommy and daddy purchased for us, but we were growing like weeds so they no longer fit by the time it was time to lay my daddy to rest. This officer's wife also gave us shoes to wear.

LT's mother, for whatever it was worth, climbed out of bed and took the three of us to the barbershop on Bergen Street to get haircuts. She paid for it, but I suspect in more ways than one given the way she flirted with the head barber. "Soup" is what they called him. Soup was tall, and black, with pink lips. He had a jheri curl in his hair and was a slick-talking bastard. I heard some of the things he said to LT's mom that day, and while LT tried not to listen, the grimace to his face indicated otherwise. LT's mom called him names like "Sugar" and "Daddy," and Soup handed her something and she took it and headed to the barbershop's bathroom. LT cringed, but Jabez and I talked as we were getting our cuts to break up the moment and to give a much-needed distraction.

I remember the twenty-one gun salute, and how the sound of the gunshots startled Jabez and me, as we stood in front of the casket on that rainy winter day. The ground was wet; the day was dreary, and inside I died another death. Jabez stood there with tears in his eyes and the teardrops never stopped falling during the entire funeral. Daddy's funeral was a graveside ceremony. He was buried right next to my mother.

Officer Culligan gave the eulogy, as he and my daddy were partners and the best of friends. He did not look well at all in the face and the extra pounds Culligan carried around his waist I'm more than certain were not good for his health.

Officer Culligan called for my father's sons to come as he and the other officers removed the flag from the casket. They began to fold it and Jabez and I walked toward the shiny, silver casket that carried my father's dead body.

"We give this flag to his sons," Officer Culligan remarked. I looked back to find LT and saw that he was standing just a few feet behind us and I walked back to grab his hand. LT's face was red as a rose and he seemed to want to collapse from the pain he was enduring. Not only did I have to be strong for Jabez, I had to be strong for LT, too because my daddy was the only daddy LT had ever known.

"Come on, LT," I said and reached out for his hand. He grabbed mine and we hugged. The three of us, LT, Jabez and I walked over to take the flag the officers gave us. As the casket lowered, Jabez and LT broke down in tears, so much so that I had to release their hands, do the honorable thing, and salute my father. It was the hardest thing I've ever had to do, but I was my father's soldier and I saluted him in honor of him and respect for him.

Now, I look at the same flag given to me on that horrible, rainy, winter day at the graveside ceremony in Newark, where his dead body laid there in a shiny, silver casket, where he rested next to my mother.

A single tear falls from my eye.

I pick up the remaining contents of my daddy's box that contains my mother's wedding ring. My daddy gave her ring to me after she died. He told me to cherish the ring, and when the time was right, to put it on the hand of a beautiful woman who will make my heart sing.

I see the picture of me, Jabez and LT from when we were little out in the middle of the street throwing a football. My mother took this picture. It's yellowing and faded, but I never lost this photo.

Unpacking is almost done as I'm finally home. This duplex is absolutely everything I could have every imagined. I am grateful to LT for his generosity. I have put up the little bit of things I had, and once the money starts to roll in, I will make my house my home.

God's breath is the wind beneath my wings. I feel the presence of my parents with me now and I pray the feeling of truly being alive doesn't flee me as it has so many times before.

Getting the job at the University is one of the biggest blessings I could have ever prayed for. This will allow me to live as close to a normal life as possible and for that I'm truly grateful.

The military did issue the first of my benefit checks of just about four hundred dollars and deemed me about thirty percent disabled. I was in the hospital for more than two months, so I've had two checks accumulated. As strange as it may seem, I purchased groceries with the money and I found a record player at the Salvation Army for only fifty bucks. I was anxious to bring it home.

I remember Jill saying that the best way to listen to jazz is on a record player with a real vinyl album. We live in a digital age where technology reigns, so I knew that getting a record player and actual vinyl albums would be a great challenge, but I managed to do it.

I took the train over to Tower Records and found the last "Kind of Blue" album by Miles Davis. Jill would play this album for me often while I was in the hospital. I still don't know how she managed to get me to let my guard down, but she did—in her own little poetic way—and I thank God for her healing powers. She was the breath of life for me when I almost forgot how to breathe.

I haven't grown accustomed to not seeing her pretty face on a daily basis. I haven't been able to sleep well without hearing her voice say, "Goodnight, Soldier," and I miss the way she made sweet hot tea for me.

The title track, "Kind of Blue" plays in my new home on my new record player. I'm kind of blue, missing my nurse. I'm kind of blue missing my brother. I'm kind of blue missing Mom and Dad, but I'm encouraged because I have a new lease on life, it seems.

I miss her...

Brewing hot peppermint tea is something I've never done a day in my life, yet I'm brewing it now. Vanilla candles that I purchased on clearance at the candle shop not too far from Tower Records, smells good, and gives my new home a warm and fuzzy feeling. The dead of winter will make its debut soon, so I welcome warm, cozy things.

She talked to me about Miles Davis and John Coltrane, which are Jill's two favorite jazz musicians. I remember how her big, almond-shaped eyes would light up whenever we'd discuss jazz and poetry. Funny, I never thought much about the two after my mother passed. I remember my mother's fascination with poetry, but I had suppressed the thoughts until Jill surfaced and reopened the wound, sort of like opening my soul.

She awakened my soul, lifted my spirit and healed my body. I'll never forget her.

She said that the "Kind of Blue" album, in which Coltrane is a stable saxophonist, is the best-selling jazz album of all time. She said it is arguably Miles Davis' best work and the world's greatest jazz album. I see why. After reading about the album, I learned that it is said, by artists of various genres, to be the most influential album of all time.

"Jay, this is the best jazz album ever made." She said to me, smiling so bright. Damn, I would kill to see that smile once again.

"Word? I thought Coltrane was your man."

"He is. I'm simply talking about the album influence." She smiled. She rubbed my shoulder.

Jill stood above me as she was checking my vitals. Her hair danced around her face and her soft, amber-colored lips were shiny and sweet and looked delicious. Her skin was all aglow like she had just come from a day spa. She smelled like something straight out of the heavenly skies.

She looked in my face, with her face close to mine and checked my pupils. I inhaled her scent. Took in all of her aroma. She moved closer to me. I grabbed her arm. Exhaled. I knew how inappropriate my thoughts were and I had a moment of weakness.

She smiled. I wanted to pull her close to me. I exhaled again. I tried to restrain myself.

"Jill." I said her name softly.

"Yes?" Her smile vanished and an intense look overcame her face. Her breathing was heavy, labored. She pulled away from me, but not by much. Her professionalism pulled away from me. I'd like to think, Jill, the woman, moved at a snail's pace to get away from me.

My face was bandaged, in part, but she didn't run from me. I was at the most vulnerable place I'd ever been in my entire life, yet, she cared for me.

"I…I…" I stuttered.

"What's it is, Jay?" she questioned, staring into my eyes.

"Thank you." I told her to ease the tension that the moment offered.

She exhaled and moved away a bit more; I pulled her arm, pulled her toward me. She let out a sigh.

"You're welcome, Jay," she told me.

Her arm was still in my grasp. She looked down at it. She looked back up at me. A slight grin crossed her face. I exhaled again.

"I'm sure you have other patients to see, Jill, right?" I questioned while rubbing my hand along her forearm. "Your skin is so soft."

"I do," she replied as she moved closer to me.

"You do, what, Jill?" I questioned, staring deep into her big, almond-shaped eyes. I wanted so badly to taste her lips, but I was the injured, weak, Iraq war veteran with no game, no money, and a damaged face.

"I have other patients to see," she said. She rubbed my shoulder. Her bracelet with the ankh on it dangled as her body swayed as she rubbed me. I saw her breasts bounce behind those nurse's scrubs.

"Okay." I told her. Slightly released her arm. She looked at her arm. She looked at me.

"I'll check on you later," she whispered. My hand reached up to remove the hair that had gotten in the way of me witnessing her angelic face in full form.

The doorbell rings and I rush to answer it. LT is waiting and I move quickly to unlock the door.

"Wassup, Fam?"

I smile and we give one another dap. I haven't seen my man since he picked me up from the hospital and gave me the keys to my new pad.

"What's good, Jay? How you liking your new digs?"

"Man, heaven sent. I'm lovin' it."

LT raises his hand in the air showing me a bottle of Courvoisier. "I brought you a little house warming gift," he says as he takes the bottle of liquor into the kitchen and places it on the countertop. He removes his jacket and tosses it on the kitchen chair. "What's this I see? You're making tea?" LT doubles over laughing.

"Man, shut the fuck up." I laugh.

I reach into the cabinet and begin to make him a cup.

"You're making *me* tea?"

"No, bitch, I'm making *us* tea." I laugh.

"What the hell has gotten into you, Jay?" he smiles.

"Nothing man, just like tea."

"Who is she?"

"There's no *she*, LT."

"Oh, yes there is. You're drinking tea and wait a damn minute…what are you playing? Is that a record player?" LT walks to the record player in the living room.

"Yes, that is a record player and that's Miles Davis playing."

LT throws his hands up in the air and starts walking in a circle as if confused and looking for something.

"Where's my friend? Where's my brother, Jerusalem Jones?"

"I'm right here, punk."

"Who is she, Jay?"

"Man, it's nothing." I hand him the tea.

"Nothing? You just handed me a cup of tea, man! You're playing jazz. And, what's that smell, Jay?"

"Man, drink the fucking tea. It's good."

He takes a sip. "Oh shit, this is good, Jay. I'll be damned."

"See, don't knock it 'til you try it."

"What's the smell, Jay?" LT presses me further.

"Vanilla candles." I'm embarrassed as I answer.

LT looks at me.

"Okay. Uhm, I just simply got some positive influence from my old nurse, Jill."

"Ah ha! I knew it! You fucked her yet?" LT claps his hands in the air like he had just figured out the meaning of life.

"Man, no! She was my nurse! Have you seen me lately? I'm walking with a slight limp, and my bandages are still on my face!"

"You like her?'

"I admire her, LT. There's a difference."

"When do the bandages come off?"

"Soon! Can't wait! Been a long haul. I'll be gold after that, minus the scarring."

"You'll be good and if the plastic surgeon is as good as we've heard, you'll be looking good as new."

"I pray so."

"So, what are you going to do about Jill?"

"Nothing."

"Why not, Jay?"

"Because I'm discharged from the hospital. Reason, season, lifetime. She was a beautiful season. She made me want to live again."

"That's deep, Jay."

"I know."

"Go get her, Jay."

"Can't."

"Why?"

"Because she was my nurse, LT. Didn't you hear me?"

"I did. But I haven't seen you this enthralled or excited about a woman in a very long time. As a matter of fact, I've never seen a woman change you for the better."

"Man, I've been in other countries."

"So what. I'm your brother. And I would know if any woman

had. I know the ladies you've fucked over the years. This one is different."

"I just can't."

"You can. And you should."

Chapter 18

Jill

Coco

"…it's just that you've been so down and out lately, that we want to give you a pick me up. We're your friends, Jill, that's what wc do."

"I know, Deseree, but really I'm not in the mood for this tonight," I tell Deseree as I watch LaLaina remove my scarf.

The three of us are seated in my oversized bathroom and LaLaina and Deseree have ambushed me this evening. The flat irons are on high, and LaLaina takes a square of my hair, moisturizes it with organic coconut oil and straightens and smoothes it out with the flat iron. I haven't worn my hair out straight since going natural and it has been years. I kind of like it.

I smile at her through the mirror. She returns my smile.

Deseree runs her fingers along the marble in my bathroom. Carrara marble tile floors, tub deck, tub splash, countertops and shower, plus a dark-wood custom vanity and mirrors compliment my master bath just outside of my bedroom.

"Jill, if nothing else, you're exceptionally talented when it comes to your home's décor." Deseree tells me as she admires the double sink in the bathroom.

"Yes, the bitch has skills," loud mouth LaLaina chimes in. She blows the steam that leaves my scalp from the combination of the flat iron meeting the coconut oil.

"Thank you, ladies. You all know I got this house as a foreclosure. Mother and Father gave me the heads up and tip and I jumped right on it; otherwise I wouldn't have been able to afford it."

"Why you still call them 'Mother' and 'Father' like that?" LaLaina questions.

"It was ingrained in me growing up. You know my mother is a 'keeping up with the Joneses' kind of woman and my father is a no balls having follower of hers. She always tried to live a life that was not meant for her and I can't imagine her ever escaping the prison she has built around herself."

"Damn!" Deseree says as she begins to lotion my legs. "Your mother seems so nice when I look at photos. She's so pretty… looks like she could be your sister."

"Thank you. I wish I had the type of love for her that you all have for your mothers. I miss something I've never had, I think."

"Yeah…probably explains why you are the way you are, Jill. Your heart is as big as gold. Your patients, and all those around you, benefit from your selfless giving. I know for me, I can say that I'm blessed to have you in my life. You've always been there for me, Jill. Whether it was just a shoulder to cry on, or if I needed rent money…you've always been there for Deseree and me. You know I love you."

Tears begin to well up in my eyes, but I don't allow them to fall. I'm already terribly emotional these days. These two women – my best friends – sensed it and came to my rescue. Deseree raises me to my feet as Jill runs her fingers through my soft, deep waves. I look in the mirror and see my two friends on either side of me, and it feels good to be loved; especially at this time of what I consider a personal bereavement.

"Wow, Jill, your body is looking good. That yoga and stretching and eating grass has done wonders." Deseree tells me. LaLaina leaves the bathroom as I begin to put on my bracelets and earrings. Grabbing the bottle of White Diamonds, I spray it on my wrists then rub them together then proceed to spray onto my neck and a small amount on my chest. Instantly my mood lifts, I can feel my energy turning around from the fragrance alone. The smell of my own skin began to jumpstart a better mood.

LaLaina returns to the bathroom with a cobalt blue dress I had in my closet and a striking pair of beige stilettos. She puts the blue dress with the bow on the right hand side up to match the length of my body. "This is going to be fierce, Jill. And with these *come fuck me* shoes, girl…"

"Really?" I question.

"Yes! Speaking of come fuck me…how's Avery, that doctor? Give him some yet?"

Deseree moves in close to me to get a bird's eye view of my response. I snatch the dress from LaLaina and put it on. I love the fit as it slides down my body with relative ease. I remember the days of praying to be able to fit into a size fourteen because at the time I bought this dress, I was nowhere near it. Talk about small victories.

"No, I haven't been intimate with him."

"You're such a prude, Jill," LaLaina says.

"No, I'm not!"

"Yes, you are!" Deseree and LaLaina both say in unison.

"He's everything a woman could want…tall, handsome, educated, no children."

"So, what's the hold up?" Deseree questions as she applies lip-gloss to my lips.

"Nothing really, just distracted, I guess."

"With?" LaLaina asks.

"Work."

"What's going on at work?" LaLaina asks.

"My patients take up all of my time."

"Well, you have to live a little. It's a beautiful thing that you give them life, but you have to remember to live too, Jill," Deseree commands.

"I'm living."

"Live more!" Deseree yells.

"I will."

"Okay, ladies, let's roll," LaLaina says trying to break up the tension, and we make our way out of the bathroom.

"You ladies never told me where we are going." I say as we hop into my truck. LaLaina is driving and Deseree sits in the back with a smirk on her face.

"Bitch, you ain't gotta know every damn thing all the damn time. You're such a control freak!" LaLaina yells.

Deseree laughs.

"Okay, well, just don't have me up in no ghetto ass club fighting with some ghetto ass women over some wanna be thug ass men. I'm way too old for that."

"We know, Jill. We'd never do that to you. Besides, you'd probably have some type of crisis of conscience and want to save a poor, lost soul in one of *those* clubs. Don't worry, we know our friend," LaLaina says with a snide look on her face.

"Good." I smile, sit back and enjoy the passenger seat of my truck. The heated seats are perfect since the winter will be kissing our lips soon. I think about what Deseree said earlier, the comments she made about my mother being beautiful. It's a shame, these women have been my best friends for so long and they've yet to really sit down and get to know my parents. They know and love Janet through and through, but mother and father never gave them the time of day.

I remember years ago when LaLaina, Deseree and I started to become really close. I would tell my mother stories about all of us cramming for exams and eating Chinese food 'til late at night. I even told her stories about how we felt about getting closer to graduation and what our life's goals and dreams were. With excitement, I told her everything about my college days and the two people who meant the most to me in getting through that time in my life. Once she discovered who they were and their background, Mother wasn't inspired to learn more. They meant everything to me, and yet, Mother didn't care about that or them.

"Are these girls from the ghetto, Jill?"

"Mom, what does that have to do with anything I've just told you?"

"You're better than that, Jill. Don't let those nigger hood rats corrupt you. You'll end up with three babies, by ten different niggers."

"Mom, that's impossible, and so are you!" I said and hung up the phone.

I look back at Deseree and think about all of the storms in life she has overcome. I glance at LaLaina and thank the Creator for sparing both of my friends, and myself for that matter, and shielding us from evil's might. We've been protected in ways we never even prayed about.

It's seven in the evening and my thoughts are making love to a fantasy as we head over to New York City. The beautiful New York City skyline comes into view as we cross the highways and byways on this cool and crisp evening.

I think of him. He would be winding down from a full day of therapy and would be so hungry by this time at night. I loved to watch Jerusalem eat. He had an appetite built for a king and while I never wanted to admit it, he had a body to match. I suppose all of those years in the service had him built like a well-oiled machine. It was not my place to bother or to comment, but my senses could not ignore his splendor.

I often imagined what he'd look like without bandages covering half of his face. His soft, jet-black curly hair, combined with that dark-dark chocolate skin, gave me the impression that something other than African lineage crept into his bloodstream by way of two ancestors fawning for one another in a time and place when they were not supposed to allow their very own flesh to collide.

Even with half a smile, his lips were indulgent; smooth in appearance, full and thick like many a good story had passed through them. Jerusalem's teeth were white and bright; his smile – even though there was only half of it to be seen – warmed my heart most days, but I never let on. I could never say a word.

He often thanked me. I wanted to say "Thank You" in return. Healing him, in many ways, healed me. It's hard to explain, but I feel alive more now than I have in quite some time.

"Jill, what's on your mind? You've been down for the last few weeks." Deseree questions.

"I promise you two, I'm okay. I guess we all have seasons in life in which we deal with things, or not. I'm good. I swear, I'm good and when and if the day comes where I'm not good, you'll be the first to know," I tell them.

I remember when he grabbed my arm. It wasn't forceful in a dangerous way, but he made a statement with the touch of his hands and his mouth didn't have to say a word. "Your skin is so soft," he said and I needed to be the adult in the room, as hard as it was. I had to allow my professionalism to take the lead. I had to put my feelings aside about the way he made me smile when I read poetry. My being so proud of him didn't matter; I was his nurse and he…my patient. Nothing more, nothing less.

I wanted to hug him and kiss him when he spoke of his mother. I remember the day he told me about her story. I remember early on, when he first arrived, he cried in the middle of the night. I rushed in to check on him.

"Sergeant Jones. What's the matter?"

"Nothing."

"Well, you're lying here in the dark and you're crying."

"Nothing's wrong."

I turned on the lights and his face was soaked, wet with uncontrollable tears. I took a tissue to his face, patted the tears from around his bandages.

"Sergeant Jones! What's the matter?"

"Today is my mother's birthday."

I said no more. I simply wiped the tears from his face. I placed tissue around his nose and squeezed.

"Blow."

He blew his nose so hard and I cleaned his nose and his face.

"How's your head?"

"It's throbbing."

I wiped his tears more.

Reaching over his lifeless body, I pressed the button for an attending nurse to come to the room. Sandy walked right in.

"Yes, Jill."

"Sandy, get me something to help Sergeant Jones sleep and something for his pain. He has no allergies. Have one of the aides bring Sergeant Jones a hot cup of tea with honey and cream. There's chamomile tea in the kitchen in my cabinet. Make it very sweet. Also, have them bring me some warm blankets."

"You don't have to do this," he said in almost a whisper.

"Sergeant, I didn't ask for your advice or opinion." I told him and continued to wipe the tears from his eyes. I went into the bathroom and grabbed a towel, and drowned it in cool water, and brought it back and placed it on Jerusalem's head – right across his forehead. I began to hum a tune and while doing so, rubbed his arms, held his hands, and rubbed them too. Blotted the tears from his eyes.

The aides came in with warm blankets and while I raised the back of his bed up so he could sit up, I wrapped him in those warm blankets. Sandy brought in the sleeping pill and something for his pain and I gave it to him with a glass of water.

"Thank you," he said right before he swallowed.

"Here's the hot tea, Jill." One of the nurse's aides told me as she handed me the cup.

"Here, Sergeant Jones, take a sip."

He did.

"Tastes good."

"Good."

He sat up, sipped his tea, and said no more. I turned off all the lights in his room and sat at his bedside. I rubbed his arm and his hand and hummed a tune. Once he finished his tea, I took the cup and placed it on his table.

"Thank you," his depleted voice conveyed.

"Shhhh…get some rest," I told him.

I got up and lowered his bed. Wiped his face. Rubbed his arms. Rubbed his hands. Hummed a tune.

We arrive at our destination. It's a place I've heard of, but have never been. It's a new supper club to the area, with a live jazz performance for the evening. We make our way to the door.

"You all shouldn't have," I tell Deseree and LaLaina.

"We had to. You've been in a scarf for weeks. You've been sounding so down and out lately. We love you, Jill, and whatever you're going through – whatever this storm is – we are going to get through this."

We all hug. I'm touched by their care. It's the kind of care I wish I had received from my own mother.

This place is so nice. Upscale to the max. Tea candles surround the club's borders, entranceways and tables. Soft lights running down the middle of the walls makes an interesting look as the top portion of the walls have sixteen by twenty posters of jazz greats – most of them are my favorites. Lights line the bar, the kind you see around Christmastime. The back of the bar is all glass from the floor to the ceiling with silver and purple lighting shining throughout.

I'm impressed.

We sit at our table, which is smack dab in the middle of the club's orchestra section. Deseree and LaLaina order drinks for all of us. Without hesitation, they order one of my favorite drinks for me, a Brandy Alexander. I could use the sweet taste of that in my life right now. I could use the alcohol's effects to take me to another place. I need the escape. My girls don't let me down.

They order dinner for me. They order appetizers and as we wait for our meals to return, the start of tonight's event appears on stage.

Joe Thomas, jazz legend, appears with his dream band, his horn in hand and a string wrapped around his neck secures it. Talk about loving your instrument.

He greets the audience and begins to play a melody that is so endearing. The crowd of onlookers and jazz lovers enjoy the medley as do I. Deseree and LaLaina must really love me because they would much rather be at an R&B concert as opposed to this. Hell, LaLaina's ghetto ass would love to be checking out Jay-Z, I just know it. Yet, they brought me here. They medicated my soul. That's love.

We munch on stuffed mushrooms and teriyaki chicken fingers. The drinks keep coming back to back and I sip on each one each and every time our server sits a fresh glass in front of me.

He plays a song and pulls out his flute. The melody is smooth and soothing and touches my spirit in only the way music can. The flute sings a particular song to me and the harmonies remind me of Jay's laughter. I hear the flute. I see Jay smiling. I hear the flute and I hear Jay laughing.

I'm overwhelmed.

I bow my head and tears pour down my face as Joe Thomas puts his heart and soul into every note of a love song. It has to be a ballad. I feel it. I sense that it is. It is taking over my soul, inside out, from the depth of my core.

"Jill?" Deseree softly questions as she rubs my back.

"I'm okay," I tell her.

LaLaina hands me a tissue. "What's wrong, honey?"

"I'm okay."

"You're not okay, Jill. Cut the shit!" LaLaina demands.

"Jill, please tell us. We want to help." I can feel the sincere concern in Deseree's words.

"I miss my patient."

"Who?"

"Jerusalem Jones."

"I remember that name," Deseree says.

"He was discharged a short while ago."

"Short as in a couple weeks, Jill?" LaLaina asks.

"Yes."

"You've been down a couple weeks, Jill," LaLaina adds with a look on her face that lets me know an inquisition is about to begin.

She wipes my tears. "What's going on, Jill?"

"Nothing."

"What happened between you and Jerusalem, Jill?" Deseree pokes at my feelings with her question.

What did happen between us? I think to myself. "Nothing, well, everything," are the words that I utter instead.

"Do you love him, Jill?" LaLaina asks.

Well, go for the jugular why don't you? My mind says. Why are they asking me questions I haven't had the courage to ask myself.

"How can I? I was his nurse. He was *only* my patient. I just miss taking care of him. That's all!" I speak words that even I don't believe.

"No, baby…this is *way* more than that," Deseree insists as she puts an emphasis on the word, "way."

"Can't be! I was just doing my job," I tell them in a tone a little louder than called for.

"Where is Jerusalem now, Jill?" LaLaina asks.

"I don't know!" I burst out in tears and start to cry uncontrollably.

"Oh, Lord, have mercy. Why don't you look up his records and find him?" LaLaina asks.

"I can't. It's inappropriate,"

"Baby, you are *way* past appropriate," Deseree says, emphasizing the word, "way" again.

Deseree rubs my back and LaLaina wipes my tears.

"Find him, Jill. I've never seen you like this before," LaLaina demands.

Joe Thomas continues to play. My friends continue to console me. My tears continue to fall. Through it all, my heart joins the aura of the night in pleading for me to ignore my head and follow my heart.

Why does my heart ignore what my mind says?

Chapter 19

It's My Thing

"**D**on't get too close, because you might get shot!" I say aloud as my head nods up and down in sync and in rhythm to EPMD's, "It's My Thing." With the recent discovery that I'll be getting a guaranteed four hundred dollars a month from the military, I decided to buy myself a truck. I was tired of borrowing LT's spare car. Although he would have given it to me if I asked, God bless the child who's got his own.

I got my own. It may not be much, but I got my own.

Sweet, black, used Cadillac -- Escalade to be precise. Very used but I will make this work. A real man's car. Black leather-wrapped steering wheel with radio controls, all wood grain throughout, which is super sexy, heated front and second row seats, tri-zone air conditioning, power lift gate, and a premium sound system with multiple CD changer, so I can go from jazz for my baby and Hip Hop for me. I got the platinum joint which has the DVD entertainment system, navigation system, heated and cooled cup holders, and power-retractable running boards.

I talked the salesman down to practically cost this past

Saturday. I told him I was newly employed to the University as a basketball coach and that I was an Iraq war veteran. I offered him tickets to the games at the University. I remember my mother telling my father, "No one sells us anything, we buy it." She said it when we were purchasing the family car; a 1982 Toyota Corolla in white. The reaction Jabez and I, and even LT had for that matter, had to our new family car was ridiculous when I think about it. We were so hyped!

Too funny. Good memories.

One of the true pleasures I've come across in life is Hip Hop. Hip Hop has gotten me through some of the worst times in my life. When words spoken by another to a beat that can't be easily removed from one's mind meet…clarification often is achieved. That's what Hip Hop does for me. Whether it's a song that reminded me of my first crush or something profound that spoke to me – and a generation of young black boys like me – there's something about Hip Hop that is incredibly dope. It is poetry in its rawest form. And, when it comes from the right artist…Hip Hop is poetry in motion.

Another pleasure of mine is being able to turn my music up 'til it makes the speakers bleed. I mean, who can listen to EPMD without the volume being on ten? I know I can't. Right…I'm not a kid anymore, but real men do real things, and this here "Strictly Business" is a symbol of a real man doing his damn thing.

I feel alive. More alive than I've felt in almost twenty years.

New crib, new whip, new limp, "Ha, ha, ha," I crack myself up sometimes. I'm trying to get that Denzel Washington strut down pat to mask this limp I have.

As happy as I am about looking forward, I am equally nervous. I'm on my way to Doctor Rodgers' office to remove these bandages once and for all. It's been a good minute since the surgery, and while very tempted, I didn't remove the bandages; not even a little. I was not going to have a hand in fucking up the progress of my face. Doctor Rodgers said the work he did was extensive, and there was no way in hell I was ruining it by being impatient. I need to be from under this cloud.

Pressing the pedal to the floor, the sunroof is open, allowing the cool, crisp, early morning – almost winter – air into my new ride. The sun is kissing me from the top today and I'd like to think it's my mother and father showing their love. My nerves have the best of me, but I have a song in my heart.

A song in my heart.

Damn, I miss that girl.

I pull up to the parking lot for Doctor Rodgers' office, and I see that it is rather empty. That's good, because right now, I don't want to be confined by anything any longer; even patients in a waiting room of a doctor's office. I step out of my truck, and my foot hits the pavement first. Stacy Adams jet black leather shoes on my feet. I threw on a white button up, a black suit jacket and black suit pants today because right after the new reveal, I have a meeting with the University of New York basketball head coach. LT already apprised them of my condition, so even with bandages and a fucked-up face, I'm determined to get this job; no matter what I look like and no matter how scared I am.

Since feeling better and being in my own home, I know in these past couple of weeks I've gained a few pounds. In a minute, I'll be back to my two hundred thirty pound frame. It's where I'm most comfortable. Even the limp doesn't destroy my mood, because at the end of the day, the doctors were able to save my leg. I'll take a limp over a stump any day of the week. I still appear to be six foot three, and I have my legs, so all I can do is say, "Thank you, God," and I have that saying on repeat in my mind and on my lips.

Two white women walk past me and they stare. I often think that when people stare, it's because of my face, but it could be the fact that EPMD is on full blast. I reach back in my truck and turn off the CD player. I smile as they look back at me again after I've turned down the music.

The jackass in me waves "Hello" and shorty winks and waves back.

Oh shit!

I wish I was on the market because the final thing missing in my life is my wife. But even though technically I am single and therefore on the market, my heart belongs to one woman and one woman only; and she doesn't even have a clue of her position as queen of my world. I wasn't in a position to run any type of game on her. I was too busy dying and wanting to die to even realize that I started to really dig her. I couldn't throw my Mack on her because she was wiping my tears. I was so wide open in her presence. She definitely had, and still has, the upper hand, even though I haven't seen her in weeks.

Reaching the receptionist's desk, I greet her with a sincere, "Hello…good morning," and tell her, "Jerusalem Jones. I have a nine o'clock appointment with Doctor Rodgers."

"Sure thing, Mr. Jones. Have a seat and we'll call you shortly."

I make my way to the first available seat, which is right in front of the television, and I catch my man LT handling the sports on the late morning news. He's adorning that big ass, fake ass, Kool-Aid smile that the ladies seem to love so much. He looks dapper, though; my brother definitely keeps himself together. Always has. Light-skinned, light-eyed ass.

I crack open the newspaper and see that the Republicans are still blocking every damn thing President Obama tries to accomplish. Seems like the same headline daily – Obama pushes, Republicans pull; or Obama goes left, Republicans go far right. *Same shit, different day.* I'll never understand the two-party system when everyone in office, and who have the privilege to serve this country, will only serve based on what side of the aisle they sit. Those that we elect into office make it a point to stay true and convicted to their positions, according to affiliations versus what's right; even if it means the detriment of their fellow Americans and the people they are supposed to serve. Hell, if I had those same selfish feelings, I sure wouldn't be sitting here with shrapnel in my leg and a face that suffered third-degree burns.

But, what do I know.

"Mr. Jones?"

"Yes?"

"Come on back. Doctor Rodgers will see you now."

I feel like I need to throw up, but I maintain my composure as I greet the nurse at the entranceway to the patient rooms in the back. The nurse tells me to follow her and I willingly oblige. We finally enter the room where I'll be seen, and she takes all of my vitals. I stare at the ceiling and exhale deeply, hoping to bring down my blood pressure, which I am sure, is sky-high due to my anxiety.

"Everything checks out, Mr. Jones."

"Thank God."

"Okay, the doctor will be right in."

I sit on the examination table and wait patiently. I like to think my anxiety is lowering, but to think that way would only be fooling myself.

"Okay, thanks," I utter as calmly as possible.

Doctor Rodgers and his assistant enter the room and my nerves are at an all-time high…once again. It's something about them damn white coats that get me every time. I'm scared to death, but again…I don't let it show. My Division Commander once told me while we were in a fighter jet on our way to Iraq, "Never let them see you sweat." This was during my first tour. I never let those words escape me. I apply it to life in general and to daily living. The only person who ever saw me sweat was LT, and that's because he's my best friend. Other than him, the only other person has been Jill, and I still have no real explanation as to why I let my guard down with her.

Doctor Rodgers has been removing bandages and cleaning my face for what seems like hours. If I didn't know any better I would swear he is a masochist and that he gets off from watching me suffer. His assistant keeps triple-checking his work and following behind him with her own set of responsibilities. *All of this for bandages?* I ask myself, but I lay here patiently, because I know one of two things; either the worst is over, or it is just beginning. I want to throw up again, but I keep my cool.

I think about Jill and I smile. Even the thought of her name does that to me. I think about her silly laugh and her strong personality. If she were here, she'd be cheering me on, reminding me that I'm a soldier and by virtue of that title, I'm a king among kings. If she were here, she'd be telling everyone what to do and how to do it, even Doctor Rodgers. If she were here, she'd be barking out orders while dishing out love. I smile when I think about how reserved, yet how feisty she is. She's an enigma of sorts and it's very intriguing. Whoever the man is in her life, he's one lucky son of a bitch. I envy him. I wish I were him.

"All done, Mr. Jones," Doctor Rodgers says as he and his assistant help to lift me off the table so I can sit upright.

Moment of truth, I feel my soul shout.

His assistant, Katie —I assume that's her name since it says it on her lab coat – is smiling from ear to ear. I want to garner a sense of comfort in her smile, but I dare not. I'm nervous all over again.

Doctor Rodgers smiles. Takes a deep, long, and uninterrupted look at my face. Why does he torture me so? *Spit it out already, Doc,* my mind screams behind un-parting lips.

He turns to Katy. "I'm good; huh, Katie?"

He chuckles, but still waits for an answer from her.

"Yes, Doctor Rodgers, you're very good. Probably the best," she smiles and looks at me.

Katie hands me a hand-held mirror and I don't put it up to my face. I lost all courage in that one instant. I want to so bad. I want to see the new me. I want to see if I look like…me. The old me. The me that I know and love. The me that I am comfortable with and want to return to.

"Go ahead, Mr. Jones," Doctor Rodgers insists, encouraging me to let the mirror introduce me to myself.

Slowly and methodically, and at a snail's pace, I lift the mirror to my face with my right hand; praying for God's grace with each inch that the mirror rises. The butterflies in my stomach are doing somersaults at an all-time high.

"Go ahead, Mr. Jones. You can do this." Doctor Rodgers says with an air of support that I know he truly feels.

"I'm trying, Doctor Rodgers. Big day, ya know?" I pause a moment longer, summonsing my inner soldier for protection.

"I do know."

Finally, I look myself in the mirror and I see my full face. My face. It's a bit foreign to me, but it is still mine. I see my face. I haven't seen my face in months. I haven't felt air on my face. I see my face. It's mine; I own it. I remember this face. It's distorted and that has come with age, time, and circumstance, but it's there. It's mine. It's my face and I love it and all that it represents, for it represents me. I recognize the person staring back at me. I know it's me and I'm happy to see, embrace and recognize the man in the mirror. I'm happy to see me.

Everything else in the room disappears. Nothing else exists. Just me and my face. The doctor disappears. The nurse disappears. The world, with all of the good and bad in it, disappears. All that remains is me and seeing my face.

My fingers trace my skin and I see and feel the damage. It's minimal. I can live with that. I cringe when I think about whether

I'll ever get a wife at this point due to my facial scarring, but I'm thankful I didn't end up like Abdul. Abdul was in Iraq with me, and most of his face was blown off. Completely blown off. Yes, he's still alive, but how much living is Abdul going to do with half a face.

I've got mine.

It's scarred, but it's there.

I'm thankful.

I see my face. It's me. I recognize this dude. He loves Hip Hop. He's grown enough to love jazz. It's Jerusalem Jones; son, brother, soldier, democrat, Iraq war veteran and simply Jay to some. I know who he is. I like him and he stares back at me with a smile that indicates he likes me too.

I rise to my feet and extend my hand to shake Doctor Rodgers'.

"I can't thank you enough, Doctor Rodgers." I tell him. Doctor Rodgers walks over to the counter and grabs what appears to be a chart. He hands the folder to me.

"Have a look, son," he tells me as he pushes the folder further towards me. The contents of the folder force me to sit down on the examining table. The same table I just got up from. I sit and I look and my eyes fill with tears.

"Doctor?" I question Doctor Rodgers and he looks at me and smiles. Although I know my experience, the injuries I sustained while fighting for this country lean toward the worst end of life's spectrum, I realize there are those who have suffered more than I have. Even in the immense experience I have gained from being a burn victim – a victim of war – there are some situations I cannot begin to imagine. Fourth-degree burns, amputation, loss of sight, loss of limbs and complete loss of function covers some of those realms.

"That was you, Mr. Jones; right after the attack when you were in the infirmary. The second set are photos of you after a few weeks of what I call, "Getting you ready.' See Mr. Jones, I've been getting you ready for months.

I can't fight the lump building in my throat. I try to man up… but my heart is weak.

"I've come such a long way," I hear myself speak although I am not conscious of doing so.

"You have…and you're very lucky. You're as strong as an ox,

you're young and you have an insurmountable will to live. All of these things played a part in your recovery. Each one of them were not only necessary, but needed."

"But you did this, doctor, not me."

"You helped."

I don't remember having a will to live early on in this process. I give credit to Jill for that. She gave me back my life. She forced me not to give up. She made me want to live.

"I can't thank you enough for saving my face…saving my life."

"I told you I was good," Doctor Rodgers smiles and gives me a wink.

"That you are, doctor. Indeed you are."

I shake his hand one last time and Katie, his assistant, is in the corner smiling with tears in her eyes. She comes over to me and hugs me. I'm caught off guard, but I return her hug.

"We'll see you in one month just for a follow up. Fill the prescription for the cream and use that nightly. Religiously. Apply the ointment as if your life depends on it because the sake of your sanity does. Keep yourself hydrated. You're going to be fine, Mr. Jones."

I smile and make my way out of the doctor's office and head to the parking lot. As I hit the button on the remote and unlock the doors to my new truck, I hear LT's words in my ear. I replay them in my mind.

"So what are you going to do about Jill?"

"Nothing."

"Why not, Jay?"

"Because I'm discharged from the hospital. Reason, season, lifetime. She was a beautiful season. She made me want to live again."

"That's deep, Jay."

"I know."

"Go get her, Jay."

"Can't."

"Why?"

"Because she was my nurse, LT. Didn't you hear me?"

"I did. But I haven't seen you this enthralled or excited about a woman in a very long time. As a matter of fact, I've never seen a

woman change you for the better."

"Man, I've been in other countries."

"So what. I'm your brother. And I would know if any woman had. I know the ladies you've fucked over the years. This one is different."

"I just can't."

"You can. And you should."

I look back at the building that houses the doctors' offices. It's connected to the hospital. I am just moments away from seeing her again. I had dreams of returning here to thank all of the people who helped me to live again. I've been dying to see Phil, my physical therapist, and Candy, the nurse's aide who ran around like a chicken with her head cut off when Jill would bark outrageous orders like getting me tea and warm blankets.

What if my face scares everyone off? What if Jill is repulsed by the sight of me? What if she doesn't even remember who I am? Looking at my watch, I have some time before I need to head over to the University of New York.

"Go get her!" I hear LT's words again.

I'm afraid, but I need to do the right thing and at the very least, thank those folk who helped me to regain my life. I don't take it for granted and I want them to know, under no uncertain terms, that I am so grateful for what they did for me.

I make my way to the hospital gift shop and see all kinds of overpriced items in here that would make great gifts. I smile when I see the flowers on display. I order a bouquet of flowers and simply tell the Asian woman to make it colorful. I ask her to attach a "Thank You" helium balloon to the arrangement.

I'm counting my pennies as I'm purchasing. The military doesn't pay its soldiers very well and while I saved, I still have to be careful until this coaching position is offered to me. I'm speaking that into existence.

"Excuse me, Miss, can I also have an arrangement made with purple roses. Also, please attach a "Thank You" balloon to that arrangement, too."

"Only purple, sir?"

"For now, yes, thanks."

"You got it."

She hands me the two bouquets and I grab something for Phil

and head to the elevator. Those butterflies have returned with a vengeance, and I look down at my belly and whisper, "Shut the fuck up. Damn."

I also whisper to myself, "Man up. You got this."

I step off the elevator and my memory does not fail me one bit. I see the physical therapy room and I spot Phil doing what he does best – helping someone to walk again. I tap on the wooden door and peek through the glass window. Phil comes over to open the door.

"May I help you?" he inquires. His eyes are so big and blue that it makes me wonder if Phil snorts coke. Inappropriate thought, but Phil looks like he just drank ten cups of coffee.

"Phil?"

"Yes."

"It's Jerusalem Jones, you…"

"Oh my God! Look at you, man!" he yells and hugs me. His grip is so strong that I almost drop the flowers. I smile.

"Man, you look great! Oh wow, look at your face!"

My heart sinks.

"Jerusalem, you look incredible! What an outstanding job they did on your face! Man, you just made my day." Phil's smile is so big it almost brightens the room. I can feel that he is being sincere.

I'm relieved.

"Phil, I just needed to come by and say how thankful I am that you took care of me. Man, I'm walking because of you. Now, I know this isn't the most manly of presents I could have given you, but it's all the hospital's gift shop had." I tell him as I hand him a box of chocolates. Phil laughs.

"Anytime, man, and I love chocolates, but you know my wife is going to finish this box tonight!"

We both laugh.

"Good seeing you, Phil."

I walk through the hallway and head down the corridor to the nurses' station. I see familiar faces. I smile as nurses and patients and people walk past me. I nod and say hello to a few onlookers who are probably wondering why I have flowers in my arms.

Finally, I make it to the station where Jill and the crew work. I see those faces that greeted mine on a regular basis for months. I smile as Candy, the nurse's aide, walks by.

"Candy, how are you?"

"Oh my goodness, is that you Mr. Jones?'

"Yes! How did you know?"

"Your voice. Your hair. Oh wow, you look awesome!"

She hugs me.

I hand her the generic bouquet of flowers. "Here, put these somewhere. I needed to stop in to say "Thank you" to everyone who helped me.

Candy yells for the other nurses to come over and talk to me. They all rush over and hug me and I can feel the love. It's warm. It's welcoming. It feels good. Scanning the area, I look for my angel and I don't see her. Instantly, my heart sinks.

"Jill, Jill!" Candy yells and I turn around.

"Jill, look who's back!" Candy screams.

Jill's eyes lock with mine and damn, I want to run away and hide with her somewhere. Those big almond-shaped eyes won't leave mine. She does not say a word, and neither do I. She stares. I stare. I could kidnap her right now.

"Jill, do you see Jerusalem?" Candy asks.

"Yes," she smiles. She walks toward me. I hand her the purple roses.

"You shouldn't have."

"I had to."

"These are beautiful."

"Read the card." I demand.

She pulls the card out and walks toward the elevators. I follow her. I once again see the full frame, the curves, the hips, the long legs that captured me months ago. I can't take my eyes off of everything I shouldn't be staring at right now. I smell her scent. Inhale every bit of her aroma. Her smell weakens me.

"I dropped a tear in the ocean. The day it comes to shore is the day I'll stop missing you, Jill. Please call me, Jay. 973-555-1417." She reads the card aloud.

"I mean every word."

"Oh, Jay."

"Call me, Jill. I gotta run."

"Jay, please don't go."

"Gotta go get this money."

"Please, Jay, don't leave."

"Call me, Jill. I'll be in my car in five minutes."
"Okay," she says to me with tears in her eyes.
	As the elevator door closes, I blow her a kiss.

Chapter 20

Jill

You Leave Me Breathless

Nothing short of amazing these last few weeks have been. I feel like I've known Jerusalem Jones all of my life. His smile is so endearing and as corny as it sounds, it really lights up my life. I'm still struggling with the idea that this may not be the best choice – going out on dates with a former patient – but he makes me feel so good that I'm having trouble controlling myself. I'm never out of control in my life. I've managed to maintain control and move forward with my goals and desires with blood, sweat and tears, and some good, hard work, and I maintain control.

I can't in this situation. For the first time in my life, I'm out of control.

Uncontrollable desire isn't defined, it simply is; and while I've never experienced it in my life, I've heard of it, just couldn't quite believe in it before. I get it now. Live and direct.

Uncontrollable desire.

I hear all the words he's saying as I reminisce about dinner last night.

I wore my hair in a bun. It's something I think he gets a kick out of. He joked about me looking like Pebbles from "The Flintstones." The black, sweetheart illusion dress from Ashley Stewart seemed to have stopped him in his tracks. The mesh neckline is see-through and while my mouth will utter the sentiments that I was not trying to turn Jay on, I know in my subconscious I was trying my damndest to do just that.

We sat at that corner table in that little chic restaurant somewhere in the mountains; some place I had never heard of – until Jerusalem entered my life – for hours. He sipped on some brown-colored liquor, smelling the aroma of the glass and its contents almost before every sip. He smiled as he watched me. I nursed a Brandy Alexander for most of the evening. Two, actually.

The beige-colored silk shirt lay over his firm chest softly. The two top buttons were undone. I think he knew that would drive me wild. He was fucking with me and I liked it. The smell of his cologne penetrated all of my senses and as I inhaled his pheromones, I gushed and released in anticipation of him. A sticky wetness announced it presence. I didn't let him in on my dirty little secret.

My eyes followed his chiseled jaw line, around his chocolate, succulent lips, and I took a voyage to his perfectly trimmed goatee. Jay's luscious lips parted to reveal a majestic set of piano keys, pure white, pristine, like Ivory straight from the Congo – the Motherland. Yes, he was born of royal seed. Brought in to my existence from Iraq via a military helicopter. Broken, bruised, almost dead, but this man, amazingly splendid in physical beauty, adeptly regal in physical supremacy, commands all attention when he enters a room. Even with a damaged face. Even from having suffered third degree burns, his swagger is undeniable.

I know his face bothers him, so I brought the issue up and got it out of the way so we can…so he can move forward with his life.

"Doctor Rodgers did an excellent job, Jay."

His mood changed swiftly. He touched the side of his face with his left hand.

"Think so?"

"I know so."

"I feel like the Elephant Man."

I cracked a coy smile.

"Don't."

"Self-conscious is all."

"Jay…"

"Yes?"

"Don't be."

"I feel like everyone in here is staring at me."

"Probably because you look so damn good."

He smiled.

"Hope so."

"I know so, trust me."

"How can you be so sure, Jill?"

"Because you're beautiful."

"Happy as hell you think so."

"Beauty is in the eye of the beholder, Jay. You're the most beautiful man I've ever seen in my life."

"You made my heart jump."

"Then I'm doing my job."

"You have always done your job. Thank you for bringing me back to life."

"Thank you for giving me life, Jay."

"The Elephant Man gives beautiful nurse new life," that'll be tomorrow's headlines.

"Confucius said something that I want you to always remember."

"Oh, tell me philosopher," he cracked a smile.

"Everyone has beauty, but not everyone sees it."

"That's deep, Jill."

"You're beautiful Jay – wonderfully, beautifully you."

A few moments passed and I could not take my eyes off him. His jet-black curly hair and that exquisite face simply captured me. His body, through that shirt, had me in a trance.

"What are you staring at?" he questioned as he took a sip of his brown liquor.

"You," I replied, as I took a sip of the chilled wine in front of me, in hopes of slowing down our time together.

Stammering over my thoughts, I try to find something to say that wouldn't make me sound like either a complete fool or a slut. I knew that whatever came out of my mouth would only reveal the truth; I'm his forever, a faithful concubine. I'm Jay's for the taking, but I'm too much of a lady to reveal that.

"It's almost midnight. Getting late," he said as he took a spoonful of his dessert – white chocolate bread pudding.

Leaning into the center of our quaint table, the votive candle illuminated my face. I whispered, "Then, we should get going."

He grabbed my hand. "I'm not ready," his voice was seductive as he drew circles into the palm of my hand with his fingertip. Although he wasn't ready, the words he really wanted to utter were, "please don't leave me." I know him. I know Jay so well.

I stared him in the eyes, and revealed, "We eventually have to go home, baby."

"You called me baby. I'm honored. I *am* home," he smiled. His fingertip slowly ran up the side of my arm.

"I enjoyed dinner, too, Mr. Jones," I say, as I lay flat on my back on my bed. The snow is starting to fall and it appears that winter is coming early November. My room is warm; and as I lay here in a raspberry-colored chemise and panties, I feel so free, so alive, and so beautiful. My fingers twirl in my hair and I take a piece and curl my locks. I smile as Jay jokes, on the other end of the phone line, about the topic of the day. He's such a clown.

"So, really, if President Obama got this country back on track and we had a surplus, the Republicans would find a way to say that having a surplus is wrong."

"Jay, stop!" I laugh aloud.

"If Obama brought back Jesus Christ himself, the Republicans would say it was the wrong timing for the second coming."

"You're such a fool, Jay! Stop! You're making my stomach hurt." I laugh more.

"I love your laugh, Jill."

"Oh, you say that to all the nurses who saved your life and baked you cookies and made you hot tea."

"Perfect!" Jay yells.

"Jay?"

"You're my cookie. That's what I'm going to call you, baby.

You're my Cookie."

My heart skips a beat.

"What are you playing over there? Let me guess, Coltrane?"

"Yes, sir. 'You Leave Me Breathless' by Coltrane. You like?"

"*You* do."

"I do what?"

"You leave me breathless, Jill. But I'm sure you know that already."

"I didn't know that, Jay."

"Let me repeat that, Cookie. You and your beautiful, sweet, delicious, fine ass…YOU leave me breathless."

"Wow."

"It's true."

"Jay, how many dates have we been on?"

"Probably a dozen or so. Why?"

"Just seems like a whirlwind."

"Is that a bad thing?"

"No…"

"What's wrong, baby?"

"I struggle a lil bit, Jay. I mean…I was your nurse and you were my patient."

"Understood. I'll pump the brakes. Just don't shut me out completely."

"I can't."

"Music to my ears, Cookie. But I just have to say something."

"What is that?"

"I've seen enough devastation in my life to know that when you find a good thing in life, you really have to cherish that good thing in the here and now; regardless of what anyone says or does or thinks. Cookie, you don't strike me as the type of person who…"

"You're right, baby."

"Oh, she calls me, baby? Hot damn!"

"You're so silly. Jay, what did you do today? I know I worked my ass off…"

"Oh baby, don't work that off, I like it just the way it is."

"Jay!" I laugh again.

"Well, before we met for dinner, I was researching online how to find my brother Jabez. I told you about him. We were separated more than twenty years ago. I was in and out of foster care. He got adopted. LT told me he found out that the adoption was by a family named Anderson. I don't see him on social media anywhere. I keep running into brick walls."

"Oh, baby. What's his date of birth?"

"December 29th, 1978."

"And yours is Christmas day; right, baby?"

"Yes, Cookie. Good memory. My mother had us around the same time even if it was a few years apart."

"How sweet."

"You're sweet, Cookie. I bet you taste as good as you look."

Jay's words soared throughout my soul, ran through my veins, and landed on both of my nipples where they now throb and ache for him. Funny, we've been out to lunch and to dinner and we've yet to kiss. We simply hug and embrace, but I think we're both too scared to take it any further.

"Thank you, Jay."

"Do you?" Jay asks.

"Do I what?"

"Taste as good as you look?"

I swallow hard. I cross my legs to extinguish the roaring inferno. The next Coltrane song comes on and I continue to play in my hair.

"Jay…"

"Tell me, baby."

"I don't know."

"I'm sure you do," he says. His voice gets deeper.

"Perhaps."

"No guessing. I believe you taste as good as you look. I want to find out for myself. Can I?"

"Jay."

"Baby, I asked you a question."

I exhale.

"Baby, answer me. Can I taste you?"

"Jay, you're going to…"

"What? Baby, if this is wrong, I don't want to be nowhere near right. Tell me, Jill."

"I'm thinking about it."

"Is someone else tasting it?"

"Absolutely not."

"Good, because that sweet, wet, hot, delicious snatch may be in between your legs…but it belongs to me, you got that?"

My panties are starting to soak.

I exhale.

"Jill?"

"Yes?"

"It belongs to me, and I can't wait to taste it."

"I see."

"You see what, baby? You see that I need you, right, Jill?"

"Do you?"

"Like the air I breathe."

"This is wrong, Jay."

"No baby, not at all. This is so right, baby."

"Do you want me, Jill?'

"Jay…"

"Do you want me, Jill, because I want you so fucking bad?"

"I do."

"Have me any way you want me, baby. I'm yours for the taking."

"Jay, I gotta go."

"Why, baby? Don't turn back now, Jill."

"I'm scared."

"Of?"

"You. This. I'm out of control. I can't control how I'm feeling. Moving too fast. I feel crazy."

"You think I don't feel like I've lost my mind, baby? I have been scratching my head over and over trying to figure out how I got to this place. I'm past the point of no return, Jill. I can't control this. I won't try to. Stop trying to define this."

"Okay."

"Do you want me, Jill?"

"I do, Jay."

"Tell me."

"I want you, Jay."

"Good girl. You know you're mine, right?"

"Yes."

"Tell me you want me to slide my tongue in and out of that hot pussy baby, because I want to suck it so damn bad."

"Jay…"

"I know you want me just as bad as I want you, Jill. No more denying. Now, tell me you want me to taste you."

"Jay…I…I want…"

"Tell me, baby. Tell me what you want. Don't be scared, tell me."

"Jay, I want you to taste me. I want you…I want you to slide your tongue in me."

"I'm going to give you all this tongue, baby. Tell me everything you want."

"I want to feel you deep inside of me, Jay. I do."

My God, I can't believe what I'm doing in this bed alone, with only my man on the phone.

"Good, girl. Real deep, baby?"

"Mmmm, real deep, baby."

"I'll take my time. Real slow, long, deep, slow strokes for you, baby. You want that?"

"Ahh, Jay, mmmmm, baby…"

"Tell me that sweet pussy is mine."

"All yours, baby."

"What are you wearing, Cookie?"

"Chemise. Panties."

"Damn, girl. What color?"

"Raspberry. Pink."

My panties are off now and my fingers are sticky from rubbing between the lips of my vagina. The constant throbbing between my thighs makes me feel as if I'm going to burst. I try to contain myself, and not let Jay know how much he's blowing my mind.

"Mmm Mmmm Mmmm. Take off your panties and chemise, baby."

"Jay, I can't."

"I'll come over there and take it off of your fine ass. You want that?"

"Baby, okay, I'll take them off."

"Good girl. Put your phone on speaker."

"Why?"

"Because I want you to get my pussy ready for me."

"It is ready, Jay."

"I want to make sure. Who else is getting that sweet pussy?"

"Nobody."

"I don't want anyone else close enough to smell it. You hear me?"

"Yes, Jay. You're getting me too wet this way. We can't do this over the phone, Jay!"

"Rub it nice and slow, then stick your fingers in all that sweetness for me. Pull it out then in, over and over again, as if I'm deep inside your love."

"Jay…" I whisper his name as the rain begins to fall.

"You've been thinking about me, haven't you baby? You've been wanting to get to know me, I feel it. I know it. You want me to love you good. You want me, I can taste your sweet ass now."

"Jay," I cry through whispers.

"I need to smell it, Jill. The thought of touching you drives me wild. The thought of having you…can I have you, baby? I want all of it, all of you. I want to taste it. Fuck it. Suck it. Spank it. Love it. Empty myself inside of it, please," he whispers.

"Jay, it's too fucking wet now," I plead.

"Baby, open your legs nice and wide and take that pussy and spread it really nasty for me," he commands.

"It's open for you, baby."

"Jill, I'm stroking this hard dick for you. I can't wait to be deep inside of you."

"Ooooh, I'm coming all over that pretty pussy, baby…Shit!"

Chapter 21

Jerusalem

In a Sentimental Mood

"Hey, babe!" I yell as I open the front door.

"Yes, baby, I'm coming right down!"

"Hurry, baby!" I yell just to push her buttons.

"Jay, you just got here, give me a minute, please."

I laugh, a quiet, soft, devious laugh as I put down my briefcase and head into my baby's kitchen. Jill gave me a set of keys and the alarm code to her semi-palatial estate. My baby has the grandest of style because her pad is laid out to perfection.

The interior of my woman's beautiful home has a lovely main floor, second floor and basement. The second floor has a master bedroom and master bath, two bedrooms, two bathrooms and a fantastic loft. The main floor has a colossal top-of-the-line kitchen, living room and dining room, with high ceilings and wood beams and a family room with a wood-burning fireplace and a game room for guests and family members.

Jill didn't skimp on any design work either and no details are left unattended. The granite in the kitchen must have cost my baby a grip. When you are around Jill, you get a full sense of her humility, her compassion and kindness. One would never dream she lives in a place this grand and luxurious.

One of the things I admire about her is the fact that she doesn't take this house too seriously. She keeps it well, protects her investment, but she doesn't boast. That's not in her character. Women nowadays are not built the way my baby is – she cares about others more than herself and that's a beautiful trait to possess. God blessed her with more than her fair share of beauty, kindness, intelligence, free-spiritedness and so much more.

Reaching in the cabinet right next to the stainless steel refrigerator, I grab two cups and pour us some water. I play with her some more.

"Hey, baby! Come on!" I yell upstairs. I know she's ready to curse me out, but she would never do that.

"Jay! You've been here three minutes, I'm coming. Please be patient!" she yells back. I know she's saying things under her breath and I get a kick out of how refined she is.

"Babe!"

She doesn't answer. I laugh and take a sip of my water. I run back over to my briefcase real quick to grab the box. The gift-wrapped box is lined with silver and has a big gold bow on top. I pray she loves what's inside.

"Babe!"

"Yes, Jay!"

"Did you wear blue like I told you, baby?"

"Oh my God, yes, Jay, I'm coming now. What's gotten into you today?"

I hear her voice getting closer so I walk to the bottom of the stairs. She finally reaches the top and my heart flutters. I inhale and exhale quickly and swallow hard. A vision of loveliness greets me. My eyes peer up to take in all that is gorgeous and charming and beautiful and…damn.

All I see are legs for days as she walks down the flight of stairs that lead from the upstairs to the lower-level foyer. She has on beige come-and-get-me heels. I've never seen her in heels that high before. She said she doesn't wear heels often because of her height. The cobalt, royal blue dress hugs her every curve, like its holding on for dear life. While I try to maintain my composure, it's hard. I swallow hard again and I smile.

"Well, hello, beautiful," I tell her with a smile. I reach my hand out for hers as she makes her way down the last few steps.

"Jay, why did you rush me?" She smiles. I lean in to kiss her on her cheek. I can't believe we haven't kissed yet.

"Bae, I was just messing with you. You look beautiful by the way. I've never seen your hair like that. It's stunning."

"You like?"

"Very much."

" LaLaina flat ironed my hair some time ago and I loved it so I wanted to do it for tonight. You said it was a special night, I had to wear blue, so I figured I'd go all the way out and make you proud."

"I am very proud of you. Proud to have you on my arm. Proud to have you as my woman."

"Thank you, Baby."

Her honey brown hair cascades below her shoulders in seductive waves and it looks like feathers or something soft. I fight the urge to run my hands through it. Her shiny, copper-colored lips match her eye makeup so well. She smells like the sweetest of sins. I could smell her for the next few lifetimes.

I escort her to the kitchen. "Come on, baby, I poured you a glass of water." I tell her and she allows me to lead the way – her hand in mine.

"Baby…water? I thought we were going out? Jay, are you tired? The meds too strong, baby?"

"No. Hush. Come here." I pull her close to me.

"Here." I hand her the box.

"What's this, Jay?" she smiles.

"Open it."

Soft, pink and white manicured nails delicately unravel the bow and open the box. Her right hand covers her mouth and she looks at me with tears in her eyes.

"Baby, you didn't have to do this!" she hugs me. Kisses me on my cheek.

"I did."

"I don't know what to say."

"Don't say anything. Here let me put it on you."

Gently, I grab her wrist and take the sapphire and diamond bracelet and secure it onto her right wrist. She looks at me and smiles. She's holding back tears of joy which warms my heart and soul to know I touched her that way. She's so good and I want her to have the best of everything. Anything that I can do to make her happy, I'm going to do. If it means I have to sacrifice and work extra hard, then that's what it means. She deserves even more than that.

"This bracelet is a symbol of my love for you and my commitment to you. I hope you like it, baby."

"I love it, baby." Her sweet scent penetrates my senses as she leans in to give me a soft, succulent kiss on my lips. It's brief. It's delicious. Her mouth tastes so sweet. Her breath, like strawberries just picked from a beautiful meadow in the country. I don't force it. I let her move away from me as she feels comfortable. All of me wants to rip her clothes off and take her upstairs, but I'm patient and I want to do this right. I want her to be my wife someday, so I have to behave. She deserves me at my gentlemanly best and that's what I'm going to continue to give her.

Our first kiss…

"Come on, baby. I have a special night planned." I tell her as we walk toward the front door.

"Okay, but baby…"

"Yes, baby?"

"This is my night to see Janet, my sister. I don't want to ruin your plans."

"Say no more, baby. You've shared so many stories about Janet that it is time that I meet her. She needs to know who her soon-to-be brother in law is. I want her approval. We can head to your surprise right after that. Okay, baby?"

"K." she smiles.

We walk out the door hand in hand and head to my truck. I open the door of my Escalade for Jill and she hops in.

"Baby, stop spending so much money on me." Jill taps my hand in a loving way.

Trying to pay attention to the road and traffic is really hard with Jill seated next to me. Her aroma is alluring. Her soft voice makes me weak, but it's her spirit that makes me yearn for every drop of her time. I am anxious about learning all the corners of her mind. I can't get enough of this woman. Part of me feels like God is blessing me in abundance because of all of the hardships I've had to endure in my life.

"Sometimes you have to speak victory during the test," I remember my mother saying that to me, Jabez and LT as she talked about the book of Haggai. "The temple had been destroyed and they had been instructed to rebuild it. And amazingly enough, after fifteen years, it still was not completed. Why? Because they were more concerned with building their own houses than the house of the Lord."

I couldn't understand it then and I'm not quite sure that applies to me now, but I remember my mother also saying, "The future of this temple will be greater than its past glory. Your latter will be your greater."

I choose to believe that I am walking in my latter with Jill by my side and it will be my greater.

"You deserve everything I can offer you, Jill." I tell her as I take her hand and kiss it.

"I feel like I have everything in you, Jay."

"Hey girl…don't ever change." I say and I smile.

"Ha, ha, ha. You know you're a clown, right?"

"So I've been told. So I've been told."

Jill and I hold hands as we reach Janet's room. Wow, Janet is a spitting image of Jill as she rests in bed. We are here pretty late, so it appears to be past Janet's bed time. Jill approaches Janet, kisses her on her forehead and Janet awakens.

"Aw, you look beautiful, Jill." Janet says with a bit of slow speech.

"Thank you. Uhm, Janet, I want you to meet someone." Jill says.

"Is that Jerusalem, Jill?" Janet questions and smiles as she raises her finger to point to me.

"Yes." Jill replies to Janet's question.

I remove my gray suit jacket and lay it on the chair next to Janet's bed. I notice pictures of Janet and Jill all around her room, it's very heartwarming. I see my baby when she was a little girl and it tickles me, but I don't say anything to Janet or Jill. I just allow the moment to touch my heart. I lean in to give Janet a kiss to her forehead. "Nice to meet you, Janet."

"I've heard so much about you, Jerusalem."

"Good things, I hope." I say as I rub her hand.

"Yes. You make my sister very happy."

"Then I'm doing my job. Listen, we're going to bring you home for Thanksgiving this year, Janet. It's been too long since I've had a Thanksgiving that I care to remember and I know you two haven't had one in the traditional sense in forever. Sound good?"

"Yes." Janet replies with a smile.

"Baby, how…"

"We'll make it happen, baby."

"Okay. Thank you, baby." Jill tells me.

"I'm going to take very good care of your sister, Janet. Jill means the world to me."

"Please take care of her."

"I will. I promise."

"Cocoa Brown's, Jay? How did you know I love this place?" Jill asks me as we valet park.

I get out of my whip, hand the valet the keys and walk over to get to my queen before one of these punk ass dudes thinks she's available. Reaching out my hand, I take Jill's in mine and we head into Cocoa Brown's. Tonight is "Love and Life" night at the club. Live jazz all night with sets from the dopest poets in between. I knew my baby would love this. It's sort of like Valentine's Day – the set up, but they do it right before the holiday season, just before Thanksgiving, is what the host told me when I called to make reservations. I reserved a VIP table with bottle service for me and my baby. Champagne will flow throughout the evening, as well as her favorite finger foods and one of her favorite dinners. I know Jill has been eating like a rabbit with her lifestyle change, but tonight is about pure indulgence for her.

The host escorts us to our corner table. The waiter follows closely behind, so by the time we have a seat, he's giving me and Jill two wine flutes with fresh strawberries in the bottom of the glass. He begins to pour champagne into both glasses.

"We hope you have great evening here tonight at Cocoa Brown's, Mr. and Mrs. Jones."

"Thank you, we will."

"Mr. and Mrs. Jones?" Jill questions with a smile.

"Speaking it into existence, baby. Name it and claim it."

"I see."

"All of this is for me, Jay? Why? You're doing way too much."

"Baby, I am not going to let you get away, so if it means spending my little military money on you, then so be it. You know I get four hundred dollars a month right? I'm rich baby." I laugh and she smiles.

"Jay, I've been thinking."

"About? What? Oh, marrying me, right?" I smile.

"No, silly, well…yeah, but Jay, your benefits seem a bit on the low end. I think I need to look into it."

"Really?"

"Yes, baby."

"I thought it was good. I was injured."

"Yes, Jay, my point exactly. I'm going to pull your medical records and make a few phone calls. Your sacrifice is worth more than four hundred dollars per month."

"Well, take care of your man, baby. I just thought that between my salary as the new assistant head coach plus the benefits, and the little I have saved up, that I could provide a good life for us."

"Baby, you will and I will help you. I just want what's best for you."

"Understood."

Our waiter, and what appears to be his assistant, comes with trays of food for me and my baby.

"Rock Shrimp Remoulade in martini glasses for you and your wife, sir?"

"Yes, sir."

Our waiter places the plate in front of us. My baby smiles.

"Jay! I can't eat all of this!" Jill screams and smiles.

The assistant places the other food I ordered for us on the table.

"Shrimp & Asiago Grits on an Edible Spoon, Cajun Catfish Fritters, Collard Green Empanadas and Okra Beignets with Cilantro Sour Cream Sauce for you and the lady."

"Yes, thank you." I tell the waiter and his assistant.

"Jay! You've outdone yourself. I don't know what I've done to deserve this." Jill tells me. She's so emotional.

"Baby, you saved my life, plus you fine as hell, that's enough."

She laughs through the tears. I take one of the rock shrimp out of the martini glass and place it onto Jill's lips. She smiles as she tries to capture it to take a bite. Her lips open and close as I tease her with the shrimp. Raising the shrimp right above her mouth, I lift higher so that her tongue seeps out of her mouth a bit more. I sit the shrimp onto her tongue and she licks it. I remove it quickly so she can't take a bite. Repeating the process, her tongue once again makes an appearance and my dick is getting hard. I'm glad she can't see underneath this table.

"That's right, baby, let me see that sweet tongue of yours."

Finally, I let her eat the shrimp and she smiles. She looks like she is in heaven. My baby can eat. I love to look at a woman who is unafraid to throw down on a good plate of well-cooked food. I appreciate the fact that she is so free with me, that she is unashamed to drink champagne, and to eat like a little pig tonight.

"Baby, you're tearing that food up." I laugh.

"Oooh, Jay, do I look greedy?"

"Yes." I laugh.

"Oh my God, I'm sorry."

"Baby, I'm teasing. Enjoy yourself."

"Whew, okay. I don't want to embarrass you."

"Baby, I don't want to embarrass you in here looking like the damn Elephant Man."

"You keep talking about my man like that and I'm going to put you on a time out." Jill says with a serious look on her face.

"Okay, baby, I'll stop. I don't want any trouble out of you."

"You damn sure don't, Jay. You're beautiful, remember?

Wonderfully, beautifully you."

"I'll keep that in mind."

"Within you, I lose myself, without you, I find myself, wanting to be lost again."

"Girl, you're going to make me lose my mind."

There's a whole lot I'd like her to do with those big, juicy lips of hers - namely use them to meet and greet every inch of my body. Thoughts of the warmth of her mouth around my dick make me slightly hard. The discomfort of the feeling is inviting.

Damn, I want her in the worst way.

I keep reminding myself every ten minutes or so that I'm not here to kiss those pretty, luscious, copper-stained lips; and that reminder has me going crazy on the inside. Unapologetically, she's built. Cornbread fed, thick, like she grew up eating shrimp and grits. She is an image that men instinctively think about and are careful to desire. Dim lights, candles all around, on a beautiful, crisp winter evening with the woman I love, in the corner of a restaurant that will become our place of the best of memories over the years. In a strange way, it is home – our own private, secluded place in the universe where she is mine and I am hers - alone. *Our home,* I think, our place of refuge where everything that is so wrong about our love affair is so unequivocally right. I have every damn right to be here with my woman, my lady, my heart, my life, the love of my life.

Sitting alluringly, she crosses one long, curvaceous leg over the other and softly feathers a loose curl from her brow.

I grab her hand. "Come on, let's get on the dance floor. They're about to play your song." I hear it coming. The band is about to do a cover of John Coltrane and Duke Ellington's "In a Sentimental Mood."

We make it to the dance floor and the melody begins. My arms wrap around her waist and she places her arms around my neck.

She smiles. Damn, I would kill a motherfucker for that smile. My hand reaches the small of her back and I pull her close to me, so close that I can feel her heart beating. We sway back and forth to the loving melody. Her big, bold and beautiful eyes lock with mine. Instantly I melt. I lean in to kiss her forehead. Her fingers travel alongside my neck, travel down to my chest. My breathing becomes erratic. I try to maintain my cool. She leans in to kiss my scar. It makes me want to cry. Her fingertips run gently over my healed wound. She kisses it again. Makes her way to my lips. She kisses me. I return her kiss. Behave myself while doing so. Her tongue enters my mouth for the first time. Our tongues dance and play and greet one another. They belong together. I feel her heat. Temperatures rising.

The music ends, yet we keep swaying. We don't say a word. We just hold on to each tightly and sway. I look into her eyes. Remove the soft runaway of hair from her face. I gently grab around her mouth, pull it closer to me, part her lips with my thumb. I seek her tongue again with mine. I take it, suck it, make it my own. She softly moans.

A poet appears on stage. I hear the words as the emcee introduces her. I don't take my eyes off of my baby to see who it is. She takes a sneak peek and immediately gets back to making love to me with her spirit. Damn, this feels so good.

"Please welcome Isis who will be performing, 'Voyage to Atlantis'" the emcee announces and the poet makes her way to the stage. I hear it all, but my eyes won't leave my woman.

"Greetings. I do hope you enjoy." I hear the poet say. I hear bass. I hear a soft high hat. I feel the rhythm. The vibe in the restaurant changes. I rock my baby side to side. She softly kisses my lips.

The poet speaks.

"The Journey…
beneath the heavens
clouds embrace in harmony
memories of you and I
fly high along midnight skies
stars shine light that flow through curtains
darkness dissolves slowly
shifting the moon under sheets

the temple emerges
urgently urges
to feel your embrace
to devour
taste your taste
you have my body bound
lost in your presence
where I can't be found
late night
yearning you
until…
hushed words inside me rose
seeped through cushioned lips where they received a breath
of life.
whispered sweet rhythms singing melodies to my King.
Fragrant roses bloomed while minutes
transformed to hours
scented the sun-kissed room.
Scantily clad thoughts cleansed by fresh water
that fell as precipitation from lust-filled clouds loomed
Liquid sunshine poured from his lips as I received a soft blown
kiss
we reminisced of a love we loved and loved in bliss
Euphoria reigned as nothing else mattered.
One sphere of existence to another, lofty emotions scattered
the rapture…
Rhyme and absolute reason fled from our grasp the very
moment our souls collided.
Our devotion failed to lack in vitality; enthusiasm unwavering.
The soul-tie vibrant; intensity clear as autumn leaves on
once dead bushes that exhaled new life for the season.
Vanquished our fears of a love unfathomed to embrace the
dawn.
Pleasantly rested in his willing arms as we drifted to sleep
only to be awakened by the light of the sun and
the sound of the living waters running deep.
Atlantis…
After self-imposed silence was outweighed by overwhelming
indulgence

I bellowed his name, long, strong, hard, like I birthed him alone
and was somehow responsible for his survival.
He interrupted my shouts and pleas to the heavens mid-air
before they could arrive and melted them with his own form of mercy.
The heat from wet orifices drew close and our tongues
danced with sin and shame then released the burden of a battle of good verses not so much. Constant sentiments of affection gave mouth to my doubts
relentless he was in his pursuit of his prey; he hunted, conquered,
proved the rest of his celestial intentions with exquisitely operating parts of his mechanism.
Bathed in his holy ocean, fervently, in bliss."

"Baby, I had a wonderful time." Jill tells me as we enter her home. It has to be about eleven at night. A late night for both of us.

"I'm happy you enjoyed yourself."

"I'll put some tea on for us and some music."

"Baby, I need to go home. Got to work in the morning."

Here she goes with those puppy dog eyes. She removes my jacket and takes it hostage into the kitchen along with my car keys. She gives me *that* look. She knows that look weakens me.

"No, baby. Tea first. Have tea with me."

"Okay, baby." I concede and succumb to her wishes.

She removes her shoes and walks over to light the fireplace. I witness the curvature of her ass swaying side to side as I recline on the plush sofa in the living room. Jill walks over to me and hands me a cup of tea. I put her cup and mine on the coffee table.

"Come here!" I demand and grab her arm. "Sit on my lap."

She smiles and straddles me. Her full breasts are sitting right in front of my face and her heavenly face is flawless. She looks sleepy, but that doesn't take away her beauty.

"Don't break my heart, okay, Jill?"

"I would never."

"Good. You're making me crazy; you know that?"

"Join the club."

I grab Jill securely and firmly in my arms and rise from the sofa with her in my grasp.

"Jay! You can't lift me! I'm way too heavy!" she tells me as her legs wrap around my waist.

"Don't worry baby, just hold on." I tell her as I walk toward the staircase. My tongue enters her mouth once again.

The phone rings and we both ignore it. We're devouring each other's tastes and smells and I inhale everything about her. She's sweet perfection all rolled into one hell of a woman. She's heavy, but I'm a soldier and I got this. My hands gravitate to her plump bottom and I grab two handfuls of it as I carry her to the staircase.

The phone rings again and Jill's concentration is broken. "Baby, that may be the nursing home for Janet. I better get it. No one calls this late."

"Okay, baby."

I let Jill down and I follow her with my eyes as she walks into the kitchen to retrieve her cell phone. She left it on the marble countertop on the island in the kitchen. She stands right there and picks up the phone. I walk behind her, grab her waist and pull her close to me. Her ass sits right on my length and I know she can feel the firmness through my dress pants. I remove her hair from the back of her neck and toss it to one side.

"Oh, hey, how are you?" she says into the phone and smiles as I kiss her on the back of her neck.

"I have company right now." she says to the person on the other end of the phone.

"Why so many questions? This is not a good time."

In a loud and forceful tone, I ask Jill, "Do you want him?"

She gets startled and turns around to look at me. I back her into the island and her ass rests firmly on the corner of it. The phone is still in her hand and the person on the other end is still on the line.

"Do you want him or do you want me, Jill?" I ask her as I kiss her lips and my tongue travels down her neck. I kiss her neck over and over again and she's giving in to me.

"Hello? Hello? Jill?" The man on the phone is yelling.

"Because I want you, Jill." I tell her and kiss her earlobe.

"Avery, I have company." she tells him.

"Do you want him or do you want me, Jill, because I want you. I need you." I tell her and my tongue enters her mouth once again.

"Tell me!" I demand as I take a handful of her ass in my grasp. I pull her close to me.

"Do you want him?" I question again as I gently tug on her nipple through her dress.

"Jay…"

"Do you want him or me, Jill, because I want you so fucking bad!"

I kiss her lips. She exhales. She's losing control.

"Tell me now! You want me, Jill or you want him?"

"I want you," she says through heavy breaths. Her tongue enters my mouth again. She's hungry. She wants her king to feed her. She needs me to nourish her. To extinguish that flame I lit between her legs.

"You want me, baby?" I question her.

"Hello? Jill? What's going on over there?" The man questions.

"Yes." Jill tells me as she licks the side of my neck.

"Then hang up the phone and have your man, baby."

Jill presses the button on the phone to hang it up.

"Turn your phone off." I tell her and she obeys my command.

"Good girl."

"Jay…"

"Are you my woman?"

"Yes. I am."

"Because you better not ever tell me I'm not your man. You understand?"

"Yes."

I grab my baby's hand and lead her to the staircase when a crisis of conscious kicks in. I laugh.

"Baby, I'm sorry. I just don't want anyone loving you but me."

"I feel the same way, Jay. We'll get through this." Jill smiles and rubs my shoulder to alleviate my discomfort.

"What Coltrane song is this?"

"How Deep is the Ocean."

Chapter 22

Jill

How Deep is the Ocean

I often dreamed about this time and space, a special place where I'd be in the presence of a living God. Envisioning Jerusalem loving me like a sculpted Adonis would, in my dreams we were a modern day Osiris and Isis, minus the brother and sister part but holding onto the heavenly and powerful love of a divine couple.

His energy is palpable, magnetic.

In my eyes, Jerusalem is a king, and I, his queen.

The energy between us is intense. Allowing impure thoughts to create fantasies, the thought of riding his dick sent waves of anticipation through me, for I knew it would be the kind of dick that can only come from a lineage of African kings. It would be the kind of dick that will make you get up in the morning and cook breakfast. It would be that slap-a-man-in-the face-just-because-it's-too-good, kind of dick. Lovely, delicious, I'm dropping all my friends for this kind of dick. Stiff, rock hard, never gets tired, only comes when I beg him to dick. Sweet, chocolate, if you're drinking, it'll make you dizzy, dick. The kind of dick that will make you lose your religion if there were set protocols in place to determine who would be deserving of tasting a piece of heaven, dick.

Glory, glory, hallelujah dick.

He was so forceful moments ago, and if I didn't know Jay the way I know him, I would think he's controlling, but I know better. Knowing my baby has fought for everything in life – his life has been unfair - I also realize that Jay's last, "Do you want him or do you want me" questions and demands have something to do with me, but everything to do with that man on the other end of my phone.

"You ain't slick, baby." I smile and tell Jay as he leads me upstairs.

He turns around and smiles. "What do you mean?"

"You were making sure that Avery knew, under no uncertain terms, that you were here and he was way over there." I chuckle.

"I hope he got the point that being way over there is in his best interest." He smiles.

Following Jay with my eyes, we make it to the top of the stairs. He's built like a well-oiled machine and I admire the strength and dedication it took for him to maintain a body like a king. He cherishes and worships his temple. He must. Otherwise, he wouldn't look the way he does.

He's physical beauty in abundance, even with damage to his face, and unfortunately, his soul.

He is some kind of beautiful.

We arrive in my bedroom and Jay pauses at the doorway. He admires the African American art on the walls as he moves slowly into my place of refuge. Removing his Stacy Adams shoes, he twirls me then pulls me close.

I smile.

"You're on a roll tonight, baby." I tell him and I smile feeling the warmth of his embrace.

"Baby, I'm just getting started."

My heart jumps.

Jay's tongue enters my mouth again with force. His strong hands wrap around me and find the zipper to my dress. He unzips it. I feel his length – his manhood as it swiftly hardens.

His heart is beating so fast.

Mine too.

My dress falls to the floor as well as all of my inhibitions. This man has me so wide open. My mind's gone half crazy and I can't leave him alone.

Jay steps back to witness me in my black lace bra and panties. They're actually boy shorts and normally I would feel self-conscious, but I don't with him. He looks me up and down and I simply stand here and play in my hair. He stares and I say something to break the silence.

"You must like what you see."

"No. I love what I see. Come here. Touch me!" he commands.

I follow his every wish and begin to unbutton his shirt. I see his gorgeous, dark, smooth, sun-kissed chest as I remove his shirt. I throw it to the side. Pressing my nose against his neck, I inhale his cologne. I linger there for a moment, mesmerized. Lick his neck. Kiss it. Suck on it a bit. His head tilts backwards.

"You smell good."

"Versace Blue Jeans."

"Smells good on you."

"Thank you, baby."

My hands move to his belt and I unloosen the buckle, unbutton his carefully-tailored dress pants and they drop to the floor. He steps out of them and smiles.

"You're going to get yourself in a lot of trouble, Cookie."

With a sexy purr, I respond, "I like trouble."

Witnessing the bulge in his boxer briefs, I know Jay is ready for me. I am ready for him.

An irresistible force is ready to meet an object ready to be moved.

"Come here." He tells me as he gives me that sweet tongue again. Tenderly, his hands rub my skin gently, down my arms and moves to my thighs, where he massages them. He's behind me now and his strength pushes me toward my king-size pillow-top bed. I lay on the bed and he lies on top of me.

Jay removes the front closure to my bra and presses my breasts together.

"I love chocolate berries," he says, referring to the erect point of my mounds. Taking one in his mouth, he uses that aroused object between animated lips to make circles. Soon, he presses them both together again and alternates between both sets of nipples, licking and sucking ever so gently.

"Jay," I whisper as the good sensation gets to me.

Jay travels down to my belly button and kisses every part of it. He licks around my navel. He removes my panties and kisses the top of my womanhood.

"I was born a patient lover, baby, so I'll start with your feet." I exhale.

I hear Coltrane's, "How Deep is the Ocean" playing on my surround sound. The melody accompanies our personal melody.

Jay lies between my legs and places my feet on his chest. He takes my right foot into his hand and kisses it. His eyes show an admiration to my feet that I have never witnessed a man show before. My big toe enters his mouth. I lay there, looking at him, moaning with the feeling he is giving me. Taking each toe, he sucks on them one by one and my body trembles. His free hand roams to my breasts and he rubs them, caresses them, and fondles my nipples. His thumb lands on my clit and he rubs it vigorously while the big toe of my left foot enters his mouth.

I moan louder and my legs shake. He removes his thumb from my womanhood and places it into his mouth.

"You taste so good."

Have mercy.

"Jay…" I whisper.

"I'm going to be late for work, baby."

"I'm sorry, Jay." I whisper.

Jay removes his boxer briefs and opens my legs wide. Wide, like he's placing one leg on the moon and one on the sun. He stares at me, then my womanhood.

"Damn, you look good, baby."

"Jay, please…" I beg.

The smile on his face lets me know that he enjoys it when I beg.

With one thrust, he's deep inside of me. I cry, he cries, and we sing a heavenly song in unison as he pulls out and puts his dick back into me. He pulls it out, witnesses how wet I've made him already, then slides it back into my slipperiness. I'm crazy.

"Is this enough dick for you, baby?" he questions while sliding in and out of me.

"Yes, baby," I cry out loud and moan.

He thrusts into me harder.

"You sure, baby?" he asks, grunting while spreading my legs further apart. Takes a nipple into his mouth. Sucks it. Loves it. Licks it.

"Oh, baby," I yell. He strokes me harder. Faster. Opens my legs wide. Pulls it out. Thrusts back into me. Tilting his back in pleasure, he closes his eyes and growls.

"Ahhhhhhhhhhhh."

My king feels mighty, because my pussy's good, real good. I give him a thrust back then roll my hips to create circles around the head of his dick.

"Baby, shit, damn, you feel so fucking good!"

Jay slides into me, hard, his strokes powerful, potent and possessive. He pulls out, goes back in over and over, dipping and dancing with delight. He's hitting my spot, and creating new ones. I'm nuts.

"Jay!" I yell.

"Give me that come, baby. Come all over me, baby."

He strokes me harder, faster.

"Oh Jay!" I yell.

I take my fingers into my mouth and rub his nipples. His head tilts back once more and he slows down with his strokes. He returns to me and looks at me, c. Oh my God he's gorgeous.

"I belong to you," he tells me. "You fucking own me!" he says as he leans in to give me his tongue. He kisses my neck. Sucks on it. Kisses my cheek. His thrusts are long, and slow. I'm so wet.

Jay bites my earlobe. Gives me delicious dick . Kisses my ear. Whisper naughty things to me.

"I love you," he says. Strokes are slow. Kisses my neck and again whispers, "I love you, Jill. Please don't ever leave me."

My emotions consume me.

Jay pulls all the way out, lifts up from my body.

"Jay," I beg.

He quickly travels down to my vagina. Lifts my legs. Spreads them wide. Places them on opposite continents. My purr of satisfaction lets him know that he's getting the job done. I want to give him a goddamn standing ovation, but I'm on my back.

He's a greedy lover. The best I've ever had.

My nails make new pathways into his back, and I'm sure the

pleasurable pain is welcomed as it represents battle scars on this battlefield of deep, intense affection.

We're making love, not war.

And with each sensational stroke he's trying to get this right.

Oh baby, you got this shit right.

He licks me like he loves me. Sucks me like his life depends on it. Smacks the side of my ass. Tastes me, teases me with that tantalizing tongue.

I come in his mouth. Generously gulping my offering, he drinks all of my nectar. Inhales my scent. Savors my ambrosia.

Jay returns to my face, lies on top of me. Whispers in my ear. "I love you, baby."

His words penetrate my soul. Tears well up in my eyes. He enters me again. He cries out to the heavens. I cry. Tears pour down my face. I can't hold them in.

"It's okay, baby. I love you," he tells me as he loves me. Makes loves to me.

"I love you, too." I cry. He kisses my tears, then goes into high gear.

Midnight grinding, heart rates climbing. He's giving me every ounce of his love like he somehow owes it to me.

We're fucking.

Fast, fantastically-furious, frenetic, fucking.

Yet within the confines of the fucking there's a deeper connection, one that transforms the act. No matter how hard he kills the kitty, the more he loves it, which redefines everything.

We're fucking, yet making love like two souls that have loved in a prior life, present and concurrent lifetimes.

We're loving, sexing, fucking, like animals born to breed.

Fucking, like we're trying to capture air we need to breathe.

"Goddamn, you're going to make me come," he tells me. I feel his dick getting harder inside of me.

"Baby, please don't, I want more." I beg.

"Cookie, please…it's too fucking good. Shit!"

Brandy Alexanders have diluted my inhibitions, which forces me to reveal my inner-most thoughts – carnal in desire, longing, needing, lusting for him. I wanted to feel this passion in a manner only Jerusalem can deliver. Oooh, I want to scream. I want to yell to the heavens, "Thank you God, for this scarred-face, big-dicked, sweet, caring, loving, black boy with his sweet, nasty ass." Euphoria is rising. Jay, covered in a serious fuck face, that life-altering state where euphoria meets a light-headed nirvana as titans clash within his soul. He's like cocaine, a drug, my drug of choice, keeping me high, scary, invigorating. He's seducing my body, one whisper at a time. I'm coming hard, in succession in response to his revelations.

"You know I could fuck you all night, girl," he murmurs in delight as he closes his eyes, leaning his head back.

"Then fuck me, Jay...all night."

"Grrrrrrrrr,"he growls.

Deep, deliberate, desirable strokes penetrating my world, as his eyes watch every moment, every caress, every in and out like a sadistic voyeur.

"Damn, I want to come all over you, Jill."

Each thrust becomes harder with intention as he makes me bounce – he rocks and rolls me in rhythm to his beat.

"Kiss me, baby," he demands as his tongue finds its way back into my mouth. He licks my lips, hot, sweet breath escapes him softly as I bite his bottom lip; my tongue lands and glides down his chin, onto his neck.

I bite it, suck it, lick it, love it.

"Mmmm," he moans in pleasure, closing his eyes for a moment. He bites my neck, whispers in my ear, "You're so good, my baby, I love everything about you."

Once again releasing, I dig my nails deep into Jay's back as I softly yell in gratification, "Jay."

He's in between, just a single step away from a place called heavenly. I feel like I want to sing his name in five different octaves, scream out an orgasmic symphony of singsong moans.

'Til the moon meets the sun to make the horizon come. I can see the sun trying to rise through my bedroom window. I could lay here for just a few minutes more, but it'll just be torture. I have to go to work. I lean in towards his face and give him a soft kiss on his cheek. I move out slowly, and his sweet smell still lingers in the air. He sleeps as sound as a baby in its mother's arms. Doesn't snore much either. I love to watch him lay flat on his back. You can tell he's really into some good sleep when that right knee gets bent into mid-air. I remember it from the hospital. It'll take a nation of millions to wake him up from one of those dead-to-the-world sleeps.

"Baby, we have work," I tell him. Gently, I whisper that into his ear. I kiss him on his cheek.

"Okay, baby," he whispers back. "The team doesn't practice until later in the morning today. What time is it?"

"It's about six o'clock."

"Get back in the bed with me, Cookie."

"Baby, I have patients this morning."

I kiss him on his cheek and crawl out of bed.

Jay has fallen back to sleep.

My shower is hot, just the way I like it. I lather up. I've always had a thing for very hot showers and exotic shower gels. Makes me feel really sexy. I'm in the shower, singing my ass off, listening to a sweet tune as I clean every inch of my body when I can sense that someone is near me. If you've ever seen or heard of the movie *Psycho*, you know damn well that this is not a good look right here. My heart races. Why? It's so silly, really. I have a big black man in the house with me, so whoever wants to slash me through my shower curtain will have to go through Jerusalem first. It's amazing how the mind can play tricks on you. Just to make sure, I pull the curtain back slightly and take a look.

"Baby, what are you doing?" Jay gives me an adorable, devilish smile. He's up to something. I know my baby.

"I was just coming in to give you a towel. You know…to help you dry off."

I give him a *yeah right* look and smile.

"Thank you, baby. You're so sweet."

Jay leans his head further into the shower and puts his nose up against my arm and inhales deeply. "You smell so good."

"Thank you, baby. Now get out honey, I have to finish up." I push him on his arm. Jay removes his head from the shower. I continue to bathe. After a few seconds, I hear the shower curtain open again. I turn around.

Jay is in the shower with me, dick in *steel-bat-status*. I look up at him, "Baby, I'm almost done. I'm getting out of here."

Before I say another word, Jay lifts me up and spreads my legs. The music in the background with the hot, steamy shower makes for a tantalizing moment.

I'm caught off guard and wet all over again. I wrap my legs around his waist and place my arms around his neck to balance myself. He's shocking me at this very moment. His look is so intense.

He wants some more pussy, I know it.

Jay places my back up against the shower wall. The water cascades over us. He pushes my head to one side and bites and sucks on my neck so strong and hard. He is acting anxious as if he's never been inside of me before, like he's ready to reach his maximum right now. Like he has something to prove.

"Oh, Jay. Baby, I have to..."

He interrupts by placing his tongue in my mouth. I love the way he shuts me up. I can still smell my pussy on his breath, and his sticky lips. He nibbles on me gently, licking and biting my neck. He grabs a hold of my breast and sucks on my nipple, tugging at it until it reaches its firmness.

I'm looking at him, he's gorgeous as he sucks with purpose, his jet black curls, rich cocoa skin is gleaming as the water beads from his smooth texture. He comes back to my face and I'm almost afraid of what he'll do next. Jay licks his lips and reaches down to his manhood. He strokes it with his hand, and gives it all to me deeply.

"Jill, Oooh, you feel so good. Oh, baby, damn, your pussy is so sweet!"

Jay keeps his eyes glued to him sliding in and out of me. The more he looks, the slower he goes. With each motion, he drives that drill deeper and deeper into me. He pins me to the wall. I can't move. He's got me wide open, dripping wet, and about to come all over him. I feel as if I am going to explode if I don't go crazy first.

I try to hold it all in. I don't want to arouse him any further. Jay comes in closer to my ear.

"Jill, don't give this pussy to anybody else. This is my pussy. You belong to me, Jill."

"Don't you give this dick to anyone else, Jay, you hear me?"
"Baby, I promise I won't."

Chapter 23

Jerusalem

Party & Bullshit

"**B**asketball drills condition your body and your mind. That's what I tell my players over at the college, you light-skinned bitch." I yell to LT as I lay up the ball into the hoop. He's out of breath and I'm full of energy and I plan to kick his ass on this court today. It's cold as hell out here on our old stomping grounds; Weequahic Park in Newark, home of "Dead Man's Hill." This notoriously ghetto basketball court is full of good memories from twenty plus years ago, including giving girls hickeys on their necks, finger fucking in the dark, shooting hoops with the boys and running that hill with my dad.

I'm fucking with LT bad.

"Give me the ball, Scarface!" he yells and I throw the basketball to him. His gray shirt-shirt and red shorts are soaked with sweat and we are out here hard like it's not gotdamn twenty degrees out here. LT dribbles and shows off like he always has, and he tries to impress some young women who are onlookers. I get up in his face and try to snatch the ball from him. One dribble leaves him out of balance and confused and he leaves an opening for me to get the ball, so I take it, run up to the hoop and make the shot.

"Eight to zero, bitch! Did you have your *Wheaties* this morning, man?" I question him and he's mad. I smile. I throw the ball to him again. He takes it and at the speed of sound, he gets past me and makes the basket. Clapping my hands, I applaud him for his efforts today.

"Good boy. You got a shot. Bout time, you light-eyed negro." I tell him and he throws the ball.

Biggie's "Party & Bullshit" is on full blast as the trunk of my new whip is the DJ today and serves as the hip hop backdrop to this game of one and one where LT and I are going in. We are hustling out here on this court, in the middle of November, in the dead of winter, it feels like.

I bend down to catch my breath and see how rusty and ashy my knees have become since being out in this cold for so long. I smile and laugh to myself thinking about Jill and how she would react to the sight of these knees. She'd go get some of that A&D ointment and cover my legs and feet with a ton of that shit to keep me shining.

"Come on, you black bastard!" LT yells and throws the ball. Game is twenty and we'll see who gets there first. You would think LT would be giving me a break since I'm newly recovered, but just like when we were kids, he's not letting up. I love him for that and wouldn't have it any other way. Only thing missing is Jabez. He'd be out here finding all kinds of ways to ruin the game, cheat his way to victory, and then brag about it for the next two weeks.

LT runs up toward me and tries to get the ball, and I fake him out and dribble right past him. I run toward the basket and look behind me to see he's coming up fast. I break, make a swift left, spin, then dribble again to gain some ground. I look back again and smile, but he's right there. I dribble like I'm being scouted for the Knicks then shoot and wait for the ball to go in the hoop. LT places his hands on his hips and watches the ball go in.

"What?" I question LT and he smirks. LT pauses and retrieves his phone from his basketball shorts pocket.

"Hello?" he says with a big smile on his face. LT knows this is not the time for one of his bitches to be interrupting our flow. I give him time, but what I really want to do is yell something gay to fuck up his macking. Instead, I run to my truck and grab two Gatorades. My baby would be whispering in my ear that with all the sweating I'm doing, I need to hydrate myself.

"Word? Oh my God, this is great news. So I need to get up to Ohio by when? Oh, wow, I have two days. No, no, no, you don't need to worry about that, I'll take care of it. Again, thank you and we'll chat soon so I can fill you in on all the details. This is a major breakthrough thanks to you and your hard work," LT says and smiles as he hangs up his phone.

"What?" he questions me.

"Nothing, man. You leaving town?" I ask as I toss him the Gatorade. He catches it, opens it, takes a sip.

"Just a quick business trip. Got a lead on a killer investment opportunity up in Ohio. Going and coming right back."

"I'll ride with you. Are you going for the weekend?"

"Nah, Jay, I gotta get on the road tomorrow morning. You have work, don't you?"

"Yes. No days off with my new assistant head coaching position. Some weekends, mainly Sundays, like today."

"Cool, Jay, well, I'll definitely hit you up once I return. Hey… there maybe something in it for you, too."

"Cool, man. Now let's get back to this game so I can get back to my baby." I smile, finish my Gatorade.

"How's that going?"

"She's my baby. Man, I fuckin' love her."

"Damn, already?"

"Man, I can't get enough of her. She's so good to me. It's been a lot longer than you think. I started falling in love with her spirit months ago when I could barely speak."

"I feel you. I ain't never heard you speak of a woman this way. Shit's got to be real if you talking love."

"She's perfect. LT, she owns me, man." I laugh. I'm embarrassed I said it, but it's true.

"Are you whipped, Jay?"

"She put that voodoo on me, man. Never had no pussy like that in my life. Greedy. She never wants me to come. Whew."

"Damn, man, so is she the one?"

"Without a doubt. She cooks like a gourmet chef…lots of Spanish food. Said she learned it from her mother and father's maid, Carolina."

"Her parents had a maid?"

"Still do. She's so not like them. Bougie. She hates it."

"She doesn't seem like it. She seems perfect for you. She's gorgeous."

"See, that's the thing. She's stunning, but she doesn't think so. Her mom brainwashed her. Fucked her up mentally with head games that made her self-conscious. But she's more than her mother ever told her she could be. She's beautiful inside and out. She's so good to me, man. I really got lucky this time. God really blessed me by putting her into my life. She reads me poetry. Plays jazz. She even took me over to Broadway to see a play. Surprised me. She does everything for me, man. She's mine to lose and I am not fucking this up."

"She's a keeper for sure, Jay. Plus you whipped, man." LT doubles over laughing.

"Man, I cannot lie. I am. It's so good."

LT is still laughing.

"Good!" I tell him. I shake my head. "So fuckin' good that LT…every time I see her my head is in between her legs. Damn, she smells so good, man. Sweet like fucking strawberries or something." I tell him again and LT is laughing so hard.

"LT?"

"What, you fool?"

"The shit is good. Fucking good. Good, man. I be laying in the bed, she's on my chest right, and I be feeling like the king of the damn world. Good." I tell him as he laughs loud and hard and I toss him the ball.

"Good."

"Jay, stop, let's play the game," he laughs.

"Good."

Chapter 24

Jill

You're My Everything

"Right there?"

"Oooh, right there, Jay."

"Oooh, I love it right there, baby."

"Baby, we're going to be late! Damn you!" I tell Jay as he holds my hips in place. He loves when I ride. Likes to see me bounce. Keeps the lights on. Rocks me hard to see everything move, vibrate and shake. Lifts me up. Pulls me back down onto him, his length, his manhood. He watches every stroke. Glazed look in his eyes. He's so hungry for me. Doesn't look sane. He's in lust. And love. Crazy. Blown.

So am I…

All reason leaves him as he kisses me fervently once more. Both of our breathing becomes heavy and hectic as he licks my lips, my neck, cups both my breasts into his hands, and sucks on my nipples.

"I'll get us there on time, baby. Oooh, you're so pretty, baby," he tells me as he watches his length slide in and out of me. "Damn, I don't want to come, Cookie. Can't hold it."

He's struggling.

Euphoria strikes him hard and he lays here, out of breath and with momentary silence. We're both under the sheets. Naked. I'm on my back and Jay has his head on my breasts. He finds comfort there. His massive hold of me seems serene. I can feel his heart beating against mine; his breathing is slow.

"My stomach knots up when I think of you. It took me weeks to change the sheets after the times I made love to you. Just to inhale your precious scent, provided comfort to my soul. You are the star of my dreams, the want in my need. The war in Iraq lead to one of those significant occurrences that no matter what life takes me through, or how much pain I endured, I'll never forget it – my meeting you. My suffering, my struggle is not in vain, because of you. I thank God for you. Every day of my life, I will thank God for you."

Jay spoke the words and I exhaled and thanked my Creator for the chance to hear them.

I run my fingers through his hair. Rub the back of his neck. Press my body harder against his. He holds me tighter. Kisses my lips once more. I get up from the bed and wrap myself in our sheet, head to my bedroom window, and peak through the blinds.

"Going to take a shower, Cookie. You're going to make us late for Thanksgiving," he laughs. I smile as I stare out of the window.

I remember my annual Thanksgiving breakfast earlier this morning with LaLaina and Deseree. It's tradition and it's something we do each and every year. Thanksgiving hasn't meant much to me, Christmas either for that matter, since Janet's accident. My mother's smug superiority and my father's continual decrease in testosterone has made two of the most important holidays of the year completely dismal for me.

But God.

Now I have Jay to share in the joy and the madness that the holidays bring.

Deseree, LaLaina and I, ate like we weren't planning to eat Thanksgiving meals later today. The Stonebridge diner has the best Thanksgiving breakfast around and that is our place each and every holiday to go to, to break bread, to reminisce and bond in sisterly love. I was given the opportunity this holiday to share why I'm thankful.

"Jay is at home in bed, LaLaina." I told her. She chuckled.

"You love him, Jill?" Deseree questioned as she ate a spoonful of her flan. Deseree eats flan each and every Thanksgiving morning, even at seven in the morning.

"I do." I tell them both. "I really do. He makes me feel so good. I love everything about him. I can't explain it, but, the more I get, the more I want."

"What about his face, Jill?" LaLaina questioned.

"LaLaina!" Deseree yelled and slapped her on the arm.

"What? I'm just asking. Damn, Deseree you are always the goody two shoes," she yelled at Deseree. The two of them are total opposites and often go head to head over topics; including me. Each one wants more of my time and more of me in general. It's all good and it's all love. I'm glad I can be the equalizer between these two.

"Yes, his face is scarred on one side. But you know what? I think it's sexy as hell!" I tell LaLaina. "He treats me like a queen. He loves me; flaws and all. I've had some damn near perfect looking men who didn't value me or appreciate me as much as Jay does. Oh, I'm happy with his scarred faced ass. He's insanely beautiful inside and out!"

"Well, I guess she shut your ass up, huh, LaLaina? That probably explains why you're manless." Deseree laughs and sips her coffee.

"You ain't got a man, neither." LaLaina joked with Deseree.

"Yeah, well, if I find me one, good like Jerusalem, best believe I'm gonna love him scars and all."

"I know that's right." I told Deseree and laughed.

"How's all the plans coming along?" Deseree asked.

"Girl, I filed an appeal with the Veterans Administration on his behalf. His face is blown off, he spends months in rehab, two tours in Iraq and he's only thirty percent disabled? Over my dead body! I gathered all of his medical records and had one of his attending physicians write a letter to support an increase in his benefits."

"Does Jay know what you've done?" LaLaina asked.

"No, but he may have a clue. Honestly, I don't care what Jay thinks about this. I know the difference between right and wrong. He's so happy to have that four hundred a month, I can't tell him anything. Poor baby." I laughed.

"Well, I pray it comes through for him." Deseree said.

"Me too. My baby needs to be at one hundred percent for all of his sacrifice. He deserves to be comfortable. That's the least the military can do. This country's government is full of waste and we spend monthly on the dumbest shit known to man and most of it is because of policy and political games. We'll go to war in a heartbeat, but our veterans are homeless? We'll send money to other countries when they are in crisis while we are in crisis over here. Not on my watch! My baby is going to get what's coming to him. I bet you if one of those legislators child's leg had shrapnel in it or if they had third degree burns, we'd see him on the evening news."

"Preach, girl!" LaLaina said.

"I'm praying for him." Deseree said.

"Now, his medical bills are stacking up. Oh, hell no! Like I said...not to my baby and not on my watch!"

"What about the other matter?" LaLaina asked.

"Considerable breakthrough. I used every connect I have and called in every favor owed to me, and I found out so much. Passed it along. It's being worked on right now. I'm so excited."

"You have a heart of gold, Jill." Deseree said.

"You do. Jay's a lucky man."

"I'm the lucky one."

"Baby, let me hear some of your passionate words." Jay asks as he drives. Of course, I have jazz in his CD player playing, and while I know my baby is a hip hop head, he yields to my wishes and allows me to hear what I want. I love that about him.

"I left my journal at home, baby."

"Well just say something poetic off the top of your head. I love the way your mind works."

"Baby, I'm not that good."

"You are. You just don't realize it," he says as he continues to drive.

We are on my way to Mother and Father's house. I had it arranged so that the nursing facility would transport Janet for the day. When Mother asked was I coming home for Thanksgiving, I told her yes on two conditions. One, that I was able to bring my man, and two, that Janet would be able to come home. She wasn't thrilled about either, but she conceded. I was able to get so much done at work and on a personal level that I feel comfortable leaving for a few days. I've never taken time off for Thanksgiving because it really never meant all that much to me before.

"Make it personal. Say what's on your heart. Your fantasies, desires or just where you are in your psyche right now," Jay says with an air of comfort and support that warms me all over. He rubs the top of my hand. "I love my baby's poetry."

"Thank you, baby."

"Welcome, baby."

I give him a smile before I begin.

"After self-imposed silence was outweighed by overwhelming indulgence, I bellowed his name, long, strong, hard, like I birthed him alone and was somehow responsible for his survival. He interrupted my shouts and pleas to the heavens, mid-air before they could arrive and he melted them with his own form of mercy. The heat from wet orifices drew close and our tongues danced with sin and shame then released the burden of a battle of good verses not so much. Constant sentiments of affection gave mouth to her doubts, relentless he was in his pursuit of his prey; he hunted, conquered, proved the rest of his celestial intentions with exquisitely operating parts of his mechanism. Tables turned as roles reversed and my Messiah - he became my savior in disguise as I forever gazed into his eyes and discovered paradise."

"That's deep baby, and very personal. You know I love you, right?"

"I do."

"I hope you never forget it."

"How can I? Without you, there's no me, there's no place for me, no use for me. Without you, I don't exist, can't exist, won't exist. Within you, Jay, I lose myself. Without you, I find myself wanting to be lost again. I'm out of control."

Jay takes my hand and kisses it. "I witnessed a lion rest in the bosom of a sheep this morning."

My God.

"Baby, the roses. Purple. I've always seen red. Lately, you've been giving me purple with one white. Help me out, baby." I tell him as I turn up the volume on the CD player. "You're My Everything" by Miles Davis. And he is, my absolute everything.

He smiles. "Purple roses mean love at first sight, Cookie. I've always loved you."

"Baby."

"The one white rose means you're heavenly. Spiritual love. Also for me it means you're one of a kind."

"Jay."

"Well, baby, you asked."

"I did." I smile.

The snow falls lightly and steadily as we head to New York to my parents' home. Jay is good at the wheel and his new ride is sturdy. I feel secure. I see traffic accidents along the shoulder of the road and I know this slippery wintry mix is to blame. I say a silent prayer for those who are afflicted by this day. I say a prayer that Janet arrives safely. I pray for me and Jay, and that we will reach our destination unharmed.

"I hope your mother can cook, Jill," he laughs.

"Carolina will do all the cooking, baby. But you know I made Thanksgiving dinner for us; so when we get home, you can eat again with your greedy, black ass. I have never met a man that can eat as much as you."

"Oh, I definitely plan to eat when we get home."

"Nasty ass! But I like that sound of that." I smile.

"What? Me eating that sweet pussy of yours? We can pull over right now if you want me to taste it again."

"Jay! No, silly! I like that sound of 'when we get home.'"

"Oh, yes, sounds good. Hey baby? What will your parents think of my face?"

"They're going to think you're beautiful just like I do. Jay, in all honesty, baby…the scarring is a bit sexy. The Most High outdid Himself when He created you. I never wanted to tell you that. I can't look at you that long without thinking things I'm much too shy to say."

"Oh my. Baby, don't say that to make me feel better," Jay says.

"I would never lie to you. You're so fine, baby. And…you're

all mine! You like that, right? I just rhymed baby."

"Ha, Ha, Ha,…you're silly, Cookie."

"Oh, Senora Jill. Look at him. He's beautiful." Carolina says and turns Jay around. He does the dance with her. He's silly like that. I stand to the side, shivering in my coat as we make our way into my parents' home.

Carolina takes our coats and throws them into the den with a swiftness. She grabs my hand and she grabs Jerusalem's hand and walks us into the dining room. She is overjoyed by our presence. She has on a lovely maid's outfit and has done her hair so lovely for Thanksgiving. Her simplicity is soothing. Her aura is comforting splendor.

My mother and father sit at either end of the dining room table and their friends are all gathered around. Some sitting, some standing in other rooms, sipping on scotch and other fine liquor. My mother rises to her feet and comes over to greet us. Some of the neighbors who watched me grow up come over under the guise of being cordial; but mainly to be nosey.

Instinctively, I smooth over my leather-like one piece jumpsuit. I decided to wear something to show off my curves. I also knew it would keep Jay on his toes. I'm so self-conscious around *her*. I try to combat it today. I know I look okay, Jay said so. My hair is straightened and hangs in soft waves around my face. I had my highlights touched up, so they're shimmering.

I smile when I see Bethany, one of our neighbors. She's drunk already. Pleasant enough. I'm so proud to show off my baby. He looks like a million dollars, and I feel like a million to have him on my arm. Dark gray slacks and a lovely gray, white and black sweater with a dash of purple is his attire for the day. He is also wearing the bracelet I bought for him about a week ago. It's white gold with onyx. Perfection to say the least.

Mother and Bethany walk toward us. Bethany hugs me and reaches out her hand to shake Jerusalem's.

"Bethany, this is Jerusalem." Her smile is welcoming as her eyes scan him from head to toe.

"Wow, what a lovely name. How are you?'

"I'm well, young lady." He's such a clown. Bethany smiles and blushes.

Mother hugs me and I return her embrace. Father walks right behind her and hugs me. Mother starts to grimace as she approaches Jay. I want to die a thousand deaths. She doesn't shake his hand. Father does.

"Good seeing you, man. Nice to meet you. I'm Jill's father."

"Nice to meet you, sir." Jay's handshake is firm but I can sense the anxiety in him from meeting my parents for the first time.

"This is my wife… Jill's mom."

Jay extends his hand out to reach my mother's. She looks disgusted and doesn't return the gesture.

"Jill, is this the PhD from the University?"

She's thinking about Avery. I correct her.

"No. This is the love of my life, Jerusalem Jones. He's an Iraq war hero and assistant basketball coach at the University."

"Nice to meet you, ma'am."

His hand is still outreached and his humility in tow. He's trying hard for her acceptance. I love him for that and hate her for not acknowledging it.

Mother doesn't say a word and simply walks away. I grab Jerusalem's hand. I feel so bad. My heart sinks. I want to cry, but Jay squeezes my hand to keep me in line. My eyes scan the room for Janet. I don't see her.

"Dad, where's Janet?"

"Oh, she's in the kitchen with Carolina."

"Why isn't she in here eating Thanksgiving dinner, father?"

"You know your mother, Jill."

I pull Jay into the kitchen and we see Janet in her wheelchair and Carolina is feeding her.

"Hi, Jill," Janet smiles with a love in her eyes that cannot be faked, no matter the circumstances. She seems happy. Jay and I walk over to give her a kiss. She smiles more.

"Jill, you enjoy your man. He's a good man. I told you, remember to feed your man," Carolina says as she moves plates around on the table next to Jill.

"I remember, Carolina," I reply as I help her.

"I make you and Jay a plate. Big plate. See it's here already wrapped. Go home. Enjoy your man. I'll take care of Janet."

"Why, Carolina?"

"Your mother is busy entertaining her guests. She doesn't see the beauty in what's happening here today. Go…go, Jill. Go be with your man. Make it a good day. Pray for your mother."

Carolina's words seem to touch her as much as they touch me. Tears form in my eyes, but I don't allow them to fall.

Anger overwhelms me and I rush into the dining room and yell to Mother.

"Your children are here, Mother! Can't you for one moment stop faking the funk in front of these people who don't give a damn about you and spend time with your children? You are repulsive!"

I storm back into the kitchen and Jay grabs me, strong, hard, boldly. I feel like a child who is about to be chastised.

Jay leans in to Janet, gives her a kiss on the cheek.

"Janet, we'll see you this week okay, sugar? I'm going to take Jill home."

"Okay, Jay, please take care of her."

"I will."

Carolina escorts us to Jay's whip. She kisses us both on our cheeks.

"Jay, baby, I'm so sorry. Mother is just a jerk."

"Baby, it's okay."

"It's not okay! She was rude. I'm so sorry. I hate her. I hate both of them!"

"Don't let me hear you say that again, Jill. Take it from someone who doesn't have a mother or father anymore. When I lost my mother, I died every day. Every feeling I had was an emergency. Every emotion was on high. I wanted to die. I didn't want to live. There's a pain…an emptiness and a sorrow that comes with losing your mother. Your mother is your lifeline, baby. She obviously has major issues and she's passed some of them down to you. But don't you ever say you hate her. I can't let you do that."

"Baby, I'm so mad!"

"I know you are, baby and this too shall pass. It's already alright."

"I've never been good enough for her."

"You're better than her. She sees how free you are. How life seems to love you. She wishes she had the courage to be like you. She's hurting. She's hurting bad. Don't let her hurt affect how you feel about yourself. I know that's hard, baby…but you are precious in God's eyes. You are my purple rose that grew from concrete. Your value does not decrease based on someone's inability to see your worth. Pray for your mother. She needs it. I love you, baby and nothing is going to get in the way of that. Not even mom dukes."

Chapter 25

Jerusalem

Paid in Full

Awakening to a howling, blood-curdling scream into the cold, brisk air, which fills my bedroom, the sound, even though it comes from my own body, startles me, causing me to sit erect to regain my mentality and composure. I'm terrified beyond belief to the point of shaking and trembling profusely. "It's a night terror, not current reality," I tell myself, but my mind could care less about the distinction as it relives the pain.

The chill in the air is offset by the warm beads of sweat dripping from the terror-filled adrenaline pumping through my body, drenching me from head to toe while warming me and causing my temperature to rise. My heart races and I inhale deeply, trying to catch breath that escapes me. The source of my screams, sweat, and tears is the same recurring invader plaguing my mind over the years without rhyme or reason. It is a mental sensation I have not been able to shake since the day I saw her in the hospital more than two decades ago. A mind-altering intruder of mine is more vivid and real than any nightmare a person could ever have, simply because it is my reality instead of being a product of an over-active imagination. Even in the realm of dreams, reality trumps fantasy. It is my mind's way of reliving the beginning source of my pain and my soul's way of reminding me never to forget.

The Evian water bottle on the nightstand next to me finds its way cleverly and productively into my hands, as it routinely does when my mind starts playing tricks on me during the night. I gulp down its purifying contents without missing a beat. Yet, no matter how hard I try to soothe the savage beast of my past, the water cannot drown the images that linger in my head no matter how fast or how hard I choose to swallow. Even as I quench the fire of my exhausting night thirst, I can't extinguish the fire ignited by my dreams—the contents of which refuses ignoring.

I still see her. I smell the scent of her Chanel No. 5, as if she is standing right next to me and I remember *that* day, as if it were *today*. I'm lost in that moment in time. My night terror ensures that I will never forget that day or *her* for that matter; despite how many minutes, hours, days, years or decades that pass. *That* day will always be *today* and she will always invade my dreams.

When the beginning of my *end* began, I was ten years old. That is the moment in time that changed my life—the point of definition known to me as the *history* of my life.

A ten-year-old does not possess the wherewithal to appreciate the blessings that make up life. A ten-year-old lives in the *here and now*; unaware of the need to smell the flowers of life along the way, or of how good life really is. If I had have known then, what I know now, maybe my life wouldn't be attacked routinely by night terrors clubbing me over the head while begging me to be thankful for what I currently have. Maybe, if I had have been a little more grateful, *she* would still be here. My dreams impose that mentality on me. They make me pose that inquiry to myself each time I awake in cold, night sweats remembering *that* day. Even as an adult, I know that rationale has no basis in fact, and was not the case then or now, yet my nightmares still make me wonder. In the instance of wanting to blame someone other than God for the fact that sometimes *shit happens* in life, my dreams still make me want to point the finger of blame at myself. That is what children do. Their minds often place blame on themselves instead of on the foundations concerning the cycle of life.

Even though I am an adult, remembrance of my mother is

still through the eyes of a child. I do not see her weaknesses; a mother is Wonder Woman in the eyes of her child. Mothers are invincible; as such, I will forever see her in that manner. I couldn't see that she, just like all human beings, had the capability of being vulnerable. My mind cannot comprehend that her life was what it was intended to be—as God made it.

I look at things concerning her through the eyes of a child missing his mother; and all I can see is invincibleness; as such, all I can do is wonder what I did wrong that might have caused her to be taken away from me. Through the eyes of a child is how I see things when it comes to my mother. The view lies in the eye of the beholder, and the day it all began and ended still invade my dreams.

I sit up still, and quiet as to not wake my woman up. This girl, my Queen, has held me down as if we have been married for decades. She has seen every part of me. I have been my most vulnerable with her, before I even knew I loved her, she got to see all of me.

I lie back down and try to get to sleep once more. As I watch the clock, I see it move from 2:57 in the morning to just 3:20 a.m. This is torture. I think about Jabez. Wonder why I can't find him. Pray he's alive. I wonder if he still loves me. I swallow hard as that question alone breaks my heart. Tears begin to pour down my eyes. Jabez. I think about the last time I saw him. My God, why did they separate us? I pray he is alive and well.

The holidays are bitter sweet for me. Bitter has overruled sweet for decades. The sweet parts take over my mind when I reminisce about Christmas when I was a child. My mother had the house smelling like sweet cinnamon sugar first thing in the morning. Jabez and I would wake up early on Christmas morning and rush to the gigantic freshly cut Christmas tree that me, Jabez and my dad had brought home the day after Thanksgiving.

Toys galore and plenty of clothes would be under the tree each and every year. By the time we were done ravaging through everything Mom and Dad had gotten us, there would be wrapping paper and bows all over the place. There was no shortage of love, presents, or sense of family then. Those times make me smile. Makes me wish and long for days like that again.

The clock reads 3:42 in the morning and I think about those

horrible holidays I spent in foster care. My mind wards off those disgusting memories of being hungry and cold, frightened and orphaned through the most formative years of my life. I hide behind tears until they flood me. I'm quiet in my sadness when I think of Mom, Dad and Jabez.

"Baby, what's wrong?" Jill turns over and asks me. She rubs my head. Rubs my shoulders.

"I'm okay, baby." I lie. I tell her that so she doesn't worry.

"No, you're not."

She sits up. Turns her nightlight on that sits on her nightstand. Everything that belongs to me is hers. My back faces her and I'm glad she can't see my eyes. She's become so good at reading me. I wipe away the last tear and force myself not to allow another to fall.

She pulls on my shoulder and my arm. She's tugging at me for me to turn over. To turn toward her. I don't. I resist.

"Baby, come here. Talk to me," she tugs more.

"I said I'm fine, Jill. Baby, trust me, I am."

"You promised you'd never lie to me, Jerusalem." she says. I hear the concern and hurt in her voice.

I turn around and see her in her pink nighty. It's soft; just like she is. We decided to stay at my place tonight because I hadn't been here in so long.

"Baby, talk to me."

She gestures for me to lay on her chest. We lay on one another's chest almost nightly. I find comfort on her breasts. Her scent calms my nerves. I follow her command and lay on her chest. I hold her tight.

"Holidays are hard." I exhale.

"I know."

"I miss my family."

"I know." She runs her fingers through my hair.

"I just wish my mother and father and Jabez were here to meet you."

A tear falls from my eye onto her breast. The wetness of the tear stains her nighty.

"We're going to have a wonderful Christmas together."

"I know."

"Your mother and father are with you. They're here with you.

I like to think they protected you over the years."

I exhale and more tears flow. "You're not supposed to see me cry, Jill. I hate that I'm so open with you."

"I'm your woman, baby."

"I know, but I'm your man and I'm supposed to be the strong one."

"You are very strong. You're my rock, Jay."

"Thank you for being here."

"I'm never leaving you. We're going to have a lovely Christmas. I'm even thinking of us going away for New Year's. Oh, baby, let's have Christmas here this year."

"At my house?"

"Yes, Jay. It's your first Christmas home and in your new home. Let's celebrate here. I'll cook. We'll have LT and Deseree and LaLaina and others over. It will be fun. I promise."

"Okay, baby, whatever you want."

She begins to hum a tune as she rubs my shoulders, runs her fingers through my hair.

My baby sang me a song and I fell back asleep. I'm sitting at the dining room table now which is adjacent to my kitchen. There is an open window in the kitchen that overlooks my dining room. Going through the mail is such a chore for me, but it is welcomed because ain't nothing but adult bills and correspondence arriving in my home. Mine. I feel good about that.

No, I don't want to see a car note every month, but it's my car. Not too fond of a three hundred dollar electric bill every month either, but the bill is for my home. I'm not sure I know anyone who wants to receives medical bills in the mail full of copayments, but I'm alive, so praise God.

Mail from the Veteran's Administration is something I open first before anything else. Especially now, given all that has happened. The envelope's return address is the U.S. Department of Veteran's Affairs with the seal on the side. It's addressed to me, so I open immediately.

Jill's phone rings and she answers it.

"Hello? Oh, yes. Really? Oh my God, that is so unbelievably beautiful! Whew, the hard work paid off. What a beautiful Christmas this will be. I'm floored, I just can't believe the breakthrough. Yes. Yep. Uh huh. Okay. Yep, stick with the plans. Yeah. Okay, bye and thanks again. Team work makes the dream work!"

"Baby, who was that?"

"Oh, the nurse's station…they uhm…got the budget approved for next year."

"Good news, baby."

"Yep!"

My baby is in the kitchen cooking up some breakfast. She put on Eric B. and Rakim's "Paid in Full" because she knows I loves my hip hop. I know my baby would rather be listening to jazz, but she did it for me. She looks so cute with that bun on top of her head, terry cloth shorts, slippers and my white T-shirt. She's preparing Bananas Foster French Toast and damn it…it smells good! They say the way to a man's heart is through his stomach, but I have to admit…I love the way she gets to my heart by way of my stomach and my dick! I'm going to end up getting her pregnant if she doesn't cut it out with all of this good loving.

My phone rings so I place the letter on my lap as I answer.

"Waddup?"

"What's good, partner?" LT questions.

"All good. My baby cooking breakfast."

"You's a spoiled ass."

"Hey, listen, don't hate."

"Ha, ha! Just checking to see what you want me to bring over for Christmas."

"Oh, yes, Jill and I decided to have it here for Christmas."

"Cool."

"You don't have to bring anything, LT. You know my baby is going to prepare a feast."

"I'll bring the liquor."

"Bet!"

"Alright man, see you on the big day!"

"Word. Later."

I read the letter's contents.

Dear Mr. Jerusalem Jones, We are in receipt of your appeal of your veteran's benefits. We have...

Wait a minute. I never appealed anything. I rise to my feet and walk toward the kitchen with letter in hand. I yell, "Cookie!"

"Yes?" she responds.

I approach the kitchen and she comes out.

"Cookie, I got this letter from the V.A."

She immediately turns around and walks back into the kitchen. I walk to the entranceway to the kitchen and stand there with letter in my hand. She won't even look at me. She continues cooking our breakfast and doesn't acknowledge my presence. I remember her doing this shit at the hospital when one of the doctors would tell her what to do and she didn't want to listen.

"Cookie?"

"Yes?" she responds, but doesn't look at me. "You need some lotion on your arms and elbows, Jay." She deflects.

"Have any idea what this appeal is about?"

I hold up the letter. She doesn't look at me.

"Nope."

I can tell she is lying.

"Look at me, Cookie!" I demand.

"I'm cooking, Jay."

"Oh, you're cooking, huh?"

There is a slight chuckle in my voice.

"Yep!" she says as she continues to pay attention to the food on the stove.

"Well, someone filed an appeal with the V.A. and it wasn't me."

"Oh my..."

She does not give me any eye contact. She's lying. We both know it.

"Uh huh, oh my. So, let me read this letter then."

"K."

Dear Mr. Jerusalem Jones,

We are in receipt of your appeal of your veteran's benefits. We have carefully reviewed your appeal and request for increased benefits along with the supporting documentation and our review board has determined that you are now *categorized as one hundred percent disabled. Your new monthly rate will be $2,820 for life. Furthermore, we received the addendum and your medical coverage through the U.S. Department of Veteran's Affairs will now be covered at one hundred percent. Your benefits will be paid retroactively for thirty-six months, your current benefits of $400 per month minus the new benefits of $2,820 which leaves a balance of $2,420 for thirty six months which makes the enclosed check a total of $87,120. Your new benefits check in the increased amount will be paid on December thirty first.*

I was all ready to kill my Cookie now; I don't know what to say. She puts down the spatula and walks over to me with puppy dog eyes, jumps in my arms and hugs me.

"Yay, baby!"

"Cookie! Is this real?" I can't believe this." I tell her as I take a seat on the living room sofa. My heart is beating so fast in my chest. She climbs on top of me and kisses all over my face.

"Baby, did you do this?"

She doesn't respond. She simply walks back into the kitchen.

"Baby, you want tea or orange juice?" she yells.

Yeah, she did it.

Chapter 26

Jill

Eye of the Beholder

I set the record player and put on Chic Corea's, "Eye of the Beholder" and although it's Christmas, the melody is so appropriate. It's soft and soothing and beautiful; just like my man. I watch Jay, as he makes sure the decorations on the tree are perfect. He is so happy today and it makes my heart melt to see him this way. I know how hard Christmas is for my baby, so for him to be smiling is a glorious thing. I prayed to the Creator day and night for Jay's soul. I pleaded for a healing for him. Little did I know that while the Creator was healing Jay, He was healing me too.

The soft melody plays throughout the living room, kitchen and dining room of Jerusalem's first floor of his duplex. With the money he got from the military, Jay did splurge a bit, but put the rest of it away. He wants us to have the home of our dreams and he's all ready to make a down payment, but I have a luxury home and I explained to him that our house is our home and that it is what we make it.

"Hey, baby, I'm taking your macaroni and cheese out of the

oven now." I yell to him and he rushes into the kitchen as I place the huge pan on top of the counter. I take a forkful and blow it off before I put it in his mouth.

"Mmmm," baby...damn that's good.

"It's five cheese baked mac and cheese for my king." I tell him as I check on the collard greens simmering with smoked turkey.

"Tell me the menu again, baby." He says and with eager open eyes, he waits for me to tell him once again what I'm preparing for us and our guests for Christmas dinner.

"Five cheese mac and cheese, collard greens with smoked turkey, arroz con gandules, sage sausage cornbread stuffing, turkey, prime rib, buttermilk biscuits, candied yams, sweet potato pie, mashed potatoes and you're making banana pudding."

"That menu sounds so good, baby." he tells me, leans in to give me a kiss.

"Thank you, baby. Just want a memorable Christmas for you." I tell him.

He walks back into the living room. I look at his sculpted legs and backside. *Damn, he's mighty fine in that sweater and jeans. His body is to die for and lucky me, I get to wake up to his fine ass every single morning.*

"You looking good, baby. Lookin' like a bacon, egg and cheese." I tell him. He laughs. Walks back toward me.

"Here, Cookie."

He hands me a rectangular box wrapped in Christmas wrapping paper.

"Oh, Jay! Thank you, baby!" I give him a hug.

"Baby, open it."

I take a paper towel and wipe my hands clean and open the gift.

"Baby, you can't do this!" I tell him as I see two airline tickets to Hawaii and a printout of a hotel reservation.

"I did it. What you gonna do about it, Cookie?" He smiles. "Merry Christmas, baby," he tells me. I kiss him. Hug him.

"Cookie, I have one more gift for you, but I'll give that to you later because I want you to finish cooking and not burn my food."

"Okay, baby."

I walk back into the living room and reach under the tree.

"Girl, you're looking good in that red jumpsuit. You better

hope no one stays over tonight because it's going to take me about ten seconds to get that off of you."

"Here, baby. Merry Christmas." I hand him a box. He smiles and opens it.

"Baby? Invicta? No!" He is so happy as he says those words. I went all out for my man and got him an Invicta watch. He deserves the best and that's what I plan to give him forevermore.

"I have one more gift, but, baby, let me finish cooking, okay?"

"K, baby."

The doorbell rings and Jay walks over to the door to open it. I watch him as he moves. He looks like a well-built athlete – a superstar who could easily go from football to basketball to even baseball. *Body for days and dick for long nights*, I chuckle to myself as I watch.

His chocolate brown hand turns the gold doorknob and he pulls the door open. It's Deseree and LaLaina and my heart sings a new tune. I'm joyful, happy, as Christmas hasn't meant much to me either for quite some time. This Christmas is sure to be one for the record books. I smile and walk toward the front door.

"Hey, y'all!" I yell as I make my way to Jay. He puts his arm around my waist.

"Cookie, these two fine young ladies must be Deseree and LaLaina."

"Yes, we are!" LaLaina yells and gives Jay the biggest embrace.

"So happy to finally meet you, Jay!" Deseree tells him as she gives him a hug.

"The pleasure is all mine, ladies. Come in. Get comfortable. Do what you want to do. The boss over here is running the show. I'm simply following orders," he tells them as they walk into the living room.

"Jay, stop…they know I don't give orders like that." I tell him as I hit him on his arm.

"Please. That's all you do is tell everyone what to do and how to do it." LaLaina says and laughs.

Jay takes their coats and places them into the den. He peaks his head out of the den area. "Babe, you spend some time with your people and I'm going to call LT to see when he's going to get here. Let me know if you need any help in the kitchen."

"Okay, baby." I respond and blow him a kiss.

Deseree rises to her feet and walks over toward the fireplace. She admires the poster-sized framed picture of me and Jay. We took that picture the night he surprised me with "Cocoa Brown's."

"Oh my God, Jill, this is lovely. You two look like a match made in heaven."

"Feels like it, Deseree. I'm so happy. Look what he got me for Christmas."

I hand Deseree the box with the Hawaii trip in it.

LaLaina walks over to view the contents of the box with my gift in it.

"Oh my God, girl! The Ritz-Carlton Kapalua, Lahaina. Jill, he's a keeper."

LaLaina's eyes well up with tears. I hug her.

"What's wrong, LaLaina?"

"I'm just happy for you is all. You deserve this."

"Don't make me cry, LaLaina. Thank you." I tell her and hug her harder.

"It's just that you've been through so much and finally… finally, you are going to get back all of the love that you have given so freely to all of us."

Tears pour from her eyes.

"Damn, y'all, it's Christmas, cut it out. I can't be over here crying and ruining my makeup." Deseree chimes in.

"Come on, ladies, let's set the table. I finished dinner. We're just waiting on LT. It's going to be a quiet and beautiful Christmas."

We walk toward the kitchen to bring out the food that I've already placed into serving dishes. Deseree takes one of my aprons and puts in on. We all huddle into a small circle in the kitchen and begin to whisper.

"Jill, you said everything worked out with LT, right?" LaLaina questions.

"Yes! Girl, I can hardly stay in my skin!"

"Oh my God, I have goosebumps!" Deseree says.

Jay walks in the kitchen and startles all three of us. We scatter like roaches and I grab a bowl and Deseree and LaLaina grab mac and cheese and stuffing. We make our way to the dining room.

"You ladies always so secretive," Jay laughs and questions. He walks over to me. "Baby, I'm hungry."

I take a fork and dig out a big forkful of collard greens and shove them in his mouth. "Eat that, baby. We're almost done setting the table, then you can eat with your greedy self. Oh, did you get LT?"

"Not yet. He's probably at one of his honey's houses getting some Christmas ass." He laughs and walks out of the kitchen.

The doorbell rings and Jay does a light jog to answer it. "Babe, that's probably LT, I'll answer it."

"K, baby." I tell him as I watch him. Deseree and LaLaina stand next to me to watch Jay answer the door. We all have our arms around the other.

Before Jay can reach the door, the door opens and LT walks in with a huge smile on his face. Jay stops in his tracks. A tall, brown, slender man walks in behind LT. The man smiles. Jay stumbles, almost falls backwards, he's off balance. Jay turns around to look at me. He reaches out his hand for me. He turns back around to look at the man. He looks at LT. LT smiles. Wipes a tear.

The man walks further into the foyer. The overhead lights shines on him. Jay moves closer to him. He moves a step closer to Jay. LT wipes away tears.

"No, no, no, no, no, no, no," Jay says and shakes his hand. The two reach for one another. They hug. They embrace. Their arms are wrapped so tightly around one another and they rock side to side while they hold on for dear life.

Loud cries and bellows escape Jabez and he cries into his big brother's shoulder. Tears pour from my eyes at record speed. I can't wipe them fast enough before another set run down my face.

The two brothers are still crying, hugging, holding on to one another. Jay grabs the back of Jabez's head and their foreheads are pressed against each other's.

"I never…ne…nev…never thought I'd see you again."

Jerusalem cries and struggles to get those words out.

"I tried to find you!" Jabez yells through tears.

"I was hoping you didn't forget about me." Jay tells his brother.

"I thought you didn't love me anymore." Jabez cries. He loses his composure. LT brings him into the living room. Sits him on the sofa. I run into the kitchen, pour a glass of ginger ale. Rush into the living room. Jay is standing there looking at his brother. I give Jabez the glass of ginger ale.

Jay walks over to me. He hugs me. Jay cries into my neck, holds me tight. I hug him harder.

"Merry Christmas, baby," I whisper in his ear. "Go sit down next to your brother."

"I love you so much, Jill." he whispers. I wipe his tears. He's getting overheated, so I take his sweater off. His wife beater isn't dingy, thank God. I hate when he throws those damn T-shirts on.

Jay walks to the sofa and sits next to his brother. "Jabez, this is Jill – the love of my life."

Jabez rises to his feet. Walks over to me. Hugs me. Lifts me up. Hugs me hard. Puts me down.

"Thank you. Thank you. Thank you. He cries as he holds my hands in his. LT told me how you tracked me down in Ohio. I don't know how you did it, but I thank God for you."

"She's good," LT chimes in.

"LT?" Jay questions and looks at his best friend and brother.

"Man, I couldn't tell you. Jill and I were caught up in a maze trying to find him."

"Oh, my God…I have my brother back." Jay says and walks over to Jabez and hugs him.

'Merry Christmas, baby brother."

They embrace once more. Jabez once again cries into his brother's arms.

"Merry Christmas, big bro."

Jabez looks at his brother, sees the damage to his face. He touches Jay's scar gently. "What happened?"

"I was in Iraq. I was injured. Almost died. Jill, she was my nurse. Brought me back to life."

"Awwwww, man. I'm so sorry."

"Don't be. She saved my life. She brought me back, my brother." Jay chokes up once again.

"Where you been, Jabez? I've been looking for you."

"Jail. In and out. I was lost after the Hamiltons adopted me. We moved to Ohio about a year after they adopted me. My adoptive mother tried to find you, and when she finally did, your foster mother would not let us visit you. Man, I begged her to adopt you!" Jabez breaks down in uncontrollable tears.

"I lashed out. I was a terrible kid. I got into so much trouble. I've been in and out of jail for God only knows how long. They changed my last name to Hamilton."

"I knew I needed to be with you." Jay cries and tells Jabez.

"For years I thought I killed mommy. I remember that I would get on her nerves so bad. I thought I caused her death."

"No, no, no, Jabez…damn." Jay grabs his brother and holds him tight. "You didn't kill mommy. You were just a lil fucker is all."

Everyone starts laughing hard, and long. Jay's comment breaks the tension. It adds relief to this monumental moment.

"Yeah, you're right, I was a lil fucker," Jabez tells Jay.

"You look good, Jabez." LT tells him.

"Man, I was in transition from the prison to the halfway house when I got word that you were looking for me, LT. They said my brother Lawrence Assange. I knew God had answered my prayers. Jail will make you one of two things, an animal or an angel. I learned so much about God while locked up," he says and turns to Jay. "All of the things Mommy and Daddy taught me, I relearned while in prison. If it weren't for those prison ministers, I'd be dead. I had no reason to live. I didn't have you. I didn't have mommy. I didn't have daddy; all I had was God," he says.

"Y'all come on and get some food. You have the rest of your lives to catch up now that you're back together. Let me feed all my mens." I try to lighten the mood as I always do.

They all smile as I say the words. Deseree and LaLaina make plates for the gentlemen. Jay introduces Deseree and LaLaina to LT and Jabez."Hey, baby?" Jay tells me as he gets up from the table and takes me over to the living room.

"Yes, baby? Baby I want you to eat."

"I know. But there's one more Christmas gift I have for you."

"Okay, baby, want to eat first?"

"Go grab the wooden box over there next to the record player."

"Okay, baby."

Jay walks back to the dining room. He stands in front of everyone.

"Bring me the box, Cookie."

"Okay." I walk over to him and hand him the box.

"Open it!" he commands.

I open the wooden box and pull out a United States flag. He

hands the flag to Jabez.

"This is daddy's flag." Jabez says.

"Yes." Jay replies.

"Cookie, look in the box." He tells me and gets on one knee.

I look in the box and see a picture of LT, Jabez and Jay from when they were younger. I also see a diamond ring and wedding band.

"Jay?" I feel like some charlotte out of a black and white movie as I feel my hand cover my heart and my tears begin to fall.

Is he really doing this?

My heart skips a beat. I surrender to its will.

Jay reaches up and takes the ring out of my hand. Jabez takes the wooden box and sits it on the dining room table. Jay places the ring on my wedding finger.

"This was my mother's wedding ring, Jill. My daddy told me to put it on the finger of a woman who makes life complete."

"Jay…" I whisper.

I cry. I want to strangle and kill him at the same time. This moment wasn't about me; yet, Jay made sure that it was.

"There is no me without you, Jill. I can't breathe without you, nor do I want to. You're my today, my tomorrow, my everything. Without you, there is no me. You…you…" he begins to cry.

"I was born again the day you kissed me. My life had meaning the day you called me your man."

"Jay…"

"I lived a beautiful life while you loved me. You nurtured me. Cared for me. Breathed life into me when I was invisible. Invisible. That is what I was until there was you."

"Jay…" Words escaped my mouth through tears. Jay cut those words off.

"I cannot be without you, Jill. The scar on my face speaks volumes of what I did for my country. It is visible. I wear it for life. Jill, without you, my life would be scarred. Please don't make me wear that badge as well. The scar of life I already wear, please don't make me wear the scar of love as well. I need you in my life, Jill. Please, baby, will you marry me?"

It took less than a second for the words to escape my mouth.

"Yes! Yes, Jay! I will marry you!" I yell to him and he rises to his feet, picks me up, kisses me.

Jabez, LT, LaLaina and Deseree all join in to embrace us.

Chapter 27

Jerusalem

Song for My Father

At my baby's insistence, everyone stayed the night after the holiday. Now, a couple days later, LaLaina and Deseree are gone and LT has gone back to work. This is the time of year LT begins his prep work of the best sports stories of the year. Jabez, well, before I could tell him he wasn't going back to Ohio, Jill let him know.

She gave him the keys to her truck yesterday, and her debit card and told him to go get some clothes and to get whatever he needed. She did all of this while still in bed with me. She's such a control freak, but I love her take-charge attitude. My baby gets the job done. I smile when I think about it.

I heard a light tap at my bedroom door. I was laying on Jill's breasts as usual. She had on the sweetest black nighty and smelled like a couple of beautiful forevers. Even when my baby is a bit ripe, she still smells divine. I knew it was Jabez at the door.

"Come in, baby bro," I yelled and he entered. His smile was all aglow.

"Maaaaaaann, I don't want to see you in bed with your woman!" Jabez yelled and laughed.

"Look here, son, this grown folk business happening in this here room." I laughed.

"Good morning, Jill," Jabez said and she replied with a beautiful smile.

"Good morning, brother."

"Listen, Jay, I am going through your closets, right now. I have to shower and change clothes. Isn't it funny how we ended up being just about the same size?"

"Yes, it is something you fake ass Morris Chestnut!"

"You got some nerve with your curly hair looking like a broke down wanna be movie star."

Jill interrupted.

"Here, Jabez." She handed him her keys and her debit card. "Take my truck and go get what you want and need."

"Jill?" I questioned.

"Jay, let him go be a man and get his own clothes. He shouldn't have to wear your funky drawers, baby."

"Okay, baby." I conceded.

"Damn, my soon to be sister-in-law has my big brother whipped. LT said you had it bad. I see it with my own eyes." Jabez doubled over in laughter.

"Man, whatever," I replied and Jabez headed out.

Now , the three of us are here, at my dining room table, having coffee and talking about old times. Jabez is more buff than I am but that makes sense since he's been in and out of jail. I thank God my baby brother did not lose his sense of self, his core values or stray too far away from the people Mom and Dad raised us to be. That has to seem weird since he has been in jail, but I know my brother and I know he has a good heart and I also believe that the reason he was in so much trouble is because the earth beneath us shattered at our feet. Another reason to thank the good Lord that we didn't end up as statistics as many black men do in this country when faced with extraordinary life circumstances.

"You look good brother," I tell him as I pat him on his shoulder. I take his plate and make my way to the kitchen.

"You look great yourself, Jay," he replies as he sips on his coffee.

Jill is reading the newspaper and eating breakfast -one that I prepared for us this morning. My baby is always cooking great meals that I had to cater to her and my brother this morning. I prepared scrambled eggs with cheese, French vanilla coffee, turkey bacon and onion bagels toasted with butter and cream cheese. Jabez cleaned his entire plate. I love watching my brother eat. I love being able to see him eat. I know he's nourished. I know he's taken care of now. Peace to my heart and soul and definitely God has given us peace in the storm.

I yell to Jill from the kitchen where I'm brewing more coffee. "Baby, you want some more to eat?"

"No, baby, I'm okay. But I want you and I and Jabez to head out. I have an idea in mind."

Oh Lord, no more surprises, Jill. I think to myself.

"Okay, baby," I tell her.

"Sounds good to me," Jabez chimes in.

"Okay, gentlemen, it's 11 a.m. now can we leave about noon?"

"Sure," Jabez and I say in unison.

I make my way out of the kitchen and hand Jabez another cup of coffee. He likes it sweet. I knew he would. He smiles as I pat him on the shoulder. He's seated. I'm standing. I look out the window and see the skies are clear and blue and there's no snow falling. This means it's terribly cold outside. Jill hates the cold. She hates driving in the snow. I honestly don't know how she's maintained all of these years.

"What are you planning to do with your life, Jabez? Any goals?" I ask to see where his head is.

"Now that I'm a free man, I want to explore some options. I learned so many things in and out of prison. Studied business. I even took some cooking classes. Learned about computers. I have many skills, Jay."

"I'm happy to hear that, man. I'll help you with whatever you need. Listen, Jabez, I want you to stay here with me. I have two extra bedrooms and the way Jill holds me hostage, I'm honestly not here that much. I want you close to me. I want to be able to be your brother. I want us to be together.

"Hey, I heard that!" Jill yells and laughs.

"I can't impose, Jay," Jabez tells me as he walks with me to the patio door. We look out into the backyard to witness the clear blue skies.

"You're not imposing. We need one another. And, I need to make sure you're fine. Just until you get on your feet."

"Deal."

We embrace and sip on our coffee.

♪

"Song for My Father" by Horace Silver plays in my truck. Jill has this on a couple of weeks ago and I instantly recognized the jazz tune. I look to Jabez, who is in the passenger seat, rocking a nice hat and a leather shearing coat. He's a good looking man, much like his brother. He gets the connection almost immediately.

"Jay, remember Mom and Dad would listen to this song?" He smiles big and wide.

"Yes! Jill was playing it and I told her about how Dad would dance up behind Mom and hug her from behind."

"Sho nuff!" Jabez yells with excitement. "Dad would twirl her around and take him into her arms and they'd dance to that tune for what seemed like hours."

"Yeah," I reply to Jabez and look in the rearview mirror to witness Jill in the backseat smiling. She has on a fur hat and fur coat, both in white. I know they're not real, although I offered to buy the real deal for her. She's too much of a good soul to wear real fur. I know that doesn't line up with who she is at the core. At this life transition, she's having a hard enough time eating meat of any kind. I didn't want to push it. She looks beautiful, though, with a fresh makeup-free face and a light bronzed colored lips gloss.

"You okay back there, baby?"

"Yes, honey."

"Jill, where are we headed?"

"Oh, to the Newark Police Station where your Daddy worked."

"Oh?"

"Yes."

"Jill?"

"Just go, baby."
"Damn, she has you on lock, Jay," Jabez screams in laughter.
I smirk.
"Okay, baby."

As we arrive, we pull up to the parking spot that's just about ten feet from the entranceway to the police station. Jill mentioned nothing about this, and to be honest, I never thought of returning. Jabez and I would walk down the street to visit Dad's place of employment when we were children, but since Dad died, I hadn't thought about revisiting a place that could potentially harbor so many hurtful memories. But since Jabez is with me and Jill is here, walking into this police station is not as hard as it would have been if the two of them were not here with me.

Jill grabs my hand and Jabez stands to my left and we walk win. Immediately I see Officer Culligan. He was the man who was my Dad's partner. He was like his best friend. He has aged, but I see him still through the eyes of a child.

Officer Culligan is at the front desk of the precinct. He rises to his feet. Walks toward us in a hurried rush and shakes his head. I can tell that emotions are overwhelming him.

"Office Culligan," Jabez greets him with a warm smile and an even warmer hug. I join the two of them and we all hug in unison.

"I cannot believe my Irish eyes," Officer Culligan says as he wipes away a tear that escape his left eye. "You boys…you boys. I've been looking for you for years upon years. It's like the two of you vanished."

"We did," I reply.

"Your Dad had a trust set up for you two and your mother. He told me to make sure if anything ever happened to him that I needed to make sure you three were taken care of. This was before your Mom died. I miss your Dad."

Officer Culligan walks to his desk and pulls out a picture

of him and Dad when they were young officers. He hands it to us. Jabez takes the photo in the old dusty frame. We all look at it – me, Jabez and Jill.

"You all take these papers, fill them out and bring them to me when you can. There's money here for you and your brother, Jerusalem. Your wife here…" he points to Jill, "well, she's relentless. She found me. She's a keeper."

"I know she is," I touch her cheek and smile. She's glowing.

We all embrace and head out of the precinct with papers in hand.

Jabez reclines in the passenger seat and mellows out to the smooth jazz that plays. Jill reclines in the backseat. I think we may all have a case of the partying too hard around the holidays blues.

"One more stop before we head home."

"Okay, baby," Jill says as she struggles to keep her eyes open. I love how she looks like a little duck when she gets sleepy. Pouty lips poke out and her eyes squint.

"No problem, brother," Jabez replies.

We make our way through the streets of Newark and finally end up at the cemetery where Mom and Dad are buried side by side. I help Jill out of the car and she holds onto my hand.

"Mom and Dad are here?"

"Yes."

Jabez is indifferent as we make our way to their gravesites. I walk forward and head to Mom and Dad's tombstones because if I don't move forward, I'm going to turn away and never come back. Jill grabs Jabez's hands and brings him over to the gravesite where Mom and Dad rest in perfect peace together.

I kneel in front of Mom and Dad's tombstones to show them respect, to honor them, to love them, to be closer to them. I haven't been this close to what was their physical presence in an earthly body since I was twelve years old.

Jabez kneels beside me. He takes my right hand into his left.

He sobs. He sobs like that young boy who lost his father and his mother way too soon in life. He cries a deep-throated, hard cry as if he is dying all over again. We both died when Mom and Dad did. I squeeze his hand. Somehow I feel like if I squeeze it hard enough, I can take some of his pain away.

"I miss them so much, Jay," he cries. He cries loud.

"Mom…Dad, when I was in a coma a couple months back, my spirit left me. I died all over again. The first time I died, is when you died, Mom. I died another death, when you were murdered, Dad. My world fell apart. And, while I was here physically, I didn't want to live anymore without you. I've been through hell, Mom and Dad…pure hell and when I was in that coma, all I had to do was let go. That's it. One tragedy after another in my life. I had plenty of reason to let go. But then, my spirit aligned with yours Mom and I felt your presence all around me. I saw you, somewhere in the darkness, Mom I saw your face. I smelled your cookies. Your perfume was in the hair. You smiled at me. Daddy held your hand. You two listened to some old jazz song. I felt the love all around me. I was finally happy again when I was near death and near you. I reached out my hand for you but you wouldn't take it. I struggled in that darkness. I couldn't understand why you wouldn't take my hand. I was walking that fine line, I realize that now…that fine line between death and life, joy and pain, heaven and hell. I wanted to die so I could be with you once again. But Mom, you told me to find Jabez. You told me to hold on. So I did. And when I finally woke up from the coma, I cried because I couldn't see your face again. In my vague awareness in the afterlife, I was loved again, because I hadn't been loved since you and Dad loved me. It was love all over again. When I opened my eyes, I died again because I lost your love once more. But, I felt your love, you and Dad's there with me and then Jill, she came along and she smelled like you and baked me cookies and she saved me. I think you wouldn't allow me to let go because you knew she would be my angel here on earth. You knew I would love again. You knew, Mom, that I would remember love because of Jill. You wouldn't take my hand because I needed to find Jabez. She found him, Mom. We're back together again, Mom and Dad. He's here. He's fine."

I wipes my eyes and reach for Jill.

"I finally get to meet my mother and father in law. I'm proud

to be carrying your very first grandchild."
I look up to my wife to be and question, "Jill?"

ACKNOWLEDGMENTS

Singin' in the Comeback Choir

"My vision and goal for Eye of the Beholder was so large that I was unable to achieve it until I grew into the woman who could. I became that woman." ~ Elissa Gabrielle

Beloveds,

To be able to release another novel and present my work to the public is an exciting feeling and although I've been down this road before, it truly feels like the very first time. Something happened along the way with the storytelling of my new release, Eye of the Beholder. The concept and idea and the goal and my dream and vision for this novel was epic and while the story itself is beautifully-simple, the themes I wanted to cover and the subject matter I wanted to address were not.

I wasn't evolved enough as a writer to pen this book until now. I had to challenge myself and the person I was to become the person I am now. You see the glory but you don't know my story. It is one hell of a story. Because of my life's journey to date, I am stronger, wiser, better and exceedingly blessed and I thank God for everything He has made me and for the gifts He has bestowed upon me. I don't take these gifts for granted.

I could have taken the easy road and I'm sure my readers would have loved the work, but because I am a student of the game; a writer who honors the written word and respects the craft of writing, I had to give you a beautiful love story – the ultimate love story that heals, that triumphs, that soars; one that is unwavering and blessed beyond measure.

The main character Jerusalem Jones was faced with all types of adversity and the obstacles laid before him on his life's path would make the average man throw in the towel. I know about that kind of adversity and I'm here to tell you that there is victory on the other side of through.

I remember when I started Peace In The Storm Publishing and for that matter, when I began my literary career, there were so many obstacles in the way, and as time progressed, the obstacles grew bigger and self-doubt tried to creep in. The keyword here is "tried."

So glad I didn't give up. He speaks through trials. I was reminded, through the trials, "Who" I am, and "Whose," I am. Made all of the difference in the world. And, whatever you're going through in life, no matter how big your problem may seem, I'm here to tell you that there is a God that is bigger than anything you're going through. So the next time obstacles confront you, you don't allow your problems to scream to you how big they are, you look them in the face and shout how big your God is!

Life is filled with speed bumps, roadblocks and stop signs. Our normal tendency is to listen to the world as it tells us to slow down or even stop, behind a belief that some things in life are out of our reach and beyond our attainment and control. The world wants to cushion our expectations and to ultimately limit our goals. But thankfully, there is a God. And with faith in Him and His mercies, He gives us pedals upon which to accelerate and a path of green lights upon which to proceed when others tell us to we can't possibly move forward. My life's journey has been an ongoing saga of having faith and believing that even though others can give me molehills of why I can't, My God gives me mountains of why I can.

Eye of the Beholder is an eclectic ensemble of jazz and poetry. It is both spiritual and sensual. It is redeeming and healing. It is triumph over adversity. It is love because I am love.

Thank you for taking the time to experience the power of love on this phenomenal journey.

Always and in All Ways,
I will forever remain,

Elissa Gabrielle

JESUS LOVES ME

"Yes, Jesus Loves Me," were next to the last words I spoke to my Mother. I sang the song in her ear, to comfort and soothe her. She loved my voice, either in conversation or in song and during her illness I often read to her, conversed with her, and sang to her. Actually, the very last words I spoke to my mother were, "Mom, I'm gonna be good." I have a way of being a wonderfully unique mischief at times, it's a badge my mom and dad gave me when I was knee-high.

I never broke my mother's heart, plain and simple. I was her baby girl, and all of the grace and class that she carried so effortlessly was passed down to me, and I wear it, proudly. I was born of blessed seed, so all I can do is say, "Thank You," to her and for her for molding me into the woman I am today. I lived to please her and to make her happy.

My life has been a storm of epic proportions, one that I wouldn't trade with my worst enemy, a vicious battle between fighting to save my mother's life to challenging doctors and hospitals as to the best protocols to allow for the best and finest care for her. I've traveled states, slept in hospital chairs, rode in ambulances, survived on coffee, and prayers, and held my mother's hand through it all. She was a beautiful trooper.

We rejoiced when treatments were successful. I was her shoulder to cry and scream on when things didn't go our way.

My nickname as a child was "Lil Grandma," or sometimes they'd call me "Tex," after my grandma who ran a brothel in Newark. She was big, bold, beautiful, a gorgeous, fiery woman who men adored, and were afraid of at the same time. She carried two guns. She would cook you a great meal with one hand, and shoot you with the next if you got things twisted. My mother was that way - you could have the shirt off her back, but don't cross her, cause you'd have trouble. I'm the same way.

I was born of blessed seed. I cannot complain...

When she could no longer walk, I carried her to the bathroom. When she could no longer feed herself, I fed her. I read to her, I sang to her, I prayed with her and for her, I was her "Tex," when she wasn't handled with extreme care.

I loved her. She loved me. She was my breath-taker when I couldn't sustain air on my own. She was my life before I had one of my own. I AM DESTROYED.

But, I'm honored to be her daughter. Grateful to have traveled this road called life with her. I'm happy to have had the courage to stand by her side and through it all. I owed her that much, at least, for giving me life.

I MISS HER SO MUCH...

If you know God like I know God, you'll understand that I carry with me a peace that surpasses all understanding. He's got my back, how can I lose? She's resting in His Heavenly arms and I know without a doubt, I will see my Mother once again.

Rest in Perfect Peace, Mom.

GRATITUDE TURNS WHAT YOU DO HAVE INTO ENOUGH…

Where would I be as a mother, wife, daughter, sister and friend without the help of these beautiful spirits who make my life worth living.

My Father for creating me.

My Mother for giving me life.

My husband for completing my life.

My children for continuing my life.

To Ruth and Loretta for being beautiful souls and for representing what angels are in human form. Shauna, my dearest cousin, for being my sister and one of my best friends. Paula, you are one of God's greatest gifts. To my sisters, Monique and Laura, I love you. To all of my nieces and nephews, know that you are so adored.

To LaLaina and Deseree, I named these characters after you and in honor of you and your incredible strength. I love you two more than you'll ever know.

Angelia Vernon Menchan, my Write or Die partner. I love you and I am so thankful that are walking this journey together.

Carol Hill-Mackey, you are an incredible woman and I am so honored to know you. I love you so very much.

Max Julien, I cannot express in words all that you mean to me. I am so grateful to have you in my life.

A special thank you to all of the readers, book clubs, literary colleagues and the literary community for supporting me and my work over the years. I cannot thank you enough for your encouragement.

To my family, near and far, I sincerely appreciate your love and support and your encouragement does not go unnoticed by me.

Thank you to the authors of Peace In The Storm Publishing who have stayed by my side and have shared the beautiful vision with me. You are talented beyond measure and I hope you never forget how blessed you are.

To all of the jazz greats who have influenced me since I was a little girl. My father, Joe Thomas, Miles Davis, John Coltrane, Ella Fitzgerald, Billie Holiday, Nina Simone, Roy Ayers and so many others who taught me about real music and how it heals the soul.

To all of the poets, the nation's truth-tellers who I walk amongst and am honored to join in sharing with the world the power of words.

Until we meet again, Beloveds.

MEET ELISSA GABRIELLE

"Today is the day to move passed your past, move closer to your dreams, rise above your detractors, feel the fear and do it anyway, stoop below your ego, get out of your own way, and allow your life to amaze you." ~Elissa Gabrielle

Empowering, Enlightening, Engaging and Inspirational, Elissa Gabrielle is a powerhouse in the literary industry. Respected by many, revered in the highest regard, Elissa Gabrielle maintains a spirit of excellence in all she does. She is known to have the Midas touch. The sky is the limit for this sassy, sundry and prolific author. Elissa Gabrielle has broken the ceiling of literary excellence with her gift in the skill of multi-genre writing. The author of multiple poetry books, numerous novels and contributor to several anthologies, Elissa has proven herself to be well-versed in artistic creativity.

Elissa Gabrielle has the uncanny ability to take newcomers and mold, shape them into literary superstars and has created multiple award-winning authors and best-selling books in the process.

Her colloquial and imaginative creations have lead to sensual and seductive inclusions in Zane's Purple Panties, Erogenous Zone: A Sexual Voyage, Mocha Chocolate: A Taste of Ecstasy, The Heat of the Night, Historie Chocolate D'Amour, Pillow Talk in the Heat of The Night, Zane's Busy Bodies: Chocolate Flava 4 and more. Elissa Gabrielle is the author of several short stories including Nights over Egypt, The Other Side of Midnight, An Appetite for Destruction and Saved by Grace.

As a Literary Entrepreneur, Elissa is the founder of the greeting card line, Greetings from the Soul: The Elissa Gabrielle Collection, collaborator and creator of The Triumph of My Soul, and publisher of Peace In The Storm Publishing. Elissa has managed to turn relatively unknown authors into household names and has molded and shaped the careers of some of today's brightest literary stars. In addition to these innovative achievements, Elissa has graced the covers of Conversations Magazine, Big Time Publishing Magazine, Disilgold Soul Magazine and has been featured in Urbania Magazine and Black Literature Magazine.

Peace In The Storm Publishing has been nominated in several categories in the African American Literary Awards Show, and has won Independent Publisher of the Year in 2009, 2010 and 2011. In addition, Elissa Gabrielle won for Self-Published Author of the Year in 2010 for her explosive novel, "A Whisper to a Scream." Elissa also won for Self-Published Author of the Year for the collaborative effort, "The Heat of the Night."

Her writing and publishing passion is rooted in her desire to give a reader's soul a rise, one page at a time and grounded in her quest to bring forth the Triumph Anthology series, an ongoing testament of faith. The first anthology in the series was the highly acclaimed The Triumph of My Soul, which will be followed by The Soul of a Man and The Breakthrough respectively. "I started the Triumph series because in life, we all fall down, but by the Grace of God, we get back up. There is always victory in tomorrow," Elissa says about the Triumph series.

Elissa Gabrielle has been named the Executive Director, Brand and Business Development for Modern Flavor Magazine.

From the novelty of her writing, to her highly-regarded greeting card line and the successful culmination of her publishing company; Elissa Gabrielle remains an ingenious and creative force to be reckoned with in terms of delivering distinct, fulfilling and entertaining literature. By pushing herself to stay a cut above the rest, Elissa Gabrielle brilliantly and consistently delivers Literary best.

Find Elissa Gabrielle online:
www.peaceinthestormpublishing.com
www.facebook.com/PeaceInTheStormPublishing
www.facebook.com/ElissaGabrielleAuthorandPublisher
www.facebook.com/IAmElissaGabrielle
http://www.linkedin.com/in/elissagabrielle
www.Facebook.com/ElissaGabrielle
http://Twitter.com/PITS_Publishing
http://Twitter.com/ElissaGabrielle
www.modernflavormagazine.com
www.elissagabrielle.com

www.ingramcontent.com/pod-product-compliance
Lightning Source LLC
Chambersburg PA
CBHW032023120726
47898CB00002BB/622